Scrooge
The Year After

1844

A Novel Wherein Ebenezer Scrooge's
New Nature is Sorely Tested

by Judy La Salle

ISBN-10: 0615669999

EAN-13: 9780615669991

Library of Congress Control Number: 2012912934

CreateSpace, North Charleston, SC

For Rod

"I will honor Christmas in my heart,
and try to keep it all the year.
I will live in the Past, the Present, and the Future.
The Spirits of all Three shall strive within me.
I will not shut out the lessons they teach."

[Ebenezer Scrooge's pledge to
the Ghost of Christmas Yet to Come]

Charles Dickens
A Christmas Carol
1843

Scrooge
The Year After

PROLOGUE

July 2, 1819

The sickroom was in hushed turmoil. Even as those in attendance did their best to save her, death loomed certain. It was fewer than five weeks since Mrs. Symons had been delivered of a son – and was recovering well – but now, a few weeks later, she was suddenly overtaken by perplexing symptoms. What began as a late afternoon headache progressed within several hours to violent stomach pains and vomiting. Incontinence followed and during the night she suffered convulsions. In the pre-dawn morning the room was already warm with summer, and she was delirious.

"Rebecca! Where is Rebecca?" she cried, unaware that her hand was being held by the very person she sought. Rebecca clasped it firmly while Mrs. Symons thrashed, spoke unintelligible phrases and called out various names. Through it all, Rebecca maintained her hold as if through the connection of their flesh she could will her friend to keep breathing. She was too distressed to weep. Instead, she offered soft, encouraging words.

"I'm here, Fan, I'm here. I won't leave, Dearest." Intensifying her grip on the other's slim fingers, Rebecca murmured, "You will get well, you'll see. Soon we'll go outside with your lovely new son, and have a nice tea on the lawn." She knew she was saying silly things, but she couldn't help it. It was all she could manage because she was speaking with her heart instead of her head. Rebecca continued to repeat things she wished were true, in a futile attempt to contradict the end she dreaded.

To one side of the room Mrs. Symons' personal maid and a servant spoke in hushed voices, snippets of their exchange only partially audible to anyone who might be listening.

"Th' poor, poor lady . . . 'n such a sweet new babe . . . old man in hiding, as usual . . . Yes . . . husband made his escape – too unpleasant for *him*, of course . . . The brother . . . doesn't know? . . . very busy making *money*, I'm sure . . . ."

Nurse Weekes was still in residence from Mrs. Symons' recent lying-in, and had summoned Doctor Devitt during the night. He was attending another case at the time and had only just arrived, too late to effect any cure. Nevertheless, the nurse related to him the progression of the ailment. He bent over his patient to examine her and, several moments later, enquired of the nurse.

"What did you give her, Mrs. Weekes?"

Somewhat offended, she stiffened. Her reply was clipped. "Only the draft of laudanum you prescribed, Doctor - exactly as you directed. Otherwise she ate and drank normally." She felt compelled to remind him that Mrs. Symons had been recovering without difficulty, even if she had been somewhat downcast in her thoughts. Mrs. Weekes could not, however, resist a question as they both turned away from the bed. It had been troubling her for several hours.

Leaning her head toward his, she whispered, "Doctor . . . these symptoms. They are . . ." Before she could complete the thought he interrupted with a warning glance. Even with a lowered voice, his tone was severe – and unmistakable.

"No, Mrs. Weekes. It is not yours to surmise. Do not give voice to your imagination." Because she could hardly question the doctor, and because she valued her livelihood, it would be as he said. She would not raise the subject again – not to him, nor to anyone.

By mid morning Mrs. Symons' pulse was weak, her breathing shallow, and she was unconscious. Her hand once again in Rebecca's, she lay very still and, by early afternoon, the struggle was over. Fan Symons, younger sister of Ebenezer Scrooge, was gone.

CHAPTER ONE

Friday, November 15, 1844

It was now nearly eleven months since Scrooge had been so painfully and so completely renewed. Last Christmas Eve the ghost of Scrooge's late partner Jacob Marley and that procession of tenacious spirits turned him the right way round, and this past year had been the best time of his life. He no longer counted his fortune in pounds silver, although he certainly still possessed a great deal of it. Instead, he counted his wealth by the degree of his enjoyment of, and his ability to help, other people. He was not perfect, but he was truly a new man. He had willingly discarded his former meanness and relegated it and all those spirits to the past. At least he thought so, until this morning, when Marley's ghost returned.

Whether vision or dream, Scrooge could not tell, but in the fragile morning light it troubled him to think this second visit from Jacob Marley, only a few minutes gone and so disturbing in its affect, might mean that Marley's soul had found no rest. Scrooge knew that was not the way things worked, but he desperately wanted to believe his own renewal had somehow freed Marley from those infernal weights and allowed him some peace – but it was not in his power to determine Marley's fate. This morning every indication was that Marley was still fettered by those cumbersome chains and money boxes, and was still a part of Scrooge's life.

Marley's ill-defined image had manifested itself just as a frosty church bell struck six o'clock. Scrooge awoke with the clanging and sensed he was not alone, even though he knew the doors were bolted. Suddenly his bed curtains flew apart, revealing Marley, still bound by all those iron trusses. His jaw was untied and he slid it slowly from side to side, as if trying to become reacquainted with the movement.

"Scrooooge," moaned Marley after a pause, emitting a guttural sound that was nothing like his voice in life. The specter held Scrooge's attention, but seemed unable to speak further. Instead, he made restricted hand gestures and manipulated his lips and tongue around words that would not come.

"What is it, Man?" cried Scrooge as he struggled against his own body, his limbs as useless as if pegged to the bed. "What is it you're trying to tell me?"

The spirit's pantomime made no sense but he finally managed a faint, "Leave . . . it . . . be." After what seemed an excruciating effort on both their parts, Marley faded, still waving both arms as much as his chains would allow, and Scrooge was left in a sweat. If this kept up, he would find these meetings very disturbing, indeed.

Scrooge was not afraid, however. As the specter diminished, he said, "Jacob, old friend, you will have to do better than that, if you want to get through this thick skull of mine, for I am entirely at sea regarding your meaning."

Scrooge shook off the unsettling images and stared, instead, at his bed curtains. Eleven months ago all that heavy embroidered linen had not held back those three visions of Christmas – Past, Present and Future – that trailed in Marley's wake into this very bedchamber. They showed Scrooge such a true and disturbing picture of himself that he was, by daybreak of Christmas, a broken, yet new, man. His purpose in life had been totally redefined and his character so altered that, on Christmas Day, a number of his acquaintance hardly recognized him. That was owing, in part, to his new, unpracticed smile – a phenomenon which made some wonder that it hadn't cracked his stony face in two.

That entire Christmas Day Scrooge had chuckled himself almost silly. It was astonishing how many things seemed to him enjoyable, even entertaining. At one point, while celebrating at his nephew Fred's home, someone's witticism struck him with so much delight it took him a full five minutes to stop laughing. In the meantime, his loud guffawing produced such a contagion of mirth that it infected the entire party and they all very nearly collapsed in their hilarity.

Since his transformation, Scrooge was also surprised to rediscover his ability to play games, such as whist and backgammon, and to solve riddles. He had easily bested those young pups during the Christmas parlor games, particularly the one, "I Am Thinking of Something," and although it was all in good fun, he liked to win and found it fairly easy to do so. It was, perhaps, partly due to his mastery of sums and figures, not to mention his almost uncanny ability to predict business trends, which, as he insisted, were little more than a reflection of human nature.

It was because of his renewed involvement with mankind and an awakened talent for puzzles that he had immersed himself in that wretched business at the Exchange earlier this year. He had eventually cracked the fraud, exposed the miscreant and testified at the hearing whereat the blackguard was convicted. In the final account, he provided funds to help restore the victim's family, but had insisted that the fact of his bequest not be blazed about. Anonymity had been a very definite condition of the gift. Scrooge did not realize the highly-placed, although distant, familial connections of the victims, and he had helped them only because they needed it, not for what they could do for him in return.

Today, blinking and scratching his chin, Scrooge sat up and kicked the heavy covers from his legs. He would rise like a sane man in his fifties and proceed with his morning ablutions. Oh, yes, he still giggled occasionally as he faced a new day, but he was quite able to control himself at this point, if one didn't count the few times he leapt from his bed, just to mark how far he could still jump.

As his feet hit the wood flooring, Scrooge ran mentally through his plans for the next twelve or so hours. He'd lived long enough to know that such schedules were likely to be blown to smithereens by mid-day, but he nevertheless tried to command some sort of order for the things he needed to accomplish. He might no longer be shackled by chains of greed, but he continued to have a business to run and employees to support. In fact, he now had several employees and was paying them a good sight more than ever before.

Fred's wife Catherine was encouraging Scrooge to engage a manservant to tend to his personal needs, but he had not done so. Truth be told, he wasn't sure he wanted someone fussing over him in such close quarters. He could certainly shave and dress himself. Mrs. Dilber, his housekeeper, seemed to manage the care of his clothing quite satisfactorily and, outside of that, she would never dare to interfere with his personal routines.

Mrs. Dilber's knock on the bedroom door came just as Scrooge was giving his cravat a final adjustment. He had shaved and combed his full, well-trimmed hair and had dressed as carefully as his new philosophy dictated. Twisting left and right in front of his mirror, he made a final assessment of his image. He was a man of imposing height, his wavy hair graying and his eyes still a clear mossy green. Since he tended more toward leanness than portliness, he exuded health and vitality befitting a younger man, and his enthusiasm for life made him all the more appealing.

Scrooge had never been a vain creature and was certainly no fop now, but he had to admit he was pleased to have overheard the wife of an associate when she whispered loudly to a friend, "Why, bless me, I never before realized what a fine figure of a man is our Mr. Scrooge." The remark did not make him conceited, but it was certainly a pleasant thing to recall. Besides, he wasn't yet ancient and could still appreciate a bit of feminine approval.

CHAPTER TWO

"Come in, Mrs. Dilber," cried Scrooge. The door swung open to admit his loyal housekeeper, who entered carrying a tray of hot tea and fresh baked bread with butter. She routinely presented him with his breakfast here in his bedchamber, because he preferred to eat as he completed his shaving. Other than on a Holy Day, he had no time to sit in his dressing room of a morning.

Mrs. Dilber's presence pleased him and he enjoyed the ease of their simple exchanges, which were generally centered on topics of practical household matters.

"What lovely aromas, Mrs. D. Your efforts always put me in good humor," said Scrooge. He noticed that she smiled when complimented and he marveled, too, at the extent to which she had improved in her management of the house. Prior to last year her household skills were definitely lacking, not to mention her general demeanor. He considered her rather a slattern then, but it saved him the odd penny, so he didn't attempt to change her habits. She had, since last Christmas, grown into her situation as he had developed in compassion and generosity. Yes, over the past year she had shown a decided improvement and he knew it was in large part a response to his more benevolent attitude as her employer. His housekeeper's regard for him was now in direct proportion to his treatment of her. It was kindly and loyal to a fault.

Mrs. Dilber was as thin as a walking stick, but she was clean and well-groomed. These days her manner seemed a bit more refined as she took pride in herself and her management duties. She also laughed a great deal more. Well, why not? She was happy in her employ and was making a very good wage, which she was determined to earn.

Under her direction the old house had undergone a transformation, as well. When Scrooge acquired the home upon Marley's death, it was a dark suite of rooms, several of them having been let out as offices. Scrooge continued the arrangement then, since it had suited his purposes and his general attitude. In those days he needed only a place in which to sleep since he took his dinners in a "melancholy tavern," where he read newspapers and went over his banker's-book. Last February, however, he re-assumed the other rooms in the house and embarked upon bringing the building back to life in the same way he himself had been brought back to real living.

The bookshelves still housed those wonderful volumes from school and from Scrooge's father's library, and he was thankful he had not sold them years ago, as he had often threatened to do. Marley always insisted he hold onto them because they might appreciate in value and, of course, money was the thing, wasn't it? He silently thanked Jacob for that advice now – not because of their monetary value, but because these days they were once again his companions and the means by which he could spend splendid hours in the company of fantastic characters in exotic settings. Thanks to Mrs. Dilber's efforts and the hours he spent with his nose in them, the books were no longer dusty.

In addition to meals so amply provided by the new daily cook, Mrs. Haiter, and the cleanliness bolstered by a charwoman, it would not be recognizable as the same sad residence. What was once dingy and depressing now fit a successful businessman, one in which its owner enjoyed hosting the occasional small dinner party and welcoming visitors. Rugs had been beaten or replaced, wood and brass fittings gleamed and the fabrics had all been brightened. These days, not one spider was allowed even to consider spinning within these walls.

Scrooge watched the housekeeper place his food on the mahogany side table and pour him a cup of the steaming brew before turning to face him, each hand braced on a thin, determined hip.

"Now, Sir," she said with a sternness she totally lacked where he was concerned, "Don'cher be goin' out of doors in this cold without somethin' in your stomach."

Taking one last look at the reflection of his shaved chin in the mirror, Scrooge replied through stretched lips, "I wouldn't consider doing so, Mrs. Dilber, particularly after you've gone to all this trouble, and I thank you for it. I don't know what I would do without you."

With that, Scrooge leaned down, took the cup and raised it to his mouth. Over the rim he noticed the housekeeper's dour expression just as she turned to straighten his bedclothes. It was not one she often displayed, and it worried him. He held the cup lower.

"You seem downcast, Mrs. D."

Mrs. Dilber turned back toward him and replied, somewhat resignedly, "Why, Sir, 'tis nothing for you to be botherin' yourself about. Just a little sumpin' me an' my Ollie is working out." She then began plumping the pillows with a bit more vigor than was necessary.

Scrooge opened his mouth to ask if there were any way in which he could be of assistance, but before he could speak, Mrs. Dilber again turned to face him and continued, wagging her head.

"'Is back's been poorly, as you know. It 'as been ever since 'e fell off'n that mews roof two year back now, but 'e won't listen to no one, 'specially me. I tell 'im e's got to see someone, but the only one 'e'll trust is that old Doc Devitt, an' 'e's mostly retired now – 'as been for oh, so many years. 'E in't the physician 'e once was anyway, 'n it's too bad."

The name was familiar. "Doctor Devitt, you say?"

"Why, yessir, 'e's the one what used t' mind the gentry, 'n all. 'Course, good hearted as 'e was, 'e treated anyone as needed it, which included my Ollie since 'e were workin' in one o' them big 'ouses at the time. Dunno if I ever said, but 'e did for Lord 'n Lady What'sit's for, oh, nigh on twenty year."

The doctor's name was indeed known to Scrooge, and not altogether pleasant in its recollection. Although he had nothing in particular against the good physician, if his memory served him well, it was he who had been the family's physician and had attended Scrooge's dear sister Fan prior to her death, following the birth of her son Fred. It had been many years, but the memory was still not one he wished to embrace. Mrs. Dilber would be unaware of that connection, however, and it would serve no purpose to mention it.

Scrooge munched on a slice of the delicious bread and asked, "I suppose that Ollie will eventually have to submit to another doctor, don't you expect? I'm certain my physician would see him, if he's willing to have the man look him over."

By then Mrs. Dilber was in the doorway, ready to depart, but she turned and said, "I thank you, Mr. Scrooge, but the way my Ollie is, 'e wouldn't let no one take a peek at 'is person without knowin' 'im for a lifetime." She waved a hand dismissively and affirmed, "No, it's Doctor Devitt or no one, that's for sure, even though the good Doctor can't do much for 'im anymore. Leastwise, I don't expect Ollie to die anytime soon! It's just a pinch of pain, but 'e does go on about it, 'e does."

"Well then, Mrs. D," said Scrooge, "I bid you have a good morn . . ." but was interrupted with a start as Mrs. Dilber threw her hands up and exclaimed, "Oh! Why, Mr. Scrooge, I near forgot!" Reaching into her pocket she retrieved a beautifully hand-written missive on heavy paper and handed it to him. "You 'ave a piece of mail that come three days past now, and was somehow overlooked. I do apologize, Sir." After assuring her there was no harm done, he said, "Thank you, Mrs. Dilber," and watched her scurry from the room.

Scrooge tore open the paper to find an invitation. The Wilkinses were hosting an evening with dancing and supper on the coming Wednesday, and requested the pleasure of his attendance. He and Dick Wilkins had been apprenticed together at old Fezziwig's and became fast friends at the time, only to lose touch later. Dick was a successful importer of goods from the Indies, while Scrooge built his bankroll in other ways. Through the years they had occasionally bumped into each other in Town and, as was his habit then, Scrooge fended off any suggestion of social entanglements.

These days, however, he was more than pleased to accept their invitation, since he was so fond of the couple, having renewed his closeness to Dick and finding that he liked his wife Priscilla very much. Scrooge's only reservation in attending the event was that he suspected Priscilla of trying to put him in the company of a certain widow, a Mrs. Purdy, who held not one ounce of charm, at least for Scrooge. The woman had a fixed place in society because of her deceased husband's rank, and was tolerable in looks, if a bit washed out. She even had a good heart, but he could abide her presence only to a point. Her laughter was like a whinnying horse and she tended to neigh at the oddest moments, securing her lack of appeal with at least one snort at the end of all that commotion. He wouldn't let that rob him of the pleasure of the evening however, and would simply make an effort to steer clear of her noisy camaraderie.

After one last swallow of Congou tea, Scrooge dabbed his mouth with a napkin and prepared to leave. He was eager to get to his offices to speak with Fred, who was now his new partner. They had one or two business dealings that required immediate attention which, should they turn out as planned, might increase their worth substantially.

Scrooge made his way down the polished wood-paneled stairway, looking about as he pulled on his gloves, and thought of what his living chambers meant to him now. Instead of a gloomy fortress where he once shut himself away to brood in his mean melancholy, it was now cheery and welcoming. He enjoyed returning home at the end of the day and it gave him a sense of stability to depart at morning.

Outside, Scrooge closed the front door and finished fitting his gloves between his fingers, enjoying the feel of soft leather against his skin. He then gave his usual nod to the doorknocker. *There you go, Marley,* he thought. This very knocker, on that pivotal last Christmas Eve, was transformed into Marley's ghostly face, right down to the spectacles on his forehead. Scrooge would never forget the eeriness of seeing his old friend's visage staring at him from all that brass, but he would be forever grateful. He was thankful, too, that Mrs. Dilber did not think it odd that he made a particular point of saying he wanted the knocker kept spotlessly cleaned and polished at all times.

Soon Scrooge was headed south on Old Broad Street, still ruminating on Marley, not only because of his ritual with the door knocker, but because this morning's meeting was still fresh in his awareness. Scrooge exhaled icy breath and reconsidered the encounter, wondering about its Divine implications. Could Marley's "ghost" be an angel disguised as Marley, in order that Scrooge could identify with and believe him? Scrooge was not an outwardly religious man, but he definitely believed in God, and was correcting his deficiency of practice by attending Christian services at St. Michael's most Sundays. As a boy he had been rather devout and the Spirits' visits nearly a twelvemonth ago were so real that he accepted, without question, that they were Providential. His logical mind just wasn't sure how to catalogue them and where, within his understanding of the Almighty, to stow this latest encounter with the likeness of Marley.

Scrooge's thoughts were interrupted by the clatter of a barrel falling from a dray in the alley behind a tavern, followed by male voices swearing. Threadneedle Street was already hectic as Scrooge crossed and walked toward Cornhill, where his offices sat at Newman's Court. He inhaled the sooty air, thinking that perhaps the cold temperature had lessened the stench of the River, and looked happily around, taking in the bustle of London's teeming humanity. Shutters were being removed from storefronts and ticket-porters were already running dispatches. By afternoon more venders of all sorts would be pushing their rickety carts noisily over cobbles, shouting their wares to the doors below stairs and windows above.

Now that he was actually interested in people, instead of merely annoyed by them, Scrooge enjoyed being out and about. Never mind the boys who skidded wildly on the ice and pitched into passers-by – they were young, enjoying life, and that was as it should be! It reminded him that he had once been young, full of innocent anticipation, and was, miraculously, once again optimistic with regard to the future.

Scrooge no longer walked with his head down as if bucking a headwind, ignoring the rest of mankind. In fact, he no longer approached his fellow beings as a soldier approaches the enemy.

He felt no need to degrade them to a lower life form in order to make it less of a crime to squash them like night crawlers. Adults and children alike had been little more than vermin to him, but now they were his equals, deserving of concern. Where he had once simply not noticed ignorance and had disdained poverty, he felt a true desire to participate in philanthropic endeavors.

That had been proven last Christmas Day, when he hunted down two men who were soliciting funds for the poor and pledged them a sum high enough to shock their sensibilities. One had pumped his hand with enough glee to stop the blood flowing until he could disentangle himself from the man's grip. Their elation, however, was not shared by everyone on the Benevolence Committee. A Mr. Ira Thorne insisted they were mistaken, that it could not have been Ebenezer Scrooge who made the pledge. He was emphatic in his argument that the Scrooge he knew would no more part with a penny for the poor than part with a penny to save one of his own kin.

"Oh, I cannot believe it of Scrooge," replied one of the less cynical members of the Committee. "I have seen and spoken with him since then, and he made good his pledge. Why, he's the most pleasant of men these days. He must be utterly sincere!"

After much debate during several meetings, Thorne eventually allowed that perhaps it had been Scrooge, but he could not be persuaded that Scrooge hadn't made the gesture with some motive to further his own ends – in other words, to fatten his own purse. So sure of himself was Mr. Thorne that he swore, "You mark my words, he's using us for fools. He does nothing that will not bring him a profit. No, it's the almighty pound he's after, I tell you, not the betterment of his fellow man, and you will not convince me otherwise!"

Today it was this same Mr. Thorne who rounded the corner just as Scrooge arrived at the same juncture, and Thorne was unable to avoid him. "Harrumph!" he growled at Scrooge, intending that the sound would do for a greeting that was required by decent manners.

"Why, it's Mr. Thorne," replied Scrooge, stopping in front of the man as if to chat. "I see we are of the same mind this morning – out early and ready to face the day." Failing to notice Thorne's curdled expression, he said, "I do hope it proves to be a good one for you." Scrooge tipped his hat and only then did he notice that Thorne barely nodded, brushing rudely by as he continued on his way. Scrooge thought, *I'd wager that fellow has his namesake in his stocking, and it's burrowing deep. Why else why would he be so sour?* Shrugging off Thorne's rebuff, Scrooge continued toward Cornhill.

Once he felt it would be safe to do so without being seen, Thorne turned and watched as Scrooge continued down the street. Thorne's mind was racing. In fact, his mind was in torment where Scrooge was concerned. It had been since last month. *You may deceive others with that ersatz humanity, Ebenezer Scrooge, but I know what you're about and you'll not have my fortune, no matter how foolish I was. I'm wiser now than I was in 1822, and I will not sit back and let it happen.*

The truth was, Thorne was terrified. More than one businessman had been ruined by Scrooge because they hadn't understood his character. Unlike Thorne, they hadn't seen it coming, but Thorne knew he was better than those idiots. He had been forewarned and had already taken steps to preserve what was rightfully his. He would see to it that Scrooge did not get one penny, no matter how legal the claim!

CHAPTER THREE

Still ruminating on the successful business he and Marley had worked so hard to create, Scrooge walked east on Cornhill, turning left into his counting house. The offices faced the ancient tower of St. Michael's Church, directly across on Cornhill, and the Church's presence offered Scrooge a certain amount of comfort and stability.

It would be difficult for many to say, precisely, what Scrooge's business dealings were, and he had always preferred it that way. Some assumed he was a usurer, while others believed him to be an accountant for various tradesmen, which was certainly one of his main endeavors. Others swore he did nothing more than advise men of commerce on their buying and selling, and some said he speculated. He was not, in fact, a banker as such, although he had been known to make loans with a percentage of interest that was advantageous to him. Certainly, he owned properties and maintained interests in various industries and commodities, and it was those diverse streams of income that had not only made him and Marley wealthy, but had also made it difficult to be type-cast and undercut from the outside.

Jacob Marley and Ebenezer Scrooge formed a simple friendship during their youth because of their shared single-mindedness with regard to business. Their collaborations in making money began small enough, and gradually grew into an empire of diversified assets. They first learned their trade of accounting and the laws of commerce, but then began acquiring businesses, as well as acting as advisors to others and, of course, being well-paid for it. Much of Scrooge's time was spent at the Exchange in order to keep his finger on the pulse of trade and to conduct some of his own, and his clients', business.

Scrooge and Marley set up in the City, in modest offices that served them well and allowed them a certain amount of thrift. Besides, it also appeared less opulent, since they loathed spending money and wished to give the impression of a certain amount of penury. It kept expectations of strangers at a minimum, even though word of mouth certainly advertised their successes and, thereby, their value to those who wished to engage their services. Their philosophy had wholeheartedly been to acquire money – not to spend it – even on their own comforts or convenience.

The shingle over the door now read, "Scrooge & Symons." It had been surprisingly difficult for Scrooge to remove the old sign with Marley's name on it, however enthused he was about his nephew's joining him in partnership. Scrooge had also been startled by the sudden wrench of his heart the moment the sign was ripped from its hinges. The old symbol had hung since the partnership was formed and continued in place after Marley's passing, growing ever more worn and dingy with each change of season. In winter it would swing and creak, waving Marley's name about with each gust of wind, as if he were still in residence. It wasn't that Scrooge was, at the time, in any way melancholy regarding the loss of his partner, and it wasn't that he hoped to keep his memory alive by leaving his name on display. It was, instead, that it would cost several shillings to replace the sign, and in those days he would sooner mislead people as to Marley's state of being than part with a ha'pence to make the update. Ten months ago, however, he was glad, if a bit sad, to replace the shingle and advertise his close association with his beloved nephew Fred, who was, now, more like a son.

It hadn't always been so. Until last Christmas Scrooge and Fred might as well have been passing acquaintances, for all Scrooge allowed him a share of his life. Scrooge's sister Fan died shortly after giving birth to Fred in 1819, and Fred's father followed suit in 1822, succumbing to some illness Scrooge could not recall. It was too bad, but there it was. He had barely known the man and simply accepted his death at the time as something to be dealt with in the form of Fred. Even with that connection, Scrooge never allowed himself to become close to his nephew because, although he did not admit it even to himself, he blamed Fan's death on the boy's birth.

Since Scrooge had the responsibility of watching out for Fred, he placed him with a Mr. and Mrs. Barnes. They were a kindly couple and brought Fred up to emulate their good-heartedness and practical approach to things. Nor did Scrooge neglect the boy's education and status in life. When Fred was eight years old, Scrooge sent him to a fine public school, for which Fred basically paid his own way since Scrooge used funds from the boy's father's estate. The Barneses were paid off to the exact farthing and Scrooge never suspected they would have taken the boy for nothing. Fred eventually entered University, where he absorbed all that a bright, attentive and winsome young man could absorb, while taking as much pleasure as possible in his youth.

Visits between Scrooge and Fred were few and far between, yet Fred somehow held a warm opinion of his uncle, having had that opinion instilled in him by the Barneses. He saw Scrooge as his benefactor and was convinced, somehow, that he was there for him, if not as a constantly available confidant, at least as his nearest relative. Having inherited a great deal of his mother's disposition, Fred instinctively knew, too, that Scrooge was not as callous as he tried to appear. Fred was undoubtedly the only one in the world who might have managed to retain a kindly opinion of Scrooge in spite of his treatment of him.

oW̃o

The interior of the offices of Scrooge and Symons was of dark wood and the rooms were lit by lamps since the thin winter light was not enough by which to work figures. As if thumbing their noses at the weather's gloom, as well as belying their frugal history, cheery fires warmed the rooms' occupants and encouraged an ample portion of good will. Mrs. Dilber had arranged for an acquaintance of hers to keep the place clean and well-ordered so that all who worked or entered within could do so in comfort. The inhabitants of the office could even see outside, now that the panes of glass were cleared of years' accumulation of grime.

Considering the size of the business, Scrooge wondered if perhaps someday he and Fred should move their offices to a better part of The City. He did not particularly like the idea of vacating the old premises but it would certainly mean a better image for Fred and would give more room for their expanding staff. Meanwhile, they had opened up two more rooms within the building, which Scrooge owned. Bob Cratchit's oldest boy Peter had been brought on to serve as a clerk's assistant, to perform all sorts of necessary, albeit menial, tasks.

Already at their stations were the ever-faithful Bob Cratchit, loyal work-bones that he was, and his new clerk, Homer Probert, who was proving himself invaluable not only as an employee, but also as a hopeful suitor to Bob's oldest girl, Martha. Not much had come of it yet, but Homer was being quietly persistent and Martha seemed willing enough to receive his attentions, however cautious they might be.

Homer looked like the Welshman he was. He was above average in height, with almost black hair and eyes the color and depth of a storm at sea. Most would call him handsome, although it was his sense of humor, once he got past his initial shyness, that generally won people over. Scrooge and Fred agreed that a few years' growth would make him a contender in the field of finance and commerce. He had been in their employ for five months now and the partners planned to raise his pay this Christmas from twenty-five shillings a week, to thirty. It would be a decent living for a young man. Yes, his prospects were good and Homer hoped they might be good enough for Martha Cratchit.

Scrooge entered the outer office, the door's movement alerting others of his arrival. So engrossed was he in thoughts of the morning's business that he did not notice that the door's lock had been broken.

"Uncle!" cried Fred, leaping up from a nearby chair before Scrooge could remove even his hat. "Thank Heavens you're here!"

"A fine greeting, my boy, and I thank you for it, but what brings such eagerness?"

Fred began gesturing toward the back offices where many business documents were generally kept. The other staff members were unusually quiet, but their relief at Scrooge's appearance was palpable. They fully expected his presence to put things right and, suddenly, everyone began speaking at once.

"First thing this morning . . . came in and . . . Look at this Mr. Scrooge! . . . because it didn't seem there was anything amiss, but

. . . sure it was locked . . . then saw . . . broken. Last night . . . who would have thought . . !"

Unable to make one ounce of sense from the cacophony, Scrooge roared, "Oh, BLAST it all!" and, with his outburst, everyone froze. They had not heard him erupt in such a manner for eleven months now, but it did the trick and order was immediately restored.

"Now, then," said Scrooge, in a much lower voice. As if addressing a schoolroom of boys caught playing with a mouse, he said slowly, in order to keep both himself and them in check, "Fred, will you please do me the favor of telling me what has happened."

"Yes, Uncle," began Fred. "Homer came to the office first, as he often does when he is in the midst of a special endeavor." Fred had begun at the absolute beginning, which was unnecessary and imparted no new information.

"I did that," chimed Homer, "and saw the lock had been disturbed and I searched for any possible intruders, but found no one." It was difficult to tell if he was sorry, or relieved that he had not actually discovered anyone, and Scrooge was not much closer to knowing what, exactly, had or had not occurred.

"It was I who first noticed it, Mr. Scrooge," interposed Cratchit. "It was when I saw my own work station, and went to yours and Mr. Fred's desks to investigate. Then I noticed it there, also." Seeing Scrooge's frown and his fingers drumming impatiently on the hat he was now holding, Bob quickly continued.

"I saw that the cabinets had been rifled, as were your offices and our clerks' desks. Naturally none of us here had done such a thing! We never would." To emphasize his reaction to the discovery, he gave an offended sniff and added, "Things were extremely untidy."

"Broken in, you say?" asked Scrooge, his voice rising as he glanced about. At an even higher pitch, as well as a greater volume, he cried, "Are you actually saying that some thief bashed his way through this door and ran his villainous hands through our accounts?" He was incensed. He was stunned. He even felt somewhat vulnerable – an emotion with which he was not familiar. As if suddenly recalling what had earlier been said, he looked at the group and repeated, "You're sure nothing was taken?"

Four voices replied in unison, while heads nodded up and down and eyes searched each other's for confirmation.

"Then let's take a good look men, and see what we can find," said Scrooge, as he deposited his outer garments in preparation for making a diligent search.

Scrooge and Fred examined their offices carefully, asking each employee for specifics, and finally decided that, although a great number of papers had been chaotically tossed and rearranged, nothing had apparently been removed. The intruder had come in by breaking the latch and was evidently searching for something in particular, but since nothing was missing, it appeared he had not found it.

Bob had already made arrangements for the door latch to be repaired, but Scrooge was ready to take even further action. He called for Peter.

"Peter, fetch a ticket porter. I believe I saw Toby Veck hanging about in the street." Trotter, as everyone called Toby, was a small, spare old man, who had gone for years with leaky shoes and not so much as an overcoat, until, that is, Scrooge's character was regenerated and he furnished Toby with better clothing. Last January he had outfitted Toby warmly and he continued to keep an eye on the man, often overpaying him for errands and ensuring that he was protected against the elements through which he ran his dispatches.

Turning to Cratchit, Scrooge instructed, "Bob, pen a short note to the police regarding what has occurred and have Trotter deliver it to the local station."

It was quickly accomplished and Scrooge retreated for the time being to his office as if to re-check the site and stand guard against any further assaults. Toby was handed a slight excess of coins, bobbed his head in thanks and trotted off to deliver the summons for a policeman. On his way out, he crossed paths with Bob Cratchit's daughter, Martha. Toby backed up, gave a sincere bow and tipped his hat. She nodded back and sensed the earlier state of pandemonium as she crossed the threshold. She entered the offices very slowly, looking about as if to forestall a potential danger. Fred spotted her and noticed her wariness.

"Good morning, Martha," he said in his calming voice. "No, don't fret, we're all harmless here, we've just had a bit of excitement, that's all." He strode to the door and took her elbow to guide her into the offices. As he did so her father spotted her, stood, and responded with a beam of parental tenderness.

"Why, it's my dear Martha!" he exclaimed, bursting with pride as he made his way to her. "What brings you here at this hour, tell me."

Martha, who began life as a goose among swans, had, during adolescence, burst forth with a degree of beauty that surprised everyone. She still thought of herself as a grey goose, however, and was unaware of the metamorphosis, so she tended not to notice when strangers cast admiring glances her way. She did not realize they were wondering who she was and wishing they could make her acquaintance. In addition to her striking dark eyes and hair, she had a natural grace and poise that would have befitted a lady of a much higher class. She managed to charm everyone she met, simply because that was not her intent.

Martha handed her father a note. "It's a recipe from the physician, Father, and Mother says you're to get it tonight, for Tim, although she thinks he would now do quite well without it." It was true that sickly Tiny Tim Cratchit's progress had been remarkable during the past several months, but his parents and

Mr. Scrooge were taking no chances. His appetite had grown, so he was taking in good food, and he was also getting a great deal of fresh air and limited exercise, all while being monitored by the best physicians in London. The former was made possible by Bob's wages having been at least doubled, and the latter by Scrooge, himself.

Martha's full attention, however, was not on her father. A good portion of it was on Homer, and he was neglecting his quill and figures to return the favor. They eyed each other while making a feeble attempt at subtlety, which was missed by no one. Suddenly Homer dribbled an ink splotch on his ledger and moved quickly to absorb it with a blotter. Too shy to speak up, both simply tried not to stare, willing the other to speak first. Finally Fred took pity on them and stepped in.

"Martha, you simply cannot go back into the cold without something hot to drink. Rid yourself of that heavy cape and step this way so I may pour you a bit of tea. That should help steer your course to the shop in time to open for Mrs. Pearce."

Martha was recently employed by Mrs. Lucy Pearce, who maintained a millinery shop on the Strand near Milford Lane. Martha had previous millinery experience, so she was proving herself quite a capable assistant, and very pleasing to Mrs. Pearce's refined customers. The great hats of earlier fashion had, within the past several years, been replaced by bonnets, and both Martha and her employer had a natural flair for trimming them. Neither liked the lavishness that many shops were promoting and their restraint seemed to be paying off since ladies of refined taste were frequenting the shop more often. They were also the women whose husbands could afford to pay what the bonnets were worth, which, in turn, resulted in an adequate wage for Martha. None of that was on her mind at this moment, however, as she stood in the same room with Homer, both of them tongue-tied and awkward.

Recalling with gratitude all those who had assisted him in his courtship of Catherine, Fred decided to play Eros and invited the others to join them in drinking some of the new Indian Assam tea.

"Miss Cratchit," said Homer finally, shyly meeting her eyes, "How nice to see you." Fred passed Homer a cup of tea, which Homer then handed to Martha.

"Thank you, Mr. Probert," said Martha, timidly aiming some of her appreciation at the wall behind his shoulder. Finally forcing herself to meet his eyes, she said, "I see you are busy. Are you feeling quite at home in your position?"

"Hah!" laughed her father, before Homer could reply. "He's so much at home he rarely puts down his figures." Poking him gently in the arm, Cratchit said, playfully, "Homer, here, pinches his quill at the same angle for hours on end, never noticing the movement of the clock. We tell him to take care, lest he wind up with Scrivener's Palsy, but we are wasting our breath. He appears not to hear us, so engrossed is he in his endeavors." Then he added, more kindly, patting Homer's shoulder, "Never you mind boy, it's only a bit of fun. Your habits do you credit."

Homer shifted uneasily and began to fidget with his inkwell. He wanted to say something clever but was forestalled when he noticed a stranger standing in the doorway, his head near bumping the top lintel. Soon all eyes had followed Homer's gaze and were fixed on a fellow who appeared to be a full two metres tall, with hair the color of autumn wheat. He resembled a Norse god and was obviously not there on financial business since he was reading from the note earlier penned by Bob Cratchit.

"I believe I am here at the request of a Mister Ebenezer Scrooge," he said in a more assured voice than was usually displayed in a person of his youth. "I am Rollo Norris of the City of London Police and I understand you have had a break-in to these premises."

Scrooge was fetched, introduced himself, and led the constable to the offices where most of the intruder's searches had taken place. He pointed out things that had been disturbed and assured the policeman that nothing had apparently been taken.

"Do you have any idea who might have done this Sir, or what, in particular they were seeking?" asked Norris.

"I'm afraid not," replied Scrooge. "That is indeed an unknown, but one I take very personally. Unfortunately, I doubt you can find a meaningful trail from this disarray and we can certainly provide few clues at this point." Almost as a warning, he added, "However, Constable, I am certain that a bit of nosing around and applying some clear thought to this matter will reveal a great deal more."

In spite of what appeared to be a dead end, Constable Norris took notes with his pencil. He was nothing, if not determined. After he finished scribbling they walked back to the front office, where the others stood waiting for whatever account each might have to give.

Scrooge reiterated, "I want to see our man captured, Constable, even though we have not parted with any property. Naturally we will assist in following up on this matter, and I expect to be kept abreast of anything you may learn. I'm certain a goodly exchange of information is the mainstay of a proper investigation." With that admonition he glanced at everyone and made cursory introductions of Rollo to Fred, Bob Cratchit, Homer, Peter and Martha Cratchit. Although it was fairly obvious to the men, Martha had no idea that Rollo took one look at her and promptly forgot his mission. The break-in could solve itself, for all he cared. His only concern was this exquisite creature standing before him.

"I believe I will need all of your names and directions, if you don't mind," he said, starting with Fred and ending with Martha Cratchit. In the confusion of the morning it did not occur to anyone that Martha was not a witness to anything. With that,

Norris said he would take his leave and let them get on with their business. He was sorry, but with so little information, it was unlikely that the intruder could be identified, although he would keep his eyes and ears open.

"I must be going, too, Father," said Martha, "if I'm to be at Mrs. Pearce's on time." She bade them all a pleasant good-bye, and started for the door.

"Excuse me, Miss Cratchit," interjected Constable Norris. "If you will allow me, I am going myself, and would be happy to see you to your destination." She was surprised, yet not displeased, and he pressed his case. "It is not out of my way, I assure you, and you would be doing me an honor."

Martha glanced quickly at her father, who gave a hesitant nod of permission, and she accepted the offer, smiling somewhat self-consciously. He stretched his arm toward the door and escorted her out, leaving each man unwilling to look in Homer's direction. It was just as well, because Homer was glaring darts. Although he said nothing, his thoughts toward the City of London Police Force were extremely unkind.

CHAPTER FOUR

Fred stood before Scrooge's desk, a thoughtful look on his face. The uproar of the morning had been quelled and he stood, waiting for a break in Scrooge's concentration. Scrooge sensed his presence and looked up. "What is it, Fred?"

"I've been thinking, Uncle. We have an intruder who searches our papers, does not steal anything of value, and does not take anything from the stacks in which he searches. It puts me in mind of something that happened only last week. I didn't mention it because it seemed unimportant, but now I begin to wonder." Scrooge was intrigued.

"Go on Fred. Perhaps we can put two and two together and deduce a sum of our own, since our policeman has evidently gone a-courting."

"So it seems," said Fred, smiling as he sat in a chair facing Scrooge's desk. "The other night Catherine's lap dog raised a ruckus and we simply could not shush him. I found the creature at the door of my study, yapping his fool head off and he would not obey my orders to stop. Then I heard a sound inside the study, so I burst in and found a window standing wide open, through which an intruder had evidently entered and quickly departed when the dog and I made such a noise. I don't know if there is a connection, but it now seems too much of a coincidence. In that instance, only my papers had been disrupted, but nothing taken. I assumed it was a simple house-breaking – a burglary that was interrupted by all that barking, for which the dog received treats from Catherine, I should add." Tracing his chin with his index finger, he said, "I have to wonder if the two incidents are not, in fact, connected."

Scrooge had been listening with growing interest and slapped his palm on his desk. "They are! They must be, and we cannot simply sit by and let it go unnoticed. Something sinister is afoot, my boy, and I believe these break-ins hint at a very real threat to our business." Pursing his lips in concentration, he said, "We must study this thing to the most insignificant detail, for we may ignore it to our detriment." He then glanced around, as if some piece of evidence might leap off the shelves into his lap, and added, more thoughtfully, "But where to start, my boy – where to start?"

"At the beginning, I assume," replied Fred, looking baffled, "if we only knew where that may be, in this tangle!"

"I have an idea," said Scrooge. "The beginning may be right here within reach, and we haven't noticed it. Follow me, my boy."

With Fred shadowing Scrooge, both headed toward Homer's desk. Homer looked up to see them charging toward him and jumped off his stool, trying to contain the fear that descends upon the newly hired in such a situation. Had he made one mistake too many? Should he not have eyed Martha Cratchit? Heaven knew he'd tried not to, but in her presence he became as wobbly as a spoonful of pickle. Instead of cowering, however, he stood bravely before his employers and asked, "Yes, Mr. Scrooge? Mr. Symons? Is there something you wish of me?" *Please God, it isn't my back side!*

"Yes, Homer, there is," replied Scrooge. "I have a task for you. I want you to put down whatever figures you are working on." Motioning with his right arm, he called, "Cratchit, my good man, take over anything urgent here! Homer, you are to do a little sleuthing."

Homer's countenance lit up like one of those new gas street lamps dotting the main thoroughfares. He was to investigate? Standing up straighter, he said, "Yes, Mr. Scrooge. I am happy to be of service, Sir! Where would you be sending me, then? Am I to speak to someone, in particular, or to follow a villain surreptitiously? I'm sure I am up to the task, Sir!"

"No, Homer," replied Scrooge, containing the smile that threatened. "Nothing that daring, I assure you." Rather than relief, Homer's face registered disappointment, but neither Scrooge nor Fred paid noticeable heed. It wouldn't do to embarrass the lad.

"Homer, I am going to assume the issues surrounding this burglary are of fairly recent origin, since they have only just occurred, so I want you to spend some time going through the counting house. In particular, go through my office and Mr. Symons' office, but do not neglect anything on which you and Cratchit may be currently working. Right now we have no motive for these burglaries, so go through every contract and every note we have penned for at least the past six months. If you have time, go back further." To Homer's puzzled expression Scrooge said, "I'm sorry, Homer, I am unable to give you more detailed instruction because I do not know what you are seeking. Only look for anything unusual. Look for patterns. Look for something that could be potentially damaging to someone, or to us."

Almost to himself he said, "I suppose we could assume it is not among the papers that the thief has gone through, but let's not omit those, either. He may have simply missed it in his haste. Just keep an eye out for any peculiar bit of information or circumstance that may point to our man, or to what he is seeking. I know it won't be easy and we may have no discoveries for our efforts, but we must make the attempt."

Homer thought the term "we" a bit overstated, since he would be the only one to undertake the task, but he was up to it. He would do his best. If there was so much as a wisp of treachery within these walls, he would unearth it!

∿

Monday, November 18, 1844

By Monday Homer was proving his diligence. He was working his way through the office, noting dates, contents and signatures. So far he had uncovered unimportant fragments of business that had been ignored or forgotten, and unearthed a contract that had been re-written because it was lost. He emptied shelves, searched files and cabinets, giving an occasional sneeze while waving bits of disturbed dust from before his face. With permission, of course, he also inventoried desks. He was assessing the contents of Fred's desk, the one that had been Marley's for so many years, and opened a drawer to itemize the contents. As he did so he noticed that the interior of the drawer was shorter than the depth of the desk, which usually suggested a hidden compartment. Feeling around, he located the trip, but held off. He would ask first. Fred was in Scrooge's office, discussing a contract, so Homer approached and stood in the doorway, waiting for a lull in the conversation. Eventually it came.

"If you'll excuse me, Mr. Symons," he said, as he shifted uncomfortably in his stance, "there is something you need to see, Sir, unless, of course, you are already aware of it, in which case, naturally, I will simply let it be because, you understand, I

32

wouldn't want to do anything that would be, or might be construed as . . ."

"What is it you are going on about, Homer?" interrupted Fred, puzzled. "Is there a problem?"

"Not a problem, no, Sir, but I have found a concealed compartment in your desk and I musn't look where I shouldn't, nor do I want to shirk my duty and not make a thorough search of things."

"A hidden compartment, you say? Well, let's have a look."

Homer showed Fred how to trip the access, allowing Fred to explore the contents. Fred felt around inside, his fingers eventually touching the edge of a piece of paper that was crumpled between the drawer and the side of the desk. He gingerly worked it back and forth, pulling carefully, until it came out.

"What have we here," he said, as he withdrew it. After reading the first line he re-folded it and said, "I'll take this, Homer, and you may continue your endeavors. Thank you for fetching me." He was grateful that Homer could keep a rein on his natural curiosity, as well as his tongue. Such discretion made an employee extremely valuable.

Fred took the letter to Scrooge. Handing it to him, he said, "We discovered this in Marley's old desk. I think you should be the one to read it and decide its final destination, whether it be to the archives, or the dustbin."

"It's in your mother's hand," Scrooge blurted without thinking. He recognized her handwriting before he realized it was addressed to Jacob Marley. *Fan wrote to Marley?* Marley was certainly well acquainted with her because of his close association with Scrooge. Well, perhaps that was it. Marley had no doubt taken care of something for her that was related to business.

"Thank you, Fred. I will read it and, as you say, decide its fate." Fred took the statement as a dismissal, which was exactly what Scrooge had intended. As Fred turned to his own office Scrooge unfolded the letter.

25 August 1818
My Steadfast Friend Jacob,

I write to you because I trust you and because I do not want to alarm my brother. He is currently so preoccupied with that canal shipment debacle that he can well do without his sister's imaginings, which is what I pray they are. I also trust you to take a bit of time to digest what I am saying, whereas Ebenezer might react without considering all, since we are so closely related and he has always been my stalwart guardian protector.

I believe you know I am not of a suspicious nature, yet I sense a threat from one in my company. It is in the things he says, and in his behavior toward me, which is, at best, irregular and occasionally somewhat aggressive. Jacob, he frightens me.

If you will do me the favor of hearing me out I will confide in you the specifics. I rely on your wisdom, as I do with my brother's. I also ask that you destroy my correspondence on this subject. Rest assured that I will also . . .

Here the letter ended, at the bottom of the back page, with no signature, as if the remaining pages had gone missing. It must be assumed that Marley placed the entire letter, or letters, in the compartment for safe keeping and inadvertently left the one page caught in the drawer when he disposed of the rest.

Someone had threatened Fan? Absurd! Yet she evidently believed it to be so. Scrooge would never know what advice Marley had given her, or if she had even followed through with the details she promised to furnish. Perhaps he never replied to her, but of that Scrooge was doubtful. The businessman in Marley would not let correspondence go unanswered, and he was, after all, like a second brother to Fan and would be concerned for her welfare. Still, if she really were afraid, why hadn't Marley said something to Scrooge?

Trying to apply reason to his racing thoughts, Scrooge decided it was most likely because Fan had not wanted him to. Marley could be tight-lipped when necessary, and he would have honored her request not to bother Scrooge, particularly if he became convinced she was not in danger. Fan was not whimsical, nor cowardly, but her lack of exposure to the greater world might lead her to misinterpret a statement or an action.

Still, Marley should have said something about the incident after she died, and named the person by whom she felt threatened. No, he wouldn't. He would have said nothing because he would not want to distress Scrooge with the fact that his sister hadn't confided in him, even though she was simply trying not to be a bother. In point of fact, he and Marley had not discussed Fan after her death unless it was absolutely necessary, such as when dealing with Fred's estate. Scrooge had not been able to bring himself to mention her name and Marley had honored that practice. That was, no doubt, another reason why Marley never said anything.

Nevertheless, no matter how he tried to explain things away, Scrooge was unsettled as he tucked the letter into his coat pocket. He would most likely dispose of it in due course, but not now. Not yet, although he couldn't have said why.

CHAPTER FIVE

Wednesday Evening, November 20, 1844

The following Wednesday found Scrooge entering the Wilkins home in Finsbury Circus. The houses were not new, but they were tall and attractive, having been designed by George Dance the Younger and built by William Montague in the earlier part of the Century. The houses surrounded an open area and the Wilkinses had been very pleased to acquire one.

Since the early winter dark set in hours ago, Scrooge crossed the street as carefully as possible, hoping to miss any dung from the carriage horses. As dark as it was outside, however, the house inside was well-lit with mirror-backed sconces holding candles of high grade, and even some gas lamps. Enormous ceiling chandeliers cast a warm, welcoming glow. Scrooge knew from experience that the party would last for hours and nothing would be lacking in terms of music and refreshment. He also knew the company would be a good mix of the upper middle class, some who were perhaps a bit higher up, and he would no doubt feel at home.

During this past year Scrooge's more genial nature had surprised not only himself, but also those of his acquaintance. As a result, his circle of friends quickly expanded. He was actually sought after as a pleasant and witty companion and, with a little polish on his once rusty social skills, Scrooge often found himself the life of the party, not only as a conversationalist, but also as a dancer. Fred's wife Catherine had seen to that, in spite of Scrooge's initial reticence.

The day she took it into her head to hone his dancing skills Scrooge tried to dig in his heels by pleading, "You are too kind, but I do not think . . ." He had literally backed away from her, sat down and attempted to put her off by simply being stubborn. He was not about to bound around the room like a young sheep, and that was that. As she approached him he bleated, "I'm not at all certain about this," but she had persisted. She did not seem to care a whit that he would be making a clumsy fool of himself. No, she would not be dissuaded, no matter the cost to his pride.

Grabbing his hand, she insisted, "Uncle Ebenezer, you are as graceful as any of those old hoodwinks who tramp around ballrooms, pretending to offer their partners acceptable entertainment. Yes," she said with determination, "you are, and I will prove it to you. Now, stand up with me, Uncle, and do your duty!" Pulling him up, she waved her hand toward her sister, who sat at the piano, and cried, "Flora! MU-sic!"

Over a period of several evenings, with Flora accompanying them, Catherine good-naturedly reacquainted Scrooge with some of the older movements, then the newer square dances, and they progressed from there. Before long he was feeling the freedom and enjoyment he had last experienced on the dance floor at old Fezziwig's, albeit these days his exuberance was governed by his somewhat less limber joints. The odd creakiness hadn't held him back though, and Catherine showed surprise as she cried, "Why, Uncle, you're as light as a feather on those ancient pins of yours!" They whirled about the floor, easily keeping tempo with the music and falling into chairs at the end of each lesson. Catherine would briskly fan herself as they laughed like delighted children who had just managed to pull off a great prank. The cost of his lessons had been minimal since only one lamp was broken when Catherine's skirt flew out on a turn and knocked it off its stand. She was right, by thunder, he could dance!

Now, thanks to Catherine, partners abounded when musicians struck up a jig, one of Strauss' waltzes, or even the new polka, which Scrooge found he enjoyed immensely and had mastered rather quickly. He rubbed his hands in anticipation as he considered that tonight he might just give his lazy knees another good workout!

Scrooge entered the Wilkins foyer and a manservant received his coat and hat before leaving him to be greeted heartily by his old friend Dick.

Shaking his hand and patting him on the back, Wilkins cried, "Ebenezer Scrooge! How good it is to see you, you old scoundrel!"

"Scoundrel, indeed!" replied Scrooge, laughing. Tapping his friend on the chest, he said, "I well recall which of us was the prankster – such as that time Fezziwig's account books were all mysteriously shelved upside-down and backwards!" At Dick's meaningful expression he added, "I knew nothing about it, of course!" They chuckled congenially, sharing the past as only friends of long-standing can do.

Pulling Scrooge slightly aside, Wilkins grew serious. In a low voice, his hand still on Scrooge's arm, he said, "Bad thing, that burglary of your offices, but I hear nothing of grand proportions was taken. Any idea what it was about, or who did it?"

"None at all," Scrooge replied, "But I've pulled in a constable from the police, although the young fellow they've sent us seems to be more interested in Cratchit's daughter than in bringing my burglar to justice." An idea suddenly occurred to Scrooge and he said, "I wonder, Dick, if perhaps you might stop by in the next few days to talk this thing over. You always did have a quick mind. Perhaps you could offer a few observations and more practical ideas than those of us who are so close to the problem. Meanwhile, keep your ears open as you move within the circles of commerce, would you?" Dick said he certainly would and they strolled up to the withdrawing room. Half way up, Scrooge asked, "How did you hear of our break-in, by the way?"

"Oh, word gets 'round, you know," replied Wilkins offhandedly as they reached the landing and were interrupted by his wife, Priscilla.

"Ebenezer, my dear," said Priscilla, using his first name as they had both done for several months now. "How glad I am to see you!" She had sincerely come to think of Scrooge as her friend, too. She enjoyed his cheerful manner and it also made her a better hostess, the more eligible men she could furnish at her gatherings.

"It is always a pleasure to be in your company, Priscilla," replied Scrooge. "I have wondered for some time now how Dick found you, and wondered even more how he convinced you to marry him. It is one puzzling knot I have not yet untangled, although it is clear who has the better share of the bargain."

Laughing, she said, "You continue to tease me, Ebenezer, and I'm delighted to be your subject. I am also very pleased you could join us." Then, before giving him time to make his way elsewhere, she fulfilled his worst fears by saying, rather too conspiratorially, "I know someone in particular who will be very glad to visit with you. In fact, here she is now." Horrified, he watched helplessly as Priscilla beckoned to her friend, Honora Purdy. Mrs. Purdy, all smiles, approached them as if primed to immediately break into a series of whoops. Near panic, it was all he could do not to plead sudden dyspepsia and flee the house outright. Had Mrs. Purdy been slightly more astute, she would have recognized his expression as one of terror, rather than delight.

"Mr. Scrooge!" she exclaimed before inexplicably, yet predictably, breaking into laughter. "My dear sir! Ha, ha-HAH! Why, we haven't seen each other for ages, you naughty man, and you know how I like to tease you, as if you can resist such jollity!" She began tapping his forearm with her fan and continued, "No, no, don't deny it, you devious man. You enjoy a little humorous provocation, and you are certainly witty enough to give some of my own back, eh?"

Thankfully, Scrooge did not need to reply because, with that, she launched into a series of brays that had several people within range turning to stare. They quickly recognized who was sounding off like a wild donkey and accepted the outburst as her usual comportment. Mrs. Wilkins smiled as if all were as it should be and excused herself to see to her other guests. That left Scrooge alone with only his wits to fend off the effusive Mrs. Purdy, but they, too, had deserted him. He could think of nothing to say that would not be dismissive or dim-witted. His former self would not have listened to the frightful woman for two seconds and would have had no qualms about rudely ridding himself of her obnoxious presence. Fortunately, these days he was made of better stuff and would find a more polite way to extricate himself from her dreadful glee. He would even attempt to manage it without hurting her feelings, which surely must be buried somewhere beneath that rather thick equine skin of hers.

"Mrs. Purdy," bowed Scrooge, "I see you are in good health and equally good humor." His remarks sounded as colorless as his feelings toward her, but there it was. He could think of nothing else to say and wondered how long he could manage a pointless conversation. Perhaps, if he asked her to dance, there would be less need to converse, but he envisioned Mrs. Purdy galloping around the floor and swallowed the urge to suggest such a thing. There was a limit to what even a renewed character could tolerate, and Honora Purdy was definitely beyond those limits!

As if on cue, his escape was suddenly made possible. Owen Purtell-Smythe, a client of Scrooge's, motioned to him from a few feet away. He was standing in a cluster of businessmen and investors and was anxious to include Scrooge in their conversation, no doubt to obtain his opinion on some matter, or other.

Trying rather unsuccessfully to conceal his enormous relief, Scrooge bowed again and said, "I hope you will forgive me, Mrs. Purdy, but I am being beckoned by an associate with whom I must pass some time and exchange needed information." Continuing before she could give even a quick whinny, he added, "I will deliver you to your friends, if you will point me in the right direction." She assented, but with obvious regret.

"Naturally you must accommodate him, Mr. Scrooge, although I am not pleased to part with you." With that she let out a short wheeze, which Scrooge took as an attempt at mirth, and he quickly and efficiently deposited her to a circle of her acquaintances.

Bowing, he said, "I leave you in good hands, then," as the entire group openly scrutinized him. To anyone else he would have suggested they might continue their conversation at another time, or enjoy a dance later, but his instincts told him Mrs. Purdy would consider it a promise – a binding contract – rather than a mere possibility.

As he made his way gratefully to the group of men he thought, *Priscilla Wilkins, what in the world are you thinking by trying to pair me with that . . . that . . . hoyden?*

"Ho, there, Scrooge!" The men greeted him in unison, all smiles. Two of them slapped him on the back as he laughed and said to no one in particular, "What a group this is! Have you, together, solved the question of the regulation of currency yet?"

"Not in its entirety," laughed one of them before adding, "but you're just the man we want to talk to." Before anyone could fill him in on the issue of their debate, Purtell-Smythe muttered privately, "Thought you might require a bit of fresh air, man – with a little less hilarity, perhaps?" Scrooge replied simply, "Yes, for certain, but I shall refrain from announcing my feelings about the lady, at least in this unsympathetic assembly." To the group he gave a noncommittal smile, said, "I will gladly add my shilling's worth of knowledge," and entered easily into the discussion. Within a quarter of an hour, the cluster was broken up as wives drew their husbands away for various tasks such as dancing, fetching drinks and gossip, and Scrooge found himself comfortably ensconced in Dick's library with Purtell-Smythe.

"Here, my good fellow," said Purtell-Smythe. "Try one of these Cuban segars. I picked them up from Lewis' shop in St. James Street and I think they're pretty fine, if I'm not bragging by saying so."

"It is not bragging to state a truth, and I thank you, Owen," said Scrooge. He took the segar, then rolled it between his fingers before placing it below his nose, to inhale the fragrance of the tobacco. "In fact, I accept it with anticipation." Placing it in his coat pocket he apologized, "But I will decline to smoke it at the moment, for I suspect we will not be allowed to complete the entire thing without interruption. You go ahead, though. You may be lucky enough to burn it to total ash before being deprived of its pleasure."

"We'll see," said Purtell-Smythe before he lit his segar with a lucifer match. Both men relaxed, inhaling the aroma in satisfied sighs. Scrooge sat in one of the leather-bound chairs and leaned back, listening to the distant music and tapping his foot.

Blowing smoke to the side, Purtell-Smythe remarked, "You should be dancing, my friend. That left toe of yours is telling me you want to be leading a lady through her paces, showing off your mastery of the latest steps." Before Scrooge could answer, a reply came from the doorway. It was a woman's voice, and one Scrooge did not recognize.

"Yes, you both should do, since the ladies outnumber the men and many a mother is surveying the room for possible partners, to place her eligible daughter on display. You do not fulfill your duty at these gatherings if you don't dance to these matrons' tunes. Someone must keep their offspring near to swooning for having pranced around more than is good for them!" With humor in her voice, she added, "I simply cannot comprehend why you would prefer your solitude and segars to such a task!"

The men had turned to see who was speaking so freely.

"Ah!" said Purtell-Smythe, as both he and Scrooge stood. "Rebecca, my dear, I should have surmised you would have a scathing opinion of our leisure. You have found our hideaway!"

The woman gracefully approached them as she replied in a playful voice that was somewhat low-pitched for someone of such delicacy, "It is much worse than that, Owen. Your long-suffering wife has sent me to fetch you for the next waltz, for she will not sit out one more, and has refused all offers to dance with anyone else, particularly poor old Major Ponder, who is at least one hundred and cannot move his feet beyond a shuffle. In short, Sir, she requires your presence."

Purtell-Smythe and Scrooge both laughed. Nodding surrender, Purtell-Smythe gestured to Scrooge and said, "Mrs. Langstone, may I present Ebenezer Scrooge, a business acquaintance and, I should hope, a true friend." With regret he snuffed his partially-smoked segar in the ashtray at hand, and added, to Scrooge, "Rebecca's late husband was a close associate of mine and we also happen to be first cousins."

Scrooge was trying hard to conceal the fact that he was stunned – quite pleasantly – by this delightful stranger. Without seeming to do so, he formed a very favorable assessment.

Rebecca Langstone was of middle age, yet her demeanor suggested a timeless vigor and enthusiasm. She was of medium height and, by all accounts, esteemed very attractive, with flawless skin, dark hair set off by unusually deep blue eyes, and the figure of a woman twenty years younger. Although he could not know it, she was a desirable guest at any gathering because of her exquisite manners, good conversation and general popularity. More than one widower had sought her hand and been rejected either because she believed it was mostly her late husband's wealth he truly loved, or simply because she found he had no sense of humor and held too narrow a view of life to take up the remainder of hers.

Following the introduction, Mrs. Langstone extended her hand and looked Scrooge in the eye with a directness that might have seemed rude from someone less sincerely candid. She said, warmly, "Ebenezer Scrooge? Why, yes – of course. Mr. Scrooge and I have previously been introduced, but it was years ago and I am certain he does not recall the occasion. It was when I was visiting your late, dear sister, Mr. Scrooge, who was my intimate friend from the time we were girls."

Fan!

Scrooge took Rebecca's hand, bowing over it, and felt that old emptiness in his chest. Here was someone who knew his sister. Coming upright he thought, yes, she would have been about her age and would, indeed, have been her friend, from the unaffectedness he witnessed in only a few moments of acquaintance. Perhaps Fan did mention her, but he couldn't recall the name or the face. *Naturally*, he thought, *we both look different now,* and Langstone would be her married surname. He resisted the urge to enquire as to her maiden name, feeling that would somehow exacerbate the insult of not remembering her.

"Mrs. Langstone," said Scrooge. "I am extremely pleased to meet you a second time, and am even more pleased that you knew my sister. There are now so few of my acquaintance who knew her well, including my nephew – who knew his mother not at all." It surprised him that he was willing to actually discuss Fan, and he shocked himself even more by continuing with, "My sister was a wonderful person, Mrs. Langstone, as I'm sure you know, since you were so closely connected with her."

Scrooge had, for years, studiously avoided any mention of his sister's name, even with his nephew, and now, here he was, for the second time in days, being forced to look at the past. So bereft had he been when she died, that to think of her brought on paroxysms of despair. This conversation was unusual for him indeed, but the entire year had been filled with extreme modifications in his habits and he found he was not only enduring, but even enjoying this exchange very much.

In fact, Mrs. Langstone reminded him of Fan – not in appearance, but in her apparent genuineness and her spontaneity. Perhaps it was also her ability to connect with others at the very point of introduction and to appear truly interested in all things about them. For whatever reason, he found himself easily responding. As they talked about the party and a few bits of recent news, the three of them drifted back toward the crowd, remaining together until the Purtell-Smythes were engaged in the next dance. Scrooge and Mrs. Langstone continued to converse.

"I hope you will not be offended, Mr. Scrooge, but after meeting you the first time, when I was just a girl, I remarked to Fan what a very serious young man you were. It struck me as odd that you seemed so stern when you had so few years behind you." Scrooge gave a mock expression of fault, then smiled and said, "I can assure you, had I known I would be called to account so many decades later, I would have been better behaved!"

Mrs. Langstone laughed before explaining, "I was not offended. Fan said to pay your manner no mind, since that was your 'business face' and had nothing to do with your true character.

I see, meeting you again tonight, that she was correct. You have nothing of that bearing about you, at all."

"I am not affronted by your appraisals of my character, I assure you," replied Scrooge, chuckling a bit. "In fact, it confirms a change – the depth of which you cannot imagine – that I have undergone since last Christmas. I no longer take myself so seriously and I certainly no longer bow to the silver god of Commerce, which I am certain I was doing when we first met. These days I enjoy the company of others, and I am doing so tonight, to a very great degree."

. Mrs. Langstone smiled, the expression enhancing her natural beauty. "Yes, Fan was correct in her assessment of your finer, hidden character." With a small sigh she said, "I still miss her. It was so sad, the way she left us, and so very unexpected. I am still perplexed by her death." With that statement she noticed Scrooge's expression of surprise. It was also an expression that suggested she had struck an alarming note, and she made a quick decision.

"Mr. Scrooge," she said with some hesitancy, "please, do not misinterpret my meaning, and I do not want to seem ill-mannered, but might I have a word with you – in private? Might we perhaps return to the library for a few moments? I promise you I will not intrude on your time for long, but there is something I feel I must share with you."

CHAPTER SIX

Scrooge was uneasy, although he could not have said why. Nevertheless, he ushered Mrs. Langstone back to Wilkins' library, closed the door most of the way and saw her seated before seating himself. She seemed suddenly disconcerted as she absently fingered her necklace. Then, with determination, she began.

"Mr. Scrooge, I apologize for what I am about to say, but now that we are met, there is a subject I must broach. Not to do so would be negligent and I would feel I had not done my best by Fan or you, nor followed through as I should."

"I am all attention, Mrs. Langstone." By now Scrooge was truly apprehensive.

"It is fortuitous that we have met, for not more than two weeks ago I was discussing Fan with her former lady's maid, Sarah Braham, who is now Mrs. Reynolds. It was an extraordinary meeting, I must say, and with your permission I will share the substance of the exchange, although I believe it will prove upsetting."

"Upsetting to me, Mrs. Langstone, or to you? I don't want to impose on you if you will find it disturbing to recount, but if it's something I should know, please don't withhold it out of concern for my feelings. I assure you they are not in the least fragile."

"It is upsetting to me, Mr. Scrooge, because it concerns my dear friend, and it will most likely prove upsetting to you because she was your sister, and because of the subject, itself. However, if you are the man Fan believed you to be, you would insist on knowing and I see no reason to put off this conversation for a more convenient time." He was now fully attentive. Hoping she wasn't making a mistake, she set her hands in her lap, wet her lips, and continued.

"On Thursday two weeks ago I was in the morning room when Simms announced a Mrs. Reynolds who, I was told, had been lady's maid to my former friend, Mrs. Symons. Naturally I remembered her, and I received her gladly."

"You say she was Fan's personal maid?"

"Yes. Sarah. You may recall her. I saw her often when I was in Fan's company. She married quite soon after Fan's death, mostly out of despair I would imagine, and emigrated to Nova Scotia with her new husband. That was the last I knew of her so I was surprised when she called on me. She remembered my unmarried name, as well as my mother's situation, and applied to her for my direction. She then came directly to my home, before my mother could alert me regarding her intended visit.

"In short, Mr. Scrooge, Mrs. Reynolds asked what, if anything, had come of Fan's death. She wondered if anyone had ever been brought to justice."

Scrooge straightened. "To justice, Mrs. Langstone? She asked if anyone had been 'brought to justice?' Please tell me how that would apply in Fan's case?"

"Mrs. Reynolds believed then, and has believed all these years, that Fan was poisoned."

"What?" snapped Scrooge, before he could stop himself. "What is this you're saying? I have never heard such a wild report! She was suggesting that someone purposely killed Fan?"

Mrs. Langstone knew she had been blunt, but sensed that Scrooge would not appreciate a hide and seek approach, so she ventured to add, "I was actually not surprised by her suspicions since I had harbored my own, immediately following Fan's death."

Scrooge's mind was reeling. It was almost too much to take in and didn't entirely "add up" in his business mind. He looked at her accusingly.

"But, Mrs. Langstone, if you suspected such a thing at the time, why did you not pursue it? Why did you not at least inform me of your thoughts?"

Without defense, Mrs. Langstone replied, "I did pursue them, Mr. Scrooge, and the outcome laid them to rest, so there was no reason to trouble you. I spoke with both the doctor and the nurse, and was reassured that Fan had, indeed, died of a severe digestive ailment, and that the suggestion of anything else was nothing less than irresponsible. Dr. Devitt also reminded me that to make such a tenuous suggestion would not only harm the family, it would be quickly proven unfounded since both he and Nurse Weekes could attest to the facts as recorded upon her death. I was in no position to prove otherwise, and had no choice but to bow to their medical expertise. Had I even doubted it, which I did not by then, I would have been ineffective in bringing such a charge in the face of their testimony." Scrooge was obviously astonished and sat waiting, almost agape, since it was apparent she had more to relate.

"My fears were assuaged by their assurances, but my recent conversation with Mrs. Reynolds has re-awakened them. To discover, even so long after the fact, that someone else had shared my misgivings made me believe I had not, perhaps, been imagining things after all. I must also assume it is Providential that you and I meet again so soon after Mrs. Reynolds' disclosures, for I had not yet convinced myself that it would be proper to seek you out and share such startling suggestions with you, particularly since there would be nothing anyone could do about it."

Scrooge had stood and was pacing the room, running his hand through his hair. "I must speak with this Mrs. Reynolds," he said, agitated, "if you will be kind enough to give me her direction."

"Naturally," she replied. "I do not have it with me, of course, but if you will call on me in Russell Square, I will give it to you."

Scrooge stood beside his chair. "I admit to you, Mrs. Langstone, that I am completely stunned. Your claims are extraordinary and the account is, by itself, enough to set me to some sort of action – I know not what – but there is more to this than you know. I count on your discretion when I tell you that your information comes on the heels of an old letter from Fan to my now deceased partner that I only recently discovered." Shaking his head as if he could not believe what he was saying, he explained, "She wrote in the summer of 1818 that she felt threatened, but it appears that Marley put the idea aside either before, or shortly after she died of what we all thought were complications from childbirth." Feeling suddenly unsteady, he said, "You have, with several sentences, destroyed years of beliefs and given credence to Fan's frightened letter to Marley. To think that it was penned so long ago and now presents such a staggering surprise so long after the fact."

Mrs. Langstone said, "I cannot imagine who would ever have threatened Fan. As far as someone actually harming her, it is unthinkable. I look back over those days and recall that Fan had quite recovered from Fred's arrival, which was not, by the way, a particularly difficult birth, and she was reveling in her role as new mother. Her friends and family were accommodating and she seemed extremely fit, although, as I said, she did have some days when she seemed quite downcast, even confused, but that certainly wouldn't be life-threatening. She then took on severe symptoms and, within one evening and the following day, left us forever."

Scrooge's fists were balled at his sides and he was unaware that he was breathing heavily through his nose.

Mrs. Langstone hesitated before asking, she hoped not impertinently, "Did Fan not correspond with you during that period of her life, and following Fred's birth? I'm certain, had she written, her letters would have given proof of her sound state of health, at least in body, following her delivery."

Scrooge nodded, trying to keep his balance as he fought the blood pounding in his ears. Indeed, she had written, and not only to him. She had written to Marley and she had been frightened of someone. He finally gulped air through his mouth and forced himself to answer as calmly as possible as he slowly sat back in his chair.

"Yes, Mrs. Langstone. I did receive letters from her, naturally, and the tone of them made me believe all was well. In fact, I cannot recall a statement in them that suggested anything amiss, so you can imagine how astounded I was at the time to hear of her sudden death."

Although he did not say so, he also knew he may have ignored hints of anything unusual because they would have required attention on his part. To himself he thought, *She did, more than once, ask me to visit her and to see my new nephew. The truth is, she very nearly begged me, but I was too preoccupied with business dealings to take leave of them and make the short trip. Instead, I put her off with written excuses that now seem sinfully shallow. Tonight, a lifetime later, I have suddenly discovered she may have been the victim of a crime I cannot ut-*

ter, even to myself. It is little wonder she wrote to Marley, and not to me, when she required authentic response.

Out loud, Scrooge admitted, "I did not converse with Fan in person between Fred's birth and her death. Yet I recall believing, through her correspondence, that she was in good spirits and she seemed well enough." Almost to himself, he said, "Perhaps she purposely kept her correspondence optimistic, to spare me worry." He had been so preoccupied with other matters that he never considered the incongruity of her good health and her sudden death. He continued ruminating aloud, feeling safe in doing so with this new, yet already trusted acquaintance.

"For all these years I have assumed Fan's death resulted from Fred's birth and had grieved accordingly, even to the extent of almost rejecting Fred outright. Anyone observing me would not have known I was suffering since my mood and treatment of others, including my new nephew, were, I am certain, no worse than usual." It was true. He had merely become more withdrawn and more intense in the details of his business, which required no emotional investment and certainly gave none in return. At the time he believed his exclusivity with commerce a safe and comfortable relationship, since the only person he truly loved was gone.

Continuing with that line of thought, he said, "It shames me to admit it, and it surprises me that I am doing so, but I allowed Fan's death, presumably from childbirth, to taint my relationship with my nephew and I was not nearly as attentive a godfather as I should have been." He smiled then and said, with obvious relief, "Thankfully, during the past year our fondness for each other has been nurtured and allowed to grow." They were both silent for a moment, until Mrs. Langstone spoke again.

"I wonder you weren't given the particulars of Fan's passing, but I do recollect, as you no doubt know, that her husband

Geoffrey withdrew immediately, even before she died, and refused to speak to anyone but his manservant. He would not even consult further with the doctor, so it does follow, I suppose, that you were not properly informed of the details of the event."

While Scrooge was lost in these new facts and how they aligned themselves with Fan's letter to Marley, Mrs. Langstone debated whether to add something about which she was unsure. Finally, as if choosing a tile on which to place a bet, she added, "As I have already implied, there was something deeply troubling her mind not long before she died. Perhaps she shared it with you, for she certainly would not tell it to me, although I did ask."

Scrooge's thoughts were a muddle and it showed in his tortured expression. "I knew of no aspect of Fan's existence that did not please her, as she had written to me on more than one occasion, stating she was particularly happy. Indeed, Fan assured me her husband, and her home, were just to her liking and even suggested, more than once, that I should find a good wife and settle down, too." Of course Fan knew of his broken engagement to Belle, but she would not broach that particular subject with him directly. She would never want to cause him pain.

Suddenly there was a commotion at the door as Dick Wilkins bounded into the room. "Oh! I beg your pardon," he exclaimed, drawing up short. He had not expected to find the library occupied and said, "I didn't realize anyone was here and only came in to retrieve something to show Purtell-Smythe. My apologies, I'll be as quick as possible."

"Do not concern yourself, Dick. We have simply been discussing a subject we did not wish to be overheard," said Scrooge. As Wilkins raised one eyebrow, he quickly corrected any assumptions Dick might be making.

"It is not what may appear, my friend. Our topic was of a sensitive nature and we required the ability to speak freely without lowering our voices since, by whispering, we would have made a loud show of ourselves." Looking at Mrs. Langstone for her agreement, and receiving it, he added, "We will, in fact, follow you out since our business for the time being is concluded." He knew Wilkins was curious, but was too much of a gentleman to pry. No doubt Scrooge would share some of this startling news with him at some point, but not tonight.

Wilkins grabbed a book from the shelf and quickly departed, with Scrooge and Mrs. Langstone following more slowly. Although neither realized it, they were not yet willing to part with each other, considering their shared revelations and the sudden bond it had forged.

A waltz began, providing the chance of a respite from their somber discussion. Without thinking long enough to talk himself out of the idea, Scrooge said, "Mrs. Langstone, since our minds are so stimulated, and since we are already on our feet, perhaps you would honor me with this dance." She quickly assented, took his arm, and they walked toward the other couples. They turned to face each other and, as he placed his hand on her waist, he felt years younger – almost giddy. He hesitated for only a second. *In for a penny, in for a pound,* he thought, and began to lead. She followed beautifully and together they moved flawlessly with the music, as if they had danced together for years. They refused to quit the floor for one more piece while dowagers on the sidelines looked down their envious noses, and men openly admired them. Scrooge's acquaintances nodded, winked and grinned knowingly as they gave each other an occasional jab with their elbows.

After they had enjoyed their second dance it was past eleven o'clock, and guests were drifting between the music, cards and supper. Even considering the tone of their earlier discussion, Scrooge was finding Mrs. Langstone's company extremely congenial, but he excused himself when another couple approached her. From there he wandered to the end of the room where tables were heavy with various foods and drink. There he stood, sipping a delicious punch made with Portuguese wine, which had been handed to him by a servant.

Somewhat removed from the social din, Scrooge had the chance to reflect on all that had been said. The conversation regarding Fan had been excruciating in its suggestion regarding her death. That possibility, with the overlaid truth of his past actions, created one of those moments he dreaded. They were the moments when he was forced to look at the man he had formerly been, with the honesty and heart of the man he was now. It was a private and a very shameful moment, but there was nothing he could do to change the past. Now the past, itself, had changed within the last two days. It was too appalling to consider, yet too appalling to ignore.

The room around him was alive with laughter and conversation, as well as the clinking of china, crystal and the silver utensils that were used for serving, but Scrooge had mentally departed from his congenial company. He was no longer of any use to Dick and Priscilla as a guest, so he bade them farewell, thanking them for including him in the gathering, and began what he decided would be a slow and melancholy walk home. He must allow himself, for the first time in years, to willingly recall his sister and to consider a new horrifying possibility regarding her untimely end.

CHAPTER SEVEN

It was half past the hour of twelve when Scrooge finally arrived home after his trek from the Wilkinses'. He had spent the time recalling his relationship with his sister and their father, Josiah Scrooge. In direct contrast to Fan's engaging temperament, the elder Scrooge's behavior had always been erratic and contemptuous. Although he treated Fan somewhat more kindly than he did Ebenezer, she was not blind to their father's character. She once described him as an ice crystal – cold, many faceted, yet brimming with the possibility of exotic rainbows, which, of course, were never fulfilled. Scrooge had received only harsh rejection from him, and the distance between them was intensified by the man locking himself away for days on end, to accommodate his volatile mood swings.

When Scrooge was a teenager their father granted Fan's wish that Scrooge be allowed to come home from school, for Christmas. It was his first visit in years, and he was pleased to think he would be remaining at home permanently. During the second week of January, however, he was summoned to his father's library, where he found the man seated stiffly behind a desk. Josiah Scrooge was not handsome and his expression of disdain marred his appearance all the more.

"Ebenezer," he growled, as if there were something distasteful in his mouth. "You have been in my house near a fortnight and I have fulfilled my promise to your sister. It is time you made your own way in the world." He relaxed a bit in his chair while Ebenezer continued to stand, not daring to sit since he had not been given permission to do so. His father continued.

"I have, therefore, arranged for you to become apprenticed to a man who can teach you about business. His name is Fezziwig and he will give you a bed and a job. If you do as you are told, things will work out for you. If you do not do well, you will not be welcome back here. Remember that. You will not be welcome back here." Ebenezer did not say so, but he reckoned he was not welcome back home no matter how he fared – be it good or ill.

Ebenezer opened his mouth to ask when he was to leave, and was silenced when his father continued talking.

"I can see no reason why you and I should be in future contact since you are, for all intents and purposes, now a man. I expect you to make a success of it and I do not want to know if you do not. Of course you may keep in contact with your sister, but I will not require it for myself."

So it was that Ebenezer Scrooge had been turned out of the family home, leaving behind his sister, the one person in the world with whom he felt a closeness, and whose heart was broken by his departure. That day Ebenezer had vowed two things. He would never be like his father and, as soon as he was a success, he would rescue Fan from that fiend! He recalled swearing to Fan emphatically, "I will always be here for you, Dear Sister, and will never desert you!" He had meant it with all his heart and had loved Fan more than he loved any other creature, yet he now wondered at what point in his life he had forgotten those vows.

As he had trudged home, Scrooge turned over in his mind the various possibilities his conversation with Mrs. Langstone had suggested, particularly considering Fan's letter to Jacob Marley, and it filled him with foreboding. He was reminded of how he neglected Fan and reneged on his promises to protect her. Guilt for these new possibilities regarding her death was pounding in his temples, pushing its way to the front of the queue of other unpleasant realities about himself he had faced during the past eleven months. Becoming a renewed man had been extremely easy in comparison with dealing with the man he had been.

Finally, in the wee hours, Scrooge managed to doze a bit, securing only a shallowness of sleep that brought no rest but, instead, another nocturnal visit.

"Scroooge . . . Ebenezer Scrooge." He awoke with a start and quickly sat up as Marley passed easily through the bed curtains, standing within the bed, his legs invisible below the mattress. The apparition was still neither clearly a dream, nor a true vision. At least Marley could once again speak, and he wasted no forewords. Instead, he directly addressed the turn of Scrooge's mind.

"My old friend" he moaned. "You embark on a dangerous tack!" Before Scrooge could respond, Marley issued an admonition.

"Your deliberations on this matter can bring no satisfactory outcome. All of your questions concern those who have been dead and buried these many years, along with their passions, which are hosted only by flesh and blood." Holding up his hand to forestall any response from Scrooge, he declared, "You do not realize what you seek, whereas I do. I wander through an Otherworld where there is no rest, and no ending in sight. The flotsam of eternally doomed souls ever surrounds me and you will not gain by exposing any of them."

"Jacob!" cried Scrooge. "Since you seem to know the nature of what troubles me, give me some answers! Tell me something to ease my mind. As you say, you frequent the place where my answers lie. Assist your old partner in some way – do not simply warn me off!"

Marley heaved an airless sigh as he shifted his weight of chains and moneyboxes and passed his hand inside one of the smaller ledgers without opening it. When he withdrew his hand, he was holding an old, faded letter. Stretching it toward Scrooge, he recited a riddle.

"Paper and pen, one faded, one bent.

Carelessly read, but verily sent."

Scrooge could make out nothing from the riddle itself nor any of what he could see of the writing on the letter, but he reached for it, nevertheless. As he did so, Marley began to fade, unable to deliver the dispatch. He seemed unwilling to go, and was still mouthing inaudible sounds as his form dissipated to Scrooge's cry of, "Wait, Jacob! Is this about Fan's letter to you?" Within seconds Scrooge was left alone, his empty fingers still outstretched toward a paper that no longer existed, a nothingness where his friend had stood. Evidently he would get no answers from Marley – only advice, which he could not take. He fell into a disappointed sleep with images of a young Fan swirling through his dreams, leaving him with the sense that he had only known his sister as a young girl rather than as the woman she had become. Within what seemed minutes, he was being awakened by Mrs. Dilber's knock on the door, to begin his morning routine.

Once he was fully awake and dressed, Scrooge considered Marley's latest visit. What was he suggesting by his riddle? It must have to do with Fan – of course it did.

Letters! They were verily sent, but carelessly read. Fan's letter to Jacob, or her letters to me? My carelessness in receiving them? Surely Jacob was not careless in his handling of her letter stating she had been threatened. Scrooge thought of the correspondence he had received from Fan and knew he had, indeed, read them, but realized, too, that perhaps he had not paid enough attention to their contents. He decided to search for the letters, if for no other reason than to put his mind at ease and hopefully conclude that Marley's riddle did not, in fact, refer to the communications between himself and his sister so many years ago.

⚜

Late Thursday afternoon Scrooge was on his knees in an unoccupied room of his home. Unoccupied, that is, if one did not consider the cast-off furniture, trunks of old clothing and some odds and ends from his father's house. They were items Scrooge had never tossed away, which attested to his true, more tender nature – a nature that had been obscured for so many years. Without giving it any real thought, he knew where the letters might be and pulled an old trunk out from under several rolled-up rugs. The trunk was not locked and as he opened it he steeled himself to view the contents for the first time in decades. There, among other items that once belonged to both Scrooge and Fan as children, such as Dora, her beloved dolly, and a Bible Scrooge carried in school, were stacks of letters, most of them tied with ribbons. He had no idea how he had come by these particular things, other than the letters, because they should have remained with her husband, following her death. Perhaps he acquired them before she married.

Almost reverently Scrooge picked up what appeared to be the oldest of the bundles of correspondence and unfolded several. They were scribbled letters written by a very young Fan, sent to him during his early days at school. They delighted him with her exuberance and her obvious worship of her big brother. The notes brought both pleasure and pain and he realized he would not part with them for any price. He scanned them somewhat quickly, then replaced them in the trunk and picked up a stack of her correspondence that was written shortly before and after her marriage to Geoffrey in 1818. He opened several, quickly glancing at the contents, until one caught his attention.

27 March 1818
Dearest Brother,

I should not be writing to you at this time because I am most likely too upset to manage my words properly and I do not wish to distress you. However, you are the one I turn to when I am unhappy as well as when I am happy, and I must unburden myself, hopefully without disturbing your well-being in the process of improving mine. I rely on your good sense and straightforwardness to set things to right in my mind.

Today, Father and I had words, which is not his usual comportment with me. It came about so quickly I was not prepared and I am still uncertain as to how or why it occurred. I merely enquired as to something to do with breakfast the next morning and he roared, saying terrible things, most of which I dare not repeat. For a full two minutes he told me I was turning out badly, that I was like our mother and how ashamed he was of me. I stood there weeping, and that seemed only to make him more angry and more indiscriminant in his accusations. Then, of a sudden, he seemed to come to himself, and without an apology or explanation he simply turned his back on me, went to his library and closed the door.

He does not frighten me, Ebenezer, but this is very disconcerting and I am glad to be marrying soon. I will no longer be living in this house and, although I suspect he will miss me, I will feel a great deal more comfortable being fully removed from his moods.

The next time I see you will be at my wedding to Geoffrey, and I rejoice that you will be with me on that day. Should Father be too unwell to stand with me, I pray you will do me that honor. I should be pleased to have you in his stead, as you have truly been for so many years now. Until my wedding day, I remain,

Your Loving Sister,
Fan

Scrooge wondered how on earth Fan had clung so tenaciously to a brother who, for all those adult years, was essentially unavailable to her. Why had she not done as his fiancée Belle had done, and released him from the burden of a relationship? Well, that was simply answered. She had no one else, at least not until she married, and Fan and Scrooge also shared a history, throughout which they had been close.

There was one small hope. Perhaps Fred had all of the correspondence Scrooge had written to Fan, assuming she had kept it. If his memory served, other than the few things he had saved with her correspondence, Fan's and Geoffrey's belongings were taken to the Barneses upon Josiah Scrooge's death, to hold for Fred until he reached his majority. The fact that Scrooge had not, himself, retained them was further proof of his aloofness and general unsociability. It was insupportable, and he was sorry.

If Fred had any letters, perhaps Scrooge would find that he had indeed given Fan at least a suggestion of support by writing to her regularly. He must request that Fred do a bit of research and take an accounting of Fan's things, if he had them. He realized the plan had to do with his own conscience, for he was hoping he had not been as neglectful a brother as he believed he had been, and perhaps his letters would prove it. He knew, only too well, the sort of person whose skin he had shed last Christmas, but he did not want to think it had included a disregard of his sister's needs.

After glancing over two or three more letters, Scrooge picked up another stack. This entire search was proving more harrowing than he could have surmised, but he couldn't stop. It was like scratching a painful itch until it bled. He had no choice. He was driven to continue.

Near some other black-edged notes, no doubt written by friends to offer their sympathy following Fan's or their father's death, was a third group of letters from Fan. These were tied with string as if it were the only thing handy, and knotted in haste. Untying them, Scrooge sensed he was standing on the edge of a precipice from which he could still retreat, or make a leap and take his chances of survival.

Scrooge opened the topmost letter and read news from Fan following her marriage. Several more were of the same cheerful ilk, and he scanned them quickly, allowing himself to hope he would find no indication of anything that had been untoward. Half-way through the group he began reading with more interest.

20 June 1818
Dearest Ebenezer,

We are having such a glorious summer! The weather has held throughout and there has been nothing to mar it. I have often suggested to you that you stop work long enough to join us for a rest, and I will continue to do so until you take seriously my proposals. We had houseguests for a good portion of the late spring, and I know you would have thoroughly enjoyed yourself to be a part of such entertainment. Only one guest has misbehaved by being somewhat too familiar with me, although I assume I am the only one who is aware of his transgressions, and I am certain you could put him in his place right enough!

My dear friend, Miss Rebecca Sotherton, has been here some time, and is such a companion to me. She is very cheerful and my special confidant. I could not ask for more, having such a close devotee, as well as my dear husband, with me in the same house. I am so grateful she and he get along well, for it would be extremely tedious were I to be caught in the middle of two warring factions (for I cannot part with him and have been unwilling to part with her for two weeks now)! No, instead they laugh and joke with each other as if they had been playmates their entire lives. I do believe I am truly blessed to have them both with me, for they are very entertaining and are a counterpoint to father's frequent moods, when he is visiting here. He seems to have worsened recently and is occasionally quite inconsolable and rather disagreeable, although I feel disloyal in saying so. Dr. Devitt lends as much support as possible.

You will recall Dick Wilkins, with whom you passed your apprenticeship at Mr. Fezziwig's. He and his new wife, Priscilla, have visited us here, he being earlier acquainted with Goeffrey. They often remain with us several nights, and have become a welcome addition to our merry party. I like them both very much although she seems a bit more reserved than he – perhaps she is shy.

Now you simply must humor your sister and set aside your business long enough to join us for a few days. I do miss you so and long to have you stay with us here in our home, for it will always be yours, too. I will look to hear from you by return post, telling me you will come to me and observe how well we do.

Until then, I send you my love and anxiously await your affirmative reply.
Fan

So Rebecca was there – and Dick! Although, on the face of it, there was nothing beyond the ordinary, Scrooge had not expected that Rebecca was an extended visitor and he hadn't realized Dick had seen Fan more than twice, while he and Dick were apprenticed at Fezziwig's. Rebecca did say she had spoken with Fan during that time, but he assumed she referred to a rather steady correspondence.

Scrooge held the letter for some moments, considering its contents, then realized he had not fulfilled Fan's requested visit. Or had he? No, surely not, for, if he had he would have recalled spending time with Miss Sotherton, now Mrs. Langstone, and would have known of Fan's connection with Dick and Priscilla. It was a testament to his obsession with making money that he could recall so little of Fan's life during those years, yet he had a stack of correspondence to prove she had made every attempt to stay involved in his life, and to remain as close as they had been in their earlier years. The letters were testimony of her love and his indifference, at least with regard to his actions. He began to read another letter.

1 October 1818
Dearest Brother,

As you know, Father has been with us for some time now and I find the need to share with you the unfortunate truth that his mind is, without doubt, failing. I had hoped that coming to live with us would revive him and that the happy company we tend to gather around us would bring a bit of contentment to his later years. He has, alas, not thrived here and I fear it is due to some misconduct on my part, or some virtue I may be lacking in my behavior toward him.

Dr. Devitt assures me I have done nothing amiss, yet, as a daughter, I feel I should somehow have the power to improve his lot in life. I should, in short, be able to give him comfort and make him happy. Yet I am unable to do so, even though he has always doted on me, at least during those periods when his behavior was conventional. His moods continue to vacillate and he is often withdrawn and unapproachable. On occasion we do not see him for days and when he does emerge from his rooms, he either growls at every attempt to engage him, or he is almost hysterical with glee, which renders him almost as removed as when he is possessed of the doldrums. He is often easily distracted and unable to sleep, wandering the halls for hours when the rest of the household is in bed. At times he seems preoccupied with the idea that he is very ill, and even Doctor Devitt cannot disabuse him of the idea.

The Good Doctor has discussed with us the possibility of an asylum, but I am fearful of such a move. I do not want him confined in some horrid stone gaol, for that is what they must be. I would be more open to such a plan were there a greater chance that he could receive true treatment.

If you have any wisdom to impart, I would be so grateful. Other than father, you are my closest living relation and I rely on you for so much direction. Perhaps that is unfair of me and I apologize if I weigh you down with my worries. I do not mean to do so. I only require the knowledge that you are there and that the one stable rock in my foundation has not moved.

God bless you,
Fan

Scrooge was distressed by the message, not only for Fan's difficulties, but more so by the fact that he suspected he had not been duly concerned by its contents. Well, he wouldn't have been, would he? He and the Senior Scrooge were not friends and had never experienced the hearty relationship so common to many fathers and sons. He had not even grieved when the old man finally died. There were, however, other points in the letter that troubled him now that he was, so long after her death, finally paying attention to, and taking his sister's words to heart. Why had Fan referred to Scrooge as her rock, rather than her husband? Just how had Scrooge responded to this obvious request for comfort or assistance? Had he, at all? He could not recall. Instead, he picked up another letter at random, and read it. It was more news of an uneventful sort.

Reaching into the trunk, Scrooge pulled out more letters and began sifting through them. He continued to peruse them quickly until he found one that stopped him short. After a quick scan of the note he rose from his kneeling position, still staring at it, and walked to a chair, where he sat and read it a second time.

> *2 June 1819*
> *My Dearest Brother,*
>
> *How my life is changed! Three days ago I was a married lady with only a husband and a home to manage and now I am a new mother, with a lovely son – your nephew and god-son – who has made my life complete. He is the most beautiful creature and of such good nature that I am unable to express my joy. You, however, being such a soul mate of mine, will no doubt understand the sentiments to which I am unable to give words.*
>
> *According to Dr. Devitt, my body is recovering very quickly, but my mind seems to be taking its time to recover. I am not sleeping well and have experienced a few symptoms I cannot explain. In addition, it is most tedious to be of no use to anyone and, although I am certain I could be moving about, Dr. Devitt has been most insistent that I remain immobile until he gives the word to rise from this bed. Rebecca Sotherton continues to attend me since I would not part with her and begged her to remain with me for the time being. She seemed easily willing to accommodate me, for which I am sincerely grateful.*

I have, in truth, become convinced of something unpleasant, and it is of such an extraordinary nature that I hesitate to put it to paper. Since you were always my confidant, I will save it and discuss it with you when we next meet, which I pray will be quite soon. I will, in the meantime, speak of it to no one, particularly my own husband. Although I do not question his devotion to me and his new offspring, he tends to react from one or the other emotional extreme of things, and rarely from the centre. Add to that the fact that he might become upset by his part in the situation, and I shall not share it with him. I dare not.

Please come to me as soon as possible, for you simply must view your beautiful godson. I long to see your face and give it a very sincere kiss. Upon your arrival we will take long walks and you may entertain me with the foibles of all your business acquaintances. I will then broach the subject meant for your ears, alone. Until then, I remain,

> *Your Most Devoted Sister,*
> *Fan*

Scrooge stared at the aged letter, unwilling to accept the possibilities inherent in its message. It seemed a lifetime ago that Fan had penned these ideas and he was only now grasping the fact that she had been recovering well, but was indeed troubled by something. Perhaps it was the man she feared – the one to whom she referred in her letter to Marley. At the time, Scrooge had most likely read the words so quickly that their meaning and their import were completely lost to him as he scribbled a short message of regret to be sent by return post before dashing to his next business meeting. The other unthinkable possibility was that he had seen it, but ignored the portent because he simply did not want to take time away from his affairs, to deal with it.

Scrooge leaned back in his chair and closed his eyes, blowing out his cheeks in a long, self-loathing sigh. *What could Fan possibly have had on her mind, and why could I not have made time to speak with her? No wonder she turned to Marley when she did!*

It was apparent that someone had indeed threatened Fan. She had written to Marley and to himself, and Mrs. Langstone confirmed something was amiss. Mrs. Langstone had also detailed the particulars of Fan's death, which had nothing to do with childbirth. What was this "unpleasant" thing to which Fan referred, and why could she not confide in her husband? She says he is devoted to her, but perhaps she believes otherwise. She also says his reactions are extreme, which meant he would either have responded with anger, or set her concerns aside as nothing worth considering. What was her husband's part in the situation? What *was* the situation and how did it, if at all, play a part in her death? Come to that, how did Rebecca Langstone, or even Dick and Priscilla Wilkins fit into all of this?

Scrooge had no idea where to start, but he must pursue the matter. One thing more was disturbing him and, as unpleasant as it was, he could not set it aside without examining himself. He had suddenly begun to wonder whether all of these years of refusing to speak or even think of Fan, including his disdain for his own nephew, were not so much a matter of his unbearable grief, but more a matter of his shameful guilt for his neglect. He was unsure, and afraid of the answer.

CHAPTER EIGHT

Friday, November 22, 1844

Scrooge decided to call on Rebecca Langstone and obtain the direction for Fan's former maid, Mrs. Reynolds. He felt as though he and Mrs. Langstone had been acquainted longer than only one evening that had consisted of intense conversation and some dancing. Yet, even with the link it had forged, it might be construed as bad manners to call, had she not extended the invitation.

At mid-afternoon Scrooge announced to Fred and Bob Cratchit that he would be out for a time, and made his way to Mrs. Langstone's front door at Russell Square. He was torn between the pleasant prospect of her good company and the distasteful subject of Fan's death, which they must, of course, discuss.

After being admitted to the front hall, Scrooge waited while a servant asked if Mrs. Langstone was "at home," and was quickly led upstairs to the drawing room where he was cordially deposited, to wait. Meanwhile, he studied his surroundings. They reflected what he already assumed would be good taste. The room was furnished in modern pieces, but ornamentation and clutter were at a minimum. Chairs had obviously been chosen for comfort as well as display, draperies did not overpower the decor and paintings were well executed. A "whatnot" on one wall contained a few pieces of china and glass that were exquisite, and their minimal display enhanced their apparent value.

"Mr. Scrooge," said Mrs. Langstone as she entered, obviously pleased to see him. He turned from the particular piece of china he had been admiring.

"I beg your pardon if I am intruding," said Scrooge, "but I wished to obtain Mrs. Reynolds' direction and I hope you will understand and grant me a few moments for one or two further questions."

"Do not reprove yourself," said Mrs. Langstone. "You certainly violate no social protocol since we do, after all, have a connection of long standing. Please sit down. I have ordered tea." She went to a side table, opened a drawer and removed a slip of paper with Mrs. Reynolds' name and direction, which she handed to him with a smile. "You see, I was ready for you."

Mrs. Langstone gestured to a comfortable chair near the fire and took a seat across from him. He had indicated he had something on his mind, but she did not immediately pry. After crossing and uncrossing his legs one final time, Scrooge came to the point.

"Mrs. Langstone, I realize I am no doubt imposing on your good nature, and I apologize in advance, but there is something I did not ask you when last we talked." He coughed nervously into his fist before continuing.

"We spoke Wednesday night of Fan and you made some surprising comments about her illness and death. As you know, you took me by surprise." After a slight pause he said, "I did not then ask you for specifics, but I would like to do so now. I am curious about the symptoms she displayed prior to her death. It is demoralizing to realize I know less than I should know as her brother, and you are the obvious one to launch me on my quest for answers. I admit I have very few facts." He did not add, *and it is my own doing.* Mrs. Langstone thought for a moment. Then, just as she was about to answer, the tea arrived. With it was a simple assortment of food. The maid set it on a small table between them and Mrs. Langstone said, "Thank you Simms. I will pour."

As the maid left the room, Mrs. Langstone reached for the teapot and began to pour a deliciously scented brew into a cup. "Sugar, Mr. Scrooge? Or milk?"

"Neither, thank you," replied Scrooge. He did, however, accept a slice of toasted bread with jam, which she offered him after handing him his tea.

"Now, Mr. Scrooge," continued Mrs. Langstone. "You asked me about Fan's condition prior to her death. I am no physician, of course, but my proximity to her during that time did allow me to observe her fairly closely. There was some melancholy, quite severe on some occasions, but it seemed to come and go. She was elated to be a new mother, and was prodigiously proud of her offspring, but I found her sobbing more than once. She seemed to feel guilty about something, but she would not discuss it with me. Nevertheless, surely none of those signs would account for her death." It was said more as a question, than a statement.

"I would concur, Mrs. Langstone," agreed Scrooge, "but do you recall any other symptoms, in particular, just before she died? You did say you thought her death was unexplained."

Mrs. Langstone thought for a moment, then said, "I will admit, I put her symptoms out of my mind purposely long ago after being assured there was nothing amiss, and I do not relish the idea of resurrecting them. I suppose it will be an unpleasant thing for both of us to recount all of the details we know between us, and to try to make something coherent out of them, but if you are to answer your questions, we must do so." The implication that they would, together, seek some answers, was not lost on Scrooge and he said, "I would be very grateful."

"Well, then, as I told you at the Wilkinses'," continued Mrs. Langstone, "Fan had recovered nicely from the delivery and had been experiencing good physical health for several weeks, albeit she had lost some serenity of mind. As I said, she did not always sleep well and seemed to be quite confused at times, imagining things that were not so. I recall, at one point, she even questioned the health of her newborn. Still, she was expecting to resume normal activities within a fortnight. I had planned to return to my parents' home, where I still resided since I was not yet married, but when she became so violently ill, I decided to stay. That is how I happened to be there at the time of her death. In fact, I was at her bedside, along with the doctor. I do not recall the whereabouts of her husband."

"He was not there?"

"He was in residence, but I believe he abandoned her room when her symptoms became so violent. Fan had previously recovered to the extent that she had been up and walking several times a day within her own apartment and occasionally to other areas of the house, before she suddenly took on such unexpected complaints." Hesitating for a moment, Mrs. Langstone said, "With regard to those complaints, I believe, initially, she could not swallow properly. Yes. That's right. I recall thinking it was something she ate, and that seemed to be confirmed to me and to her maid. Later, she could not keep food down and, if you will excuse my graphic description, became incontinent. She complained of stomach pains and seemed to have a fever because her bedclothes became so wet they had to be changed several times."

Scrooge was aghast at the descriptions, but he had to know.

"We were all beside ourselves at that point and Dr. Devitt, who had been called to address the turn of her health, arrived much later, but before her first sign of catalepsy. She was in a state that he seemed unable to correct and, within a matter of hours she was gone. It was a shocking situation and I recall Dr. Devitt remarking that it should not have happened, but he said nothing else. As I reflect on it, he was very tight-lipped about the whole thing and was hesitant to speak to any of us although, as I told you, he did speak to me briefly when I confronted him. I believe he was as upset as the rest of the household for I know he was extremely fond of Fan."

Scrooge had sat still throughout the recitation, asking very little and seeming not to react. He was deeply affected, however, and stared, trance-like, until Mrs. Langstone finished. Both remained silent for several moments as he absorbed what he had heard and she recovered from relating it. Finally he spoke.

"I thank you for your explanation, Mrs. Langstone, although I believe the telling of it has cost you. For that I apologize, but I cannot see how we can dismiss the sinister possibilities this presents. I understand now why you thought something was amiss." Then, as an afterthought, he asked, "Do you recall anyone else who was there, or anything out of the ordinary that might have caught your interest?"

Mrs. Langstone sat for a moment before saying she could think of nothing else that occurred. Looking at the ceiling, she ticked off on her fingers the fact that the only persons present had been herself, Fan's maid Sarah, the nurse, some housemaids who came and went and, of course, Doctor Devitt. She could not, unfortunately, recall the name of the nurse. She did say, "I recall that Fan's father was living with them at the time, but he remained in his rooms during the crisis and flatly refused to come out, even when Fan became so ill."

Not caring that he might sound unkind, Scrooge said, "That sort of behavior was not unusual for him, even in the best of times," and she nodded her understanding.

"That was the case every time I visited," confirmed Mrs. Langstone before continuing.

"There was also that young Mr. Edmonds, the son of Geoffrey's godfather. I did not care for him. He was an extremely vain young man – very conceited. He visited off and on throughout the spring and summer but departed a few hours before Fan became so ill, so he was not there at the time of her death." Lifting her index finger, she seemed to recall something else.

"Oh, Geoffrey also had a party of card players in the previous evening, which was very common practice for him, and they played late into the night. It was the usual crowd of men – mostly businessmen and some gentlemen. One of them – was his name Irving? Ike? – it was something that began with an 'I', I believe, visited with Fan prior to playing. He often did that. I thought it a bit strange that he defied custom by doing so, although he tended to do things his own way and was, we all thought, a bit forceful when it came to pushing himself to the forefront of things."

"I must assume my sister would refrain from offering any reproof, however. My guess is that she simply tolerated his attentions and made the best of it."

"Yes, that was it, exactly. I very nearly said something myself, but she asked me not to and said her inconvenience was a small thing compared to upsetting the entire household.

"As I'm sure you know, Mr. Scrooge, the odd and most significant thing is that Fan's symptoms would not normally accompany childbirth." Without realizing she was entering forbidden territory, she asked, "Did you and your wife have children?" He tightened his grip on the cup. *Dear Lord in Heaven! What is it about this woman that I am forced to relive and even reveal some of the most unpleasant aspects of my life whenever I am in her company!*

Scrooge cleared his throat and squirmed in his chair. "Actually . . . no, Mrs. Langstone," he said, more curtly than he had planned. Trying for a spot of humor to lighten his retort, he added, "I am not married. I have spared some good woman a very unpleasant time of it by never entering into the wedded state." He had never in his adult life felt the need to explain his actions to anyone, yet he found himself continuing, wishing he could clamp his mouth shut before any more words escaped of their own volition.

As if he were possessed by some babbling spirit, before he knew it Scrooge was saying, "I was betrothed once, in my youth, but it was not to be. She was a lovely woman, but I was foolish and I let her go." He gulped hard. Curse his brain, had he actually said that? He couldn't believe it, yet he found himself saying and doing things of a very peculiar nature since last Christmas, even when he didn't want to. *Blast this Rebecca Langstone! Blast Marley, and blast all those Spirits of Christmas! I may be a better man because of them, but I've become as foolish as a schoolgirl.* Sometimes he actually missed his Old Self, the Scrooge who could at least control his tongue! Although Mrs. Langstone failed to notice, he felt himself blushing for the first time in forty years.

In response to this information, Mrs. Langstone nodded slightly and said, simply, "I see. I assumed you were a widower." She did not pursue the matter and did not spray him with flustered apologies, which would have only embarrassed them both. She simply poured more tea and offered him another slice of toast. For that he was grateful, even though he might as well have been sitting there in his nightshirt, for the amount of exposure he was feeling. She gave no indication of noticing, and he silently blessed her for her discretion. Perhaps, thought Scrooge, they could eventually develop a cordial acquaintance. That is, if he could get by a few things where she was concerned – her keen perception, for one.

CHAPTER NINE

Saturday, November 23, 1844

It was Sarah Reynolds, herself, who answered the door. Scrooge had, of course, seen her many years before, but he had no clear recollection of what she looked like, nor could he have described her. He did seem to recall that she was a small, demure young woman, which was a far cry from the person who now stood before him. Mrs. Reynolds was still pocket-sized in height, but had managed to grow a great deal in width. Her hair was almost totally gray, but it was a handsome shade of silver and had been fashioned very becomingly. Alert brown eyes peeped out of a dimpled face that was easy to read. It was obvious, once he introduced himself, that she was delighted to see him.

"Mr. Scrooge!" she cried. "My dear mistress's brother! Yes, Mr. Scrooge, I am that happy to see you and you are very welcome in my home. Come in. Come in!" She swung the door wide and ushered him into her immaculate parlor. The room was well furnished with modest pieces that were not new, but had obviously received good care for many years and would, no doubt, serve for many more.

"Now you sit right there, Mr. Scrooge, and make yourself comfortable," she effused, pointing him to a comfortable stuffed chair and seating herself across from him. She leaned back and studied him. "I have not seen you since . . . why, it must have been no later than 1818, and that's a lifetime ago, isn't it?" Laughing, she said, "You would at least think so, to look at me, and I see you have aged a bit yourself, although . . ." tilting her head to one side as if to assess him, she nodded approvingly, "it does suit you, I reckon. Yes, Mr. Scrooge, it suits you very well."

It was clear that Mrs. Reynolds had not been in service for many years because she no longer displayed the deferential manner of a maid. Perhaps the fact that she had lived away from England had also had an effect on her attitude. Living in a society with fewer class distinctions had no doubt blurred the lines for her. It did not matter to Scrooge, however, since he found her outgoing nature charming. He smiled, thanked her and made himself as comfortable as his mission would allow. She gave him enough silence to permit him to begin speaking, and he did so, feeling his way carefully.

"Thank you, Mrs. Reynolds, I am pleased you think the years have not harmed my appearance and I appreciate, even more, your willingness to speak with me. I am glad to find you in health and your outlook bright. I believe my sister relied on your natural humor to bring, as she said more than once, 'a certain amount of merriment' to her existence, particularly when she needed to be cheered. She said you had the ability to make her feel better with one simple statement that exposed the silliness of things, and you would both laugh heartily."

"Yes, we did that, Mr. Scrooge, and I thank you for saying I lightened her days. She said as much to me, many times.

However, I will admit to you that, although the girth of my body may suggest that my life continued in jolliness, it has not always been so. I won't bore you with my entire life's history, but I will say my time in Nova Scotia was not what I expected when I allowed Robert Reynolds to talk me into going. Oh, it was a nice enough living, but I am happy to be home again, in England, where I belong. We had no children, you see, so when Robert died – he was tossed from a horse he was breaking – I sold our home and came back to be near my brother and two sisters and their families. I cannot complain about my married life, however, for Robert was a good man. He provided well and was kind. He was . . . a very decent man."

Scrooge could be astute and he suddenly felt sorry for her. *She did not love him,* he thought. *He was a good man, and she praises him as an apology for not caring more.* It was apparent that she remembered her husband with kindness, but had been disappointed in not finding the happiness she had expected. He thought it sad that she spent twenty-five years with a man she most likely respected, but did not adore. Perhaps she would have loved him more had she borne his babes, but Scrooge had no such experience in those areas, at least not personally, so he could only guess.

"Now, Mr. Scrooge," said Mrs. Reynolds, shifting a bit in her seat. "I did not expect to see you, but I can guess how you came to know of my being in London, and especially to know exactly where I am living. I did call on Mrs. Langstone to ask if anything ever came of my mistress's death. So you see, I have deduced your purpose in coming here today, and you mustn't be shy about approaching the subject. We may easily discuss my mistress – your sister – for we both loved her and anything untoward must not be left unaddressed, for her sake."

Scrooge gave a small nod and said, "I still find it a bit difficult to broach the subject directly, Mrs. Reynolds, since I have refrained from talking about her all these years. Yet your and Mrs. Langstone's suspicions on this subject have shocked me into doing so. I understand from Mrs. Langstone that you believe my sister died by someone else's hand, and I would like to know why you think that."

Mrs. Reynolds was no longer smiling but her displeasure was not with Scrooge. She compressed her lips before speaking.

"I'll tell you why, Mr. Scrooge. Mrs. Symons was in good health following her lying-in. She ate normally, from the same kitchen as the rest of the household, and generally the same food, yet she supposedly became afflicted with a stomach ailment which no one else within miles seemed to have contracted. Nor were her symptoms those of a trifling infection. She took them on just like those rats we used to poison when I was a girl. I could describe it for you, but I would rather not."

"You needn't, Mrs. Reynolds," said Scrooge quickly. "Mrs. Langstone recalled for me the hours prior to my sister's death, and it is true they resembled far more than a common stomach ailment."

Crossing her arms as if she would brook no argument, Mrs. Reynolds said, "That is why, Mr. Scrooge – that is why I believe someone put poison in something she ate or drank and no one, including you, will ever disabuse me of the idea." Having put it thusly, Scrooge could understand her suspicions.

"I'm sure you wonder that I would have such strong opinions and why I would harbor them for so many years, but my mistress was more than merely my employer. She took me from a home full of poverty and despair, trained me and lifted me above my original station in life.

"I served your dear sister willingly, Mr. Scrooge. Many servants were tied to   unfeeling, uncharitable employers and stayed because they had nowhere to go, but I would have stayed with my mistress for half the wage, which would still have been generous.

She was kind and she always made certain I dressed well. That may sound trifling to you, but many servants wore ragged hand-me-downs and worn-down shoes while their employers donned new silk. She even ensured that I had a private and very comfortable room, not meager like some I could name. I think that is why I paid particular attention to her, always trying to serve as I ought. I paid attention, too, to how she was treated by others. Not much got by me, in that regard."

"And did you see something that was amiss, Mrs. Reynolds? Something that suggested she had an enemy, or someone who wished her harm?"

"No, Mr. Scrooge. I did not. In fact, it was quite the opposite. People – men and women alike – were drawn to your sister. She was able to make each of them feel special because she listened to them and anticipated their needs. I never once saw her put herself first, and that's the truth. I can't say that about anyone else I've ever known. I think that is one reason I've never been able to put my suspicions down. She, of all people, did not deserve what I believe happened to her!"

"Mrs. Reynolds, I realize your situation did not allow you to be directly involved in most of her social interactions, but are you aware of anyone who might have harbored some unseemly feelings where my sister was concerned? Something inappropriate, or unfitting? Something suspect?"

"Well, I don't know how it would help in this instance, but the most inappropriate was a young man who made a terrible nuisance of himself. I don't recall his name, but he fancied himself better suited to her than her husband and didn't seem to mind who knew it. Then there was that peacock of a man, Ira Somebody." *Ah,* thought Scrooge. *Ira. The name that began with an "I", according to Mrs. Langstone.*

"He tried to make it appear that he was simply being courteous to the wife of an acquaintance, but I knew he was besotted.

I never understood why Mr. Symons allowed those two men to annoy her so, but I believe he either didn't notice, or didn't take their actions seriously. He never saw any of it as a threat to him, at any rate, and I suspect that was all that mattered. He would not have noticed her discomfort."

"Are you saying he was deficient as a husband?"

"Well, Mr. Scrooge, I am saying he was more interested in his own activities than those of anyone around him, and that made him less aware of anything unpleasant that might be occurring with his wife. If you will forgive me for saying so – and I do not include you since I have no knowledge of your personal habits – he was typical of his gender." Scrooge did not know how to respond since he could not argue, nor defend. Instead, he asked another question.

"If, as you say, people were fond of Fan, why would someone poison her?"

"I cannot say why anyone would want to harm her, I can only tell you how I think it was done. As I said, I believe poison was placed in your sister's food or drink, Mr. Scrooge, as sure as we are sitting here so many years later, discussing it!"

Scrooge paused before asking, "And did you speak to any-one of your suspicions?"

Mrs. Reynolds nodded emphatically. "I did. After my mistress died I was so grief-stricken and devastated I was nearly struck dumb. All I could do was lie in bed and sob. I couldn't eat or leave my room for the rest of that day, that night and the entire next day. Later I cornered Nurse Weekes, since she and I had got on well together, and I told her I didn't like the look of things. I asked her what she thought of Mrs. Symons' death, and she said I shouldn't suggest anything amiss, that it would only cause trouble for us both. She also said the doctor knew what he was doing and that there was nothing she, nor I, could do to change things. We were both servants you see, holding no sway, and there was an end on it. Still, I never got over it, nor did I ever believe it was anything but well-planned murder!"

Coming to a decision, Scrooge stood up to take his leave and said, "Well, Mrs. Reynolds, if that is true, I will do my best to up-end Heaven and Earth to find the fiend who did it, no matter how long ago it was done!"

Rising with him, Mrs. Reynolds said, "I would be obliged if you would do so, Mr. Scrooge. We owe that to her."

CHAPTER TEN

Saturday Evening, November 23, 1844

Scrooge was determined to speak with Dr. Devitt as soon as possible. It had been years since he had seen or spoken to the man, but Mrs. Dilber provided his last known direction, and he would begin there. Someone would hopefully be able to put him on the trail to the doctor's current whereabouts.

It was coming on evening by the time Scrooge arrived at the house near Mitre Street. The humble structure was in pathetic disrepair, as was the entire neighborhood, and Scrooge held little hope of locating the doctor within. Still, he must make the attempt. He had to rap solidly with the rusted knocker several times before the door was answered, and then it was opened only partly by an older woman who looked as dilapidated as her surroundings.

"What is it y' want," she growled, wary.

"I'm seeking Dr. Devitt, if you please. My name is Ebenezer Scrooge and he was our family physician for many years, although that was some time back. Does he still reside here?"

"'E does, but 'e don't see new patients no more. 'E's not able, considerin' 'e's no better off 'n most o' them. Tsk, tsk. Why d'ya need to see 'im, Mr. Scrooge?"

"It is a personal matter and I would very much appreciate it if you would ask him to give me a few moments of his time."

"I'll ask, but don't 'old yer breath," she muttered, then slammed the door, leaving Scrooge waiting on the step. He stood there for several moments before the door opened again with a long creak and the housekeeper, or whatever she was, allowed him in.

"'E says 'e can see ya, but I'm sayin' don't count on no long conversation. 'E's taken to drink, the poor man 'as, 'n he don't last long of an evening. I'm Mrs. Cooke, 'is housekeeper. Been with 'im for several years now an' it don' seem right to leave 'im just 'cause 'e's 'ad a bit o' bad luck. So I stick by 'im, but 'e's not well. No, 'e's not well at all. Wouldn't be right to desert 'im now, would it?"

"No, Mrs. Cooke, it surely wouldn't," replied Scrooge. He was unhappy to hear that the family's former physician was doing so poorly but since she seemed likely to go on without letup, he interrupted with a question.

"How does the doctor support himself, and you?" It was none of his business, of course, but it was one of those things that seemed to pop out of him in conversation these days.

"Oh, 'e 'as a few patients what give 'im a bit o' food for payment, an' a few relatives contribute to 'is welfare by sending the odd pound or two, when 'e crosses their minds. My daughter also 'elps me out a bit." With that speech Mrs. Cooke led Scrooge down a creaky unlit hall into what must have once been a parlor. One small lamp provided little light, and many shadows. The room was dirty and worn, and reeked unpleasantly of gin, unwashed bodies and all of the odors inherent in an unkempt old house inhabited by misery. The doctor sat at a table and looked at Scrooge with rheumy eyes. Scrooge would not have recognized him.

"Doctor Devitt?"

A hoarse voice replied, "I am what remains of that man, yes."

"I believe you knew my family, Doctor – the family of Josiah Scrooge – and I would ask only a few moments of your time to obtain some answers, if you please."

"Sit down, Mr. Scrooge. You are . . . Ebenezer, I believe. Yes, I recall. You are Fan's older brother. Fan Symons."

"I am that," replied Scrooge, "and it is Fan I have come to ask you about. I will be as brief as possible since your housekeeper tells me you are somewhat indisposed."

With that the doctor cackled, a dry sound resembling ignited kindling. "Is that what you and Mrs. Cooke call it? I wonder at that," he said as he picked up his cup and took a long drink. "Now, tell me, what is it you want to ask about that precious, ill-fated creature, Fan Symons? I'm afraid I haven't much to share."

"This is rather difficult, Doctor, but, as you may recall, I was not with Fan when she died. I always assumed her death was ow-ing to the birth of her son, but I have come across some informa-tion recently that indicates that was not so."

"No?"

"No. In fact, I was given a fairly detailed description of her death by someone who was at her bedside when she died. According to that person, Fan was entirely well, had delivered her child without complications, then suddenly complained that she could not swallow properly. She became extremely ill, began retching, and was incontinent. She also had stomach pains and a fever. I am told she experienced catalepsy and died fairly soon thereafter." Scrooge did not want to suggest it, but he must ask. "Doctor, are those the symptoms of anything untoward?"

The Doctor hesitated and Scrooge was ready to ask the question again when the doctor asked, an edge to his voice, "What, exactly, are you suggesting, Mr. Scrooge – Fan's brother?"

Scrooge persisted, treading lightly. "Without casting any doubt as to your care of her, Doctor, I must ask if you believe there is any possibility Fan was given poison, either accidentally, or on purpose, by some unknown person."

As much as his bent frame would allow, the doctor sat up straight, suddenly on the defensive. Squinting, he growled, "Why do you come here, asking me these questions?"

Scrooge cleared his throat. "As I said, I have been given reason to fear that my sister did not die in the manner I once assumed. I enquire simply because I need to know, and you are the best one to ask."

"You need to know? Ah. You need to know. Your words remind me of the chant of a nursery rhyme that has no meaning. What would you need to know of something that happened a lifetime ago? It cannot affect you one way or the other, no matter what occurred. It's been too long to matter to anyone and I cannot even recall the small egg I ate this morning, assuming it is now evening, nor can I recall my own history, much less yours or your family's. It has all faded to the consistency of a dense fog since I have lost my good practice and taken up residence in this bottle of gin."

As he spoke he raised the bottle between them, making the gesture of a toast, and said, "I speak rhetorically, of course, when I refer to 'this' as my current abode! Nevertheless, it is where my essence resides. Would you care to join me? It is not a pleasant place, but perhaps a short visit would do you little harm." Cracking a small ugly smile, he said, "An extended stay, however, might prove as lethal for you as it has for me."

Leaning forward, Scrooge said, "Dr. Devitt, it is not my intention to bring you distress, but I am seeking answers and you are the only one who . . ."

"Cease this harassment!" squawked the doctor, his face screwed into an expression of anger and pain. Having so exerted his lungs, he began a coughing fit that shook his flimsy frame with a vengeance. When it abated he managed to cry, in between a few sharp hacks, "I will not re-visit those years! As God is my witness, I will not recite anything, even for you. Particularly not for you, Fan's Brother! Now get out!" He felt for and lifted a wooden cane that was leaning against the table and banged it several times on the tabletop as he called to his housekeeper.

"Mrs. Cooke! Mrs. COOKE!!" When she appeared in the doorway, he snapped, "Mr. Scrooge is leaving. Show him to the door. Quickly, woman!" As she and Scrooge turned to go the doctor sniffed, his coughing finally under control. Without looking at Scrooge, he said, somewhat more kindly, "Leave off, Mr. Scrooge. You cannot bring back the dead, no matter how they died. Let them be. It's best for all. Now I bid you good night."

There was nothing for it but to go, his information not only scant, but discouraging. The only thing Scrooge had learned for certain was that the doctor's life was entirely wasted, apparently due to circumstances he was unable, or unwilling, to overcome. Scrooge had no choice but to follow Mrs. Cooke out, but he was far from satisfied. Once beyond the doctor's hearing, he asked for, and was given, the address of Fan's nurse, Mrs. Weekes. Two coins loosened the housekeeper's tongue well enough.

❧

Sunday, November 24, 1844

Scrooge used the direction given by Mrs. Cooke and located the home of Nurse Weekes on Sunday afternoon. His knock was answered by a severe woman, probably no older than Scrooge himself, who somehow managed to convey a great many more years from her bleak appearance and attitude. With narrow eyes and thin lips, she hissed, "Yeesssss?"

"Are you Mrs. Weekes, perchance?"

"I am . . . not," she said, her cold stare still fastened on him.

The horrid woman had placed Scrooge in the position of wanting to ask, "Then who in flaming blazes are you, madam?" but he resorted, instead, to curtly saying, "It's Mrs. Weekes I'm seeking. Does she reside here?"

"She does, but she's unwell. You cannot see her." As she started to close the door, in desperation Scrooge did something very unlike him and he did it without thinking. He stuck his foot in the door. He knew it was a trick used by disreputable men and never in his life ever imagined he would have the need, nor the impudence, to resort to such behavior. Nor had he ever heard mentioned how vulnerable a foot used for such purposes could feel. Nevertheless, he kept it there. Truth be told, he wasn't sure he could remove it. He had no choice but to proceed.

As much in fear for his limb as his desire to speak with the nurse, he insisted with a louder voice, "It is very important that I see Mrs. Weekes, Madam. My name is Ebenezer Scrooge and I have a few questions I would like to put to her regarding a patient of Dr. Devitt's she once nursed." Then, to counteract the impression his foot might be giving, he attempted to soothe her by saying, "Mrs. Cooke, the doctor's housekeeper, gave her name and direction to me."

With his last remark she relaxed her hold on the door, opened it slightly and said, "Mrs. Cooke, you say? Well, I suppose, in that case . . . My sister isn't much above a corpse, though. She can't talk nor anything. Had a fit of apoplexy several weeks ago and isn't likely to recover." He stepped back, planting both feet safely beneath him, and she looked him over without subtlety. She decided, evidently, that he was most likely a gentleman, overcame her reticence, and invited him in.

"She won't be able to talk to you, nor really answer any questions, but sometimes she can give a 'yes' or 'no' by twitching a finger. You can try if you like, but I don't expect you'll get much from her."

Down a dim yet reasonably clean hallway she led him, to a room at the back of the house. Whatever it had been before, it was now definitely a sick room. Windows that may have once faced a garden were hidden by heavy covers and the air within was heavy. It was a room without dignity and without a future. Had he not needed information so desperately he would have thanked his hostess, backed away and taken his leave straightaway. It was almost too much for him, seeing the unfortunate Mrs. Weekes lying on a bed that looked anything but comfortable. Her face was somewhat contorted and she lay as still as if she were already in her coffin. He thought, *We men are not endowed with the aptitude to tend sickness. It is simply not in our nature,* but he drew from some deep reserve of courage and approached the bed as he was led by Mrs. Weekes' sister, who seemed not to have the aptitude, either.

"Bessie," she barked, "This gentleman is here to ask you a few questions. I told him you can lift a finger, so do your best." Turning to Scrooge she said, "If she lifts a finger, it's 'yes.' If she doesn't, the answer is 'no', at least that's how we've been doing things for a time now. It's all she can manage, but you'd better ask her now because she probably won't live that long."

Appalling woman! Scrooge was seething, but he chose not to admonish her in front of the invalid. He pitied Mrs. Weekes and did not want to add to her discomfort by creating a hubbub with her sister. Her eyes were almost wild with fear, but they calmed somewhat when Scrooge smiled kindly at her and began to speak.

"Mrs. Weekes," he said gently, "I am Ebenezer Scrooge, brother to Fan Symons, who died following childbirth in 1819. Dr. Devitt informed me that you were her nurse during her lying-in. Do you remember Mrs. Symons?"

Slowly, her left index finger made a small movement.

"Thank you. I know you cannot tell me anything other than a yes or no, but was there anything at all unusual about her death?"

Again, after a moment, he noticed a small movement of her finger.

"You'll never get anywhere at this rate, Mr. Scrooge, and she'll never be able to help you. She's as good as dead, herself, you know." The woman really was frightful and it was all he could do not to take her to task. Still not wanting to upset Mrs. Weekes, he said, instead, "I certainly do not want to abuse her, so I will ask only one more thing." Turning back to the form on the bed, he asked, "Mrs. Weekes, did you have reason to suspect anyone of wishing my sister harm?"

Her finger did not move, but her eyes were wide again – dark pools of some eerie unknown. Was it fear? Anger, perhaps? Guilt? He could not tell, but the interview had to be ended. He could not put her through this, no matter what he needed to know, and she could certainly not tell him what she had seen or what she believed. He was only increasing her suffering as well as increasing his own anxiety. She was unable to articulate, and he was totally unable to interpret.

As he earlier realized, Scrooge had not the propensity to tend the sick. Nevertheless, he leaned down, touched Mrs. Weekes' arm gently and said, "Thank you for helping me, and God bless you." She thanked him with her eyes and he turned to go. He hated leaving this helpless woman to her cold-blooded sister, when a thought stopped him. Perhaps he could arrange that Mrs. Weekes receive some company of a higher order than her old crone of a caretaker, and Rector Colin Gifford of St. Michael's was just the man.

Although the sister was anxious to rid the house of Scrooge, he returned to the bed and asked, "Mrs. Weekes, would you like me to ask my rector to visit you?" Glancing at her left hand he saw the finger move twice, and took her reply as a definite affirmative. "So be it," he said, gently patting her arm once more before turning to his sour-faced hostess.

"Your sister wishes the rector to visit her, so I will give him your direction." She began what may have been an argument, for which he was in no mood. Using the tone he had once found so formidable in business dealings, he raised his voice and boomed, "It is imperative that you do him, and her, the courtesy of allowing visits and give them all the time together they require." A spark of fear crossed the woman's face before she nodded and said, "Of course. It will be as you say." Scrooge gave her a handful of coins with the admonition, "Buy some good broth and other foods appropriate for an invalid. The Rector will be checking to see that she's decently fed and well cared for." Leaving the room, he added, "See to it," and was pleased to see her bob a small, involuntary curtsey.

CHAPTER ELEVEN

Monday, November 25, 1844

The offices of Scrooge and Symons were doing all they could see to do for the time being regarding the burglaries, with Homer delving through piles of contracts and business notes, yet they were still no closer to the truth of the matter. They felt vulnerable, realizing they were under scrutiny from an unseen enemy. Fred remarked that he felt like an archery target must feel as it awaits the next dart. It was an apt analogy and described why they must discover what the burglar was seeking, and soon! Scrooge had determined that he would speak with Dick Wilkins, for additional ideas.

Yet, even with all of the recent activity of trying to unearth the reasons for their break-ins, plus their usual counting house business, Scrooge was most preoccupied with Fan's death. It was utterly perplexing and was becoming an obsession. His need to know – to understand – what had happened to his sister so many years ago was intensifying even though he wasn't sure he wanted to know the absolute truth. First there was that letter Fan had written to Marley, then Marley's ghost warned him off. Mrs. Langstone thought the matter suspect and Mrs. Reynolds insisted Fan's death was murder. Fan's doctor had tossed Scrooge out, leaving him with even more reason to question. Nurse Weekes harbored some questionable or even terrifying memory regarding Fan's demise, but there was no getting to it since her seizure had left her unable to communicate.

Perhaps he should heed the caution given by Marley and simply let it go, but the doctor's behavior had stoked the fire of his suspicions. Why wouldn't the doctor speak of Fan's death? What was he hiding, or what did he fear? Was he protecting someone, perhaps Scrooge himself? He had said Scrooge was the one person, in particular, with whom he would not discuss Fan's death. Perhaps he was, after all, just a bewildered old inebriate who had nothing of import to reveal. Yet, the doctor's thinking seemed clear enough, and he was still articulate, never mind that his life was muddled beyond repair. No, Scrooge could not let it go. In fact, he had already decided to share with Fred his misgivings and suspicions, and he would seriously consider whatever advice Fred gave.

At one o'clock Scrooge said to his nephew, "Put away those figures, my boy, and let's go fill our bellies at the George and Vulture." He needed to speak with Fred alone, although he had no idea how to approach the things that had been weighing so heavily on his mind. Naturally Fred was happy to tend his appetite and converse with his uncle, so the two donned their greatcoats and hats and walked quickly to the nearby ale and pie house on Cornhill.

The interior was warm and delicious odors permeated the air. They quickly found an empty and fairly private table and Scrooge realized he was very hungry. He ordered sausages with mashed potatoes for them both, with ale to wash it down. Later they could enjoy some apple pie with cinnamon sugar and fresh cream. Meanwhile, they would talk.

After they had been served, Scrooge stuck his fork into his mashed potatoes, lifted it halfway to his mouth, and held it there. His mind was hungrier than his stomach.

"Nephew, I need to share my thoughts with you on a certain subject, although I must warn you, it is not entirely pleasant. It has to do with a quest I have begun regarding your mother's death. There are unanswered questions and, the truth is, I now suspect she died by someone else's hand."

Fred had just popped a chunk of sausage into his mouth. He stopped chewing, pushed the morsel into his cheek and spoke around it, "Foul play, Uncle?" He quickly finished the sausage and swallowed before asking, "Are you saying she did not depart this world as a direct result of my arrival into it? I don't understand."

Scrooge put down his fork, the potato untouched, and said, "Let me explain. It began with the letter you found in Marley's old desk. I assume you did not read it in its entirety, so I will tell you it was a letter from your mother to Jacob stating she felt threatened by a certain man. She actually said she was afraid, but she didn't want to bother me. I was, as usual, 'busy' with business. I assumed Marley took care of it since nothing came of it, but then I met a Mrs. Langstone, who said she suspected your mother's death was odd, and that your mother's personal maid was convinced she had been murdered. As a result, I found and re-read some of your mother's letters to me during that time. Something was definitely bothering her, but she was well enough in body, I believe." Fred was, by now, so engrossed he had also stopped eating. Scrooge finally ate his forkful of potatoes and they both took several more bites before he continued.

"I called on Mrs. Langstone to ask for the particulars of your mother's death and it seems yours was a normal birth, but some time later she suddenly took sick with a stomach ailment and died within a day or two. Mrs. Langstone described the symptoms – how they appeared so suddenly and took Fan so quickly – and said she was not satisfied at all that it was a mere inflammation of the digestive system. Then, when I spoke with Mrs. Reynolds, your mother's personal maid, she was emphatic in her belief that your mother was poisoned, but she has no tangible evidence.

"That is why I visited old Doctor Devitt, who attended your birth, as well as your mother's death. He is totally pickled by gin and was, unfortunately, extremely unhelpful – even hostile. Then I called on your mother's nurse, Mrs. Weekes, who was, due to an apoplexy, physically unable to give the slightest fragment of useful information. I am forced to explore other paths and I require your help, if you are up to it."

"Of course, Uncle, I shall help by whatever means possible. Have you any suggestions?"

"I do. It seems to me you had some of your parents' belongings at some point. If they are still in your possession, they may contain clues regarding your parents' lives at that time."

"I do have some trunks," thought Fred aloud, "although I am a bit embarrassed to admit I've never been into them. Perhaps my disinterest was due to never having really known either of them. Of course, I knew 'of' them since Mrs. Barnes spoke to me quite often of my mother, and occasionally my father. She always referred to my mother as, 'That Angel from Heaven'."

"That she was, my boy, that she was, which is one reason I must discover more about her death now that I believe it was not what I always assumed." He looked intently at his nephew.

"Fred, I have two requests of you. I would like to read the letters I wrote to your mother, if they are in your possession. I admit to you that I fear I did not give adequate correspondence for several years and I want to see exactly what I did provide her in the way of support through my letters. I am also asking you to simply sift through whatever you have of both your parents' possessions, and keep an eye out for anything unusual – anything that strikes you as out of the ordinary. Can you do that?"

"I can, Uncle, and I will. Hopefully we will be better at digging for clues in this instance than we have been in discovering who burgled our premises!"

"Quite right," said Scrooge. Having formed a plan, they tucked into their meals to work their way towards the dishes of pie and cream that had just been placed on the table.

They ate in silence until Fred made a suggestion.

"Uncle, considering the symptoms Mrs. Langstone described, you really must call on the doctor again, and question him further. With a little pressure he may be willing to answer your questions and put your mind at ease." Neither said so, but they both knew it was also possible he would say something that would grieve Scrooge beyond measure. They both knew, too, that Scrooge was willing to risk it. He had to because he would somehow feel like a coward to turn away now, as if he could be dissuaded simply because the truth might be unpleasant.

"You're right, my boy – and I had planned to do that very thing. I will re-visit the doctor and push him a little harder. He may be able to quell my imagination and answer my questions with one statement. These fears of mine need to be laid to rest. If worse should come to worst, I must bear it as best I can, but I will admit to you that as distressed as I was over losing your mother in childbirth, discovering that she had been such a piteous victim in death would be overwhelming."

Fred offered to write to Mrs. Barnes and ask for the names and directions of his mother's housekeeper and any other household servants, including the cook. Perhaps they could cast some light on things as they were in the Symons household at that time.

"Good idea," said Scrooge. "Let's pray they can be found, that they are more willing to talk than poor old Doctor Devitt, and more able to speak than poor Nurse Weekes!"

With a mischievous expression, Scrooge slyly declared, "I also hope to find a reason to call on Mrs. Langstone, again." Fred smiled, and they both laughed. It felt good to laugh again, although Fred noticed his uncle's mirth was not reflected in his eyes, which remained disturbed. At least he could be his uncle's ally in his investigations, and provide needed support.

.

CHAPTER TWELVE

Tuesday Evening, November 26, 1844

Fred located his parents' trunks and prepared himself to open them for the first time. He had not said so to Scrooge during their luncheon, but Fred seriously doubted there had been anything sinister about his mother's death. He found it difficult to reconcile his uncle's current obsession with what he, himself, knew about his mother. Or, rather, what he always thought he had known about her. Hadn't he been told how she died? As he thought about it, no, he hadn't. He had made many assumptions early on, much as his Uncle Scrooge had done, then he put it all aside as he grew and created a world of his own. Perhaps, had his mother lived longer, he would have been more curious, because then he would have had the memory of a real person on whom to attach his inquisitiveness. As it was, all he knew was what he had been told. He now realized how little that had been.

What sort of woman was his mother? His uncle and Mrs. Barnes certainly believed her to be above reproach in all areas, yet she was like an unfinished portrait, with only the bare outlines having been sketched, giving no actual representation of the person herself. Oh, he knew she had been beautiful, both in appearance and demeanor, and he knew her death was a terrible blow to his father, or so he believed, but what made him think that? Had his father ever said so to anyone? Not that he could recall, but he could recall very little about his father, as well. He had been too young.

As a baby and a toddler Fred had been cared for by servants, with little contact with his father, and then his father died when Fred was three years old. Perhaps that was why he had always considered his Uncle Scrooge more of a parent. Perhaps that early inattention from his father was also why he had had so few expectations with regard to the attention he should receive from Scrooge. In those earlier days he was never put off by Scrooge's emotional and physical distance and felt a connection with him, regardless. He learned his basic outlook and optimism from the Barneses and he had his uncle to thank for placing him with them.

Mr. Barnes did not live to see Fred marry, and Mrs. Barnes now resided with her sister near Rye. The correspondence between them was not frequent, but it was dependable and she remained a stable and uplifting presence in Fred's life.

Fred had very little tangible proof of his mother's existence, other than whatever was in the trunks. They no doubt contained clothing and other personal articles that had belonged to his parents and his grandfather, but he did not know, since he had never looked. The Symons' housekeeper packed them away following each death and stored them until they could be forwarded to the Barneses. She thought Fred should someday have the items, but he was never interested enough to explore within. He would do so now, since he had promised his uncle he would.

Having located the trunks, Fred opened one, quickly realizing it contained his mother's possessions. Since he had no idea what his search was about, he began sifting through the contents. There were books, clothing, and some small trinkets such as childhood jewelry, perfume bottles and a mirror. He held up a dress and saw how small his mother had been and was struck with an unexpected pang of having missed out on so much where she was concerned. Until the moment of actually touching the garment and holding it up to see the form of the woman she had been, he had not felt the vacuum her absence had made in his existence. It was a hole that had evidently never quite been filled, even though Mrs. Barnes had given him a great deal of love and guidance as a child.

Fred carefully folded the dress, placing it and two others aside while he picked up some of her other belongings. A small book of poetry was inscribed from a man, which struck him as odd since the date indicated it was given to her after her marriage. He decided to include it with any letters he might find that had been written by his uncle.

Finally, Fred recognized his uncle's handwriting on several packets of correspondence. He would hand them over to Scrooge, as promised.

With that, Fred replaced the items in the trunk and closed it, assuring himself he would return to his search the following day. Or the day after that. Well – this week, for certain.

∾✵๛

The next morning Fred placed the letters and the inscribed book of poetry on Scrooge's desk, saying, simply, "I found these among my mother's things, Uncle, but I don't know that they contain anything that will help you in your search."

"Ah. I thank you," said Scrooge, pulling them toward him. He seemed subdued, but Fred's intuition told him not to enquire. "Your quick response does you credit, Fred, and I'm in your debt." Although he was not expecting the letters to prove anything about Fan's death one way or the other, Scrooge prayed they would at least show that he was not such an unfeeling and neglectful brute as he suspected he may have been.

Once he was alone, Scrooge could not wait and began glancing through the stack that sat there creating so much suspense. The first contained his letters to Fan while he was at school. They were filled with gossip about his courses, his prowess at sporting events, the students and the instructors, and told of his dreams for when he would be a man. Each letter proved the closeness between brother and sister. Satisfied that their relationship had been reciprocal at that time, he set them aside and sifted through another packet. It contained some of his letters to Fan between the time he left his father's home and 1817.

> *6 July 1817*
> *My Dearest Sister,*
>
> *I am in receipt of your most recent letter and believe you are overly concerned. You are an old companion of our father's moods and his propensity to outlandish behavior, and I truly believe you would be best off to leave him be. He is no good for company when he is so indisposed. I would come to you if I thought it would do any good, but he has no use for me and would no doubt bar the door to his library the moment he learned I was within the walls of the house. It would solve nothing.*
>
> *Pray do not trouble yourself over the man. Leave him to himself and carry on with your life, please do. I am here for you if you need me.*
>
> *Your Faithful Brother,*
> *Eben.*

Scrooge picked up yet another of his letters and began to read. It was clear his mind was on other things when he penned it.

> *1 Aug 1817*
> *Fan,*
>
> *You simply must refrain from thinking the worst. Father will not benefit from your worry, nor, unfortunately, from your efforts on his behalf. Pray, do not trouble yourself to this extent. Put your energies into your own life. They are wasted on his!*
>
> *I hope to hear you have done so in your next correspondence and will do all in my power to assist.*
>
> *Yours — E.*

Scrooge read the letters with self-disgust. What platitudes! What quickly-penned discourtesy. How had he dared to treat Fan in such a self-serving and worthless manner! To say he was there if she needed him was an outright lie, and then to sign it with phrases such as, "Your faithful brother" was an affront to her intelligence. In this last letter he had not even had the manners to show some affection. No, he had not been there for her. He was counting his money and planning his next subterfuge on some unsuspecting victim. Her problems had amounted to nothing to him since they could not enrich him by at least a shilling! He should have gone to Fan immediately and given her his support and some practical suggestions. He should have helped her with their father, not because their father had earned any such efforts, but because she needed them. He should have.

Skimming over several that were much the same in content, he came across one that caught his attention.

15 Oct 1817

My Dear Fan,

I am exceedingly busy at this time but must let you know you and your present difficulties are constantly in my thoughts. I pray things will work out with Father, but I believe he is traveling a path from which he can no longer veer. Do not distress yourself, Dearest. If you feel the need to leave his home, I will gladly have you here, with me. You've only to say the word and it will be arranged.

I await your response.
Your Loving Brother,
Ebenezer

He felt a degree of relief at seeing what he had written therein, although he had to admit that even this letter, which was an attempt to offer assistance, was not particularly loving, nor even as supportive of her emotions as it should have been. Its content was too brief to convey as much as it should have, even though he had at least made the offer of assistance and had actually treated her concerns as valid. Obviously she had not called on him to remove her from their father's home, but he was reassured, a bit, to have made the suggestion. Perhaps, hope against hope, she had not thought him totally untrustworthy and unavailable.

Scrooge picked up the book of poems. It was small, penned by a female poet. A hand-written inscription inside read simply, *For Fan. A female poet? Why not. Extraordinary women are to be admired. Ira T.*

Ira T. Could it actually be Ira Thorne? If so, Thorne had known Fan and had admired her enough to give her a gift, in spite of the fact that she was a married woman. What abject boldness! It was apparent he meant the allusion to extraordinary women as a compliment, but it was an affront. It was a presumptive insult that should not have been borne, although Scrooge knew Fan would not make an issue of it, particularly to her husband. She would, instead, attempt to wait out the situation, allowing it to cool, like an unwanted bowl of porridge. Perhaps this was the "unpleasantness" Fan mentioned in her letter that was proving so upsetting. If so, how did it come into play with her death, or did it?

His mind was in turmoil, making it difficult to put these thoughts aside and return to work, but that is precisely what Scrooge, ever the businessman, did.

Later that day Scrooge approached Homer's high perch in the front office.

"Homer," he began, "what have you found, or not found, in your search of our business papers?" He knew there was little chance of discovery, but they had to try.

"Oh, Mr. Scrooge, Sir," said Homer as he quickly climbed down from his stool to stand before his master. "I have almost completed my investigations and there were only two or three things I found that were simply mistakes, it seems. At least, that's what Mr. Symons and Mr. Cratchit told me when I showed them. There were some wrong dates and a few incomplete or inaccurate figures, but they've put them to rights, Sir.

"I did think, Sir," continued Homer, "that perhaps we had a problem with one of your northern clients, but it turns out it was nothing more than a misplaced contract, which we later found."

"Well," replied Scrooge, "keep at it until you've finished going through everything. I apologize if we've wasted your time, my good man, but I'm sure you are being thorough. At least, thanks to your efforts, we can assume we either have nothing this burglar believes we have, or we still do not know where to look."

As he started to go, Scrooge looked back and said, "Homer, should you have any other ideas on this thing, be sure to share them with Mr. Symons or myself. We rely on you to be level-headed and vigilant!"

"Yes, Sir, Mr. Scrooge. I'll do my best!" replied Homer. After climbing back onto his stool, Homer sat with his back a little straighter and began sifting through yet another pile of papers.

CHAPTER THIRTEEN

Wednesday, November 27, 1844

Ira Thorne sat at his desk in the office of Thorne Shipping. He had created the Company in 1820 with only one small boat, large enough to carry small shipments of cargo between the Continent and London. The Company thrived under his hand and had, by now, even branched into operations between Great Britain and America. British trade was increasing rapidly and Thorne Shipping was among the largest shippers of both goods and passengers, although, for the latter, it was mostly steerage. His clippers were among the best and the fastest, and he was also involved in the tea trade, which he believed would prove extremely lucrative.

One of the reasons Thorne had been so successful, besides his dogged determination and boundless energy, was the fact that he was careful. He hadn't always been so, but in 1822 he learned a hard lesson and discovered the value of caution and prudence. He followed rules, did not even approach a gaming table, and did not drink to excess.

As Thorne Shipping increased in size and variable cargoes, the loss of a ship could be ruinous. So, unlike some of the others, Thorne insisted that his ships be laden correctly and carry loading marks according to Lloyd's Register. They were classed by the Register and all Classification Society suggestions were followed. Thorne had, in his maturity, realized that profits were not worth the risk that an overloaded craft must take, even if he could eventually make good the losses through insurance. He was an astute businessman and knew that recouping a financial loss through insurance did not necessarily equate with regaining good will from a customer who had not received his merchandise.

The Company was now expecting the arrival of a shipment of sugar products from the West Indies, which was usually cause for cheerful anticipation, but Thorne was anything but cheerful. He was despondent. The simple fact was that he no longer felt secure. He had been extremely pleased with his life until a few weeks ago, when he was abruptly threatened with the loss of all he had worked so hard to accumulate. It came to light through his son, Julian, who had no idea of the potentially devastating news he was delivering to his father that Tuesday night this past October.

On that particular evening Julian and his wife Marian had been taking supper with the Senior Thornes and Julian's younger sister, Leah. As usual, the company was very congenial since both Mr. and Mrs. Thorne liked Marian very much. There were no grandchildren yet, but that would surely come, in time. All was as it should be.

The blow was delivered without warning, very simply and quite innocently.

Between mouthfuls of turbot, the younger Thorne looked up and said, "By the way, Father, do you recall my old school chum, Fred Symons?" As he savored the excellent dish, Thorne searched his memory, and gave a slight wag of his head. He remembered a Symons alright, but it could not be the same family. The Symons he had known, and despised, was well-deservedly dead and had been for at least two decades. His death and the years in between were one reason Thorne felt so safe.

"I ran into Fred at Lloyds the other day," said Julian, "and he is the same congenial fellow he ever was. I was once again quite taken with him and I hope to renew our acquaintance. He was always a great sport at school, and a very loyal friend."

Mr. Thorne said, disinterestedly, "The name is not uncommon, but I do not recall him. Perhaps we never met. What is his father's name?"

"Oh, I don't think I ever knew. I never asked because his father is dead – has been most of Fred's life – certainly long before we met. I think he died when Fred was quite young, and he had already lost his mother to some illness or other, so his childhood was really quite bleak." Thorne put down his fork with a clatter and turned ashen. His son failed to notice, and continued speaking.

"He seems to have fared well enough, though, and is really a decent fellow." Then, as if to prove Fred's worthiness, Julian added, "In fact, he's doing quite well. He has gone into business with his uncle and is now a partner – Scrooge and Symons – yes, that's the name, on Cornhill Street. I'll have to stop by some day and pay my respects."

Impossible! "Scrooge, did you say?" Thorne felt as if he were seeing the room through a tunnel. His knuckles were white in his lap as he stared intently at his son, trying not to panic. Then he repeated, making an effort not to sound disconcerted, "Ebenezer Scrooge? He is this fellow's uncle?"

"Why, yes, come to think on it, I believe he did say it was Ebenezer. I understand Mr. Scrooge is an astute businessman, so hopefully the partnership will be profitable for Fred."

Profitable! No one knows how to make a profit better than Ebenezer Scrooge and this partnership may be more lucrative to him than you would like, fumed Thorne. *With his business acumen and his ruthlessness, he could easily wind up with your entire fortune!* Thorne did not voice his thoughts, and the conversation moved on to other topics, but he was only half listening and had lost his appetite entirely. He must ask.

"How is Scrooge Fred's uncle? How are they connected?"

"I don't know, Father. Perhaps it is only an honorary title since, as far as I know, Fred has no living family."

It was too much! After all these years, here was Geoffrey Symons' son – and to think he was Scrooge's nephew, or close associate of some sort! He could imagine no worse news and no worse partnership. This opened the way for disastrous possibilities, depending upon what Scrooge and his nephew knew, and when and how they would strike. Scrooge could grab all Thorne had built – and Thorne knew he would – if he did not take care. He determined to make the first move, and to do it anonymously, with caution. No one must be able to decipher a connection.

It was immediately after dinner that night in October that Thorne began to form his plan and he eventually saw it put into action, but so far it had failed. The appropriate men had been hired through third parties, and they had searched Fred's home and Scrooge's offices, but to no avail. Now Thorne was becoming desperate. He could not afford to sit back and wait. He would soon have to resort to more drastic action, which he was willing to do. Truth be told, he was willing to do most anything short of murder to preserve his hard-earned enterprise. No, Scrooge and that nephew of his would not have anything of Thorne's! He would not hand it over to that coldblooded villain, Scrooge – or, as he had often referred to him – "Ebenezer Scourge."

As Thorne wrestled with his fears and devised strategies to thwart a possible loss, the offices of Scrooge and Symons were bustling. It was now Wednesday afternoon and Dick Wilkins stopped in as requested. He asked Scrooge, "So, my friend. What more have you learned about this burglary of yours? Any idea yet who did it, or why?"

"None at all," replied Scrooge, shaking his head, "although we believe it is tied, somehow, to a recent break-in of Fred's residence. Nothing was taken there, either. We assume it was because Catherine's lap dog started barking and successfully interrupted the house-breaker. Now, however, I'm thinking it is something else, entirely. I suppose, as does Fred, that someone is looking for a particular item. I wish we knew what it was and who wants it."

Fred nodded in agreement, saying, "Since it seems they've not yet found it, I suppose there is the possibility that we might find it first – if we actually have it, that is. Unfortunately, there is also the possibility that we won't recognize it if we do stumble upon whatever it is." Dick was intrigued and had been biting his lower lip in thought. "You need to flush them out!" he ventured.

Scrooge decided to share an idea he had been entertaining.

"This is a peculiar puzzle, men, but it brings an idea to my mind. Apparently this item is something that is extremely important to someone, and he (or she) doesn't want us to have it. Naturally they don't realize we have no idea what 'it' is. Interestingly, if we look at this from the other way round, that may, perhaps, give us the upper hand." He took on a conspiratorial expression, glancing at each man in turn.

"What do you say to making them think we not only have it, but we are going to . . . I don't know, exactly . . . we are going to do something with it that they don't want done. If we let it be known that the article is in this office and that we are planning to do something with it, we might, perhaps, force their hands and grab their thieving wrists in the process."

Scrooge, Dick and Fred looked at each other, considering the merits of the proposal. Finally Scrooge called to his faithful clerk. "Bob Cratchit! Come here, man, we need you!" As Bob made his way to the group, Scrooge commented, "No one is more level-headed than Cratchit. We'll pick his brain on this."

Bob appeared, looking apprehensive, and was told of the idea for flushing out the burglars. After he had listened, he was asked to give his opinion. He thought a moment and began, somewhat timidly, to make a suggestion.

"I agree with your thoughts on this matter, Mr. Scrooge. Whatever it is, it must be something that is of great worth to whomever is in possession of it, or it is something you can use against them, or they want to use against you. Given that, we must assume it involves profit and loss, or reputation. I agree they apparently do not wish whatever it is to be made public, and they may not be certain of their right to have it, or they would simply walk through the door of these premises and ask for it. I also agree that that is your bait." Warming to his subject, he continued.

"If you wish to force an action, as Mr. Scrooge says, put it about that you will be making a remarkable announcement on a date certain and that the announcement will come from this office. That will suggest that the item lies within these walls and they may once again try to obtain it before exposure occurs. If you limit the dates to one or two, it would be a simple matter to lie in wait, and catch them within that time frame."

The group considered what had been said. Somewhat hesitantly, lest he appear presumptuous, Cratchit suggested, "I am very curious as to the nature of this thing and would be most happy to be included in the venture." Wilkins nodded in agreement and said he, too, would like to be included.

Scrooge and Fred both shook their heads and Scrooge spoke. "I would not ask it of you, Bob. Your good wife would not appreciate it, were I to place you in harm's way, nor would your Priscilla," he said to Dick, "so we will not even consider involving the two of you in the matter. You have both contributed by helping us devise a plan, and that will serve us well. However," he added, "perhaps, Dick, you could play a part by immediately putting the news about at the Exchange, and a few other choice locations. You know, get people talking. It won't take long to spread. Surely our burglars will get wind of it within hours, if they are a part of the business community. If not, we've lost nothing by coming up with an empty trap."

Donning his coat and hat, Dick agreed by saying, "I will start my tongue wagging this minute, and perhaps they may strike even tonight!"

Having said that, Dick left with his commission to speak loudly and widely about how the offices of Scrooge and Symons would, the next day but one, make a startling announcement that would astonish the business community of London.

"Let's only pray it works," said Fred. "We can manage to lie in wait for two nights, and it will be worth the investment of time if we actually manage to catch these scoundrels. Besides," he added, "I want to know what it is they think we have!"

"It is my thought," cautioned Scrooge, "that we should not involve the Police. There are those of them who are no better than the rogues they arrest and we do not want this scheme foiled. We will naturally turn our man over to them, once we have him securely in our grasp!" The others agreed and it was decided that Scrooge, Fred and Homer would lie in wait inside the offices that night, and the next if need be, in hopes that their suspects would be desperate enough to make another move.

CHAPTER FOURTEEN

Wednesday Night, November 27, 1844

There was little moonlight that night as Scrooge, Fred and Homer met at Fred's house and walked the distance to the office. It was past nine o'clock so they were not likely to be noticed. A bit of weak illumination emanated from a few windows, but most streets were dark. Still, their caution drove them to considerable stealth. Had they been spotted by the local constabulary they may have been mistaken for being up to no good and their entire endeavor sabotaged by being brought before a magistrate, themselves!

Keeping to the shadows, they turned a deserted corner and avoided the frail light from an upstairs window by hugging the brick wall of the building. Upon hearing a sudden burst of voices, they quickly hid themselves in a fetid alleyway as two drunks stumbled boisterously from an ale house. Several blocks later they started to cross a dark passage when, from their right came a fierce, ungodly scream and a small body struck Fred's back with a "Whump!" With a yelp Fred drew up short, prepared to fight for his life, but it was only a tomcat that had leapt from an eave onto his shoulder, quickly scampering off into the black distance. The animal was well away before Fred realized he was crouched, fists ready and head down. His stance caused Scrooge and Homer to charge into him from behind, buckling and pushing. Fred was knocked to one knee as they exchanged a few hushed oaths to cover their fright.

Fred quickly regained his footing and whispered, "Sorry, Uncle. Homer. I apologize. My fault – and that blasted feline's." He tried to ignore his heartbeat as it banged away like a savage war drum, and they continued walking.

"It's alright, m'boy," murmured Scrooge as he patted him on the back. "No harm done and we're almost there."

Within minutes they had reached Newman's Court. Scrooge drew a key out of his waistcoat, turned it as quietly as he could, and they slowly entered the dark interior, creeping quietly as if the burglar might already be within. Scrooge had never noticed the sound of the door's hinges during the day, but tonight they let out a startling squawk and he made a mental note to get them oiled. Each of the men knew the rooms by heart and made his way to the post he had previously agreed to occupy, to crouch on the floor behind his own desk. Scrooge and Fred would be further back in the offices and Homer would man his own station near the front door, which he had already closed and re-locked.

The night amplified every sound from within and without. Noises that would have been masked during the workaday were sufficiently magnified to give a slight sense of vulnerability. Footsteps echoed outside the door, scampering by as if being chased, but no one followed. A woman's high, shrill laugh slashed the cold air like jagged glass, followed by low conversation with a male voice until they both died away. Amazingly, they could even hear carriage wheels on the stones a full street away. A dog barked in the distance, and their old building carried on a monologue of its own, with grumbling creaks and groans.

By midnight the need to stretch their muscles became so intense they could hear each other rustling about. They were like dogs circling in their beds and at one point Fred stood and tiptoed into the other office, to join his uncle. It did not occur to them that things might not go as they had planned, since this was one of two nights it must happen if they had, indeed, set a good trap.

At half-past twelve Scrooge emitted some muffled snores as his chin slid slowly to his chest. Fred grinned to himself in the darkness, assuming his uncle's advanced years made it easy for him sleep in such a position. After several snuffles Scrooge awoke with a snort just as someone began picking the door lock.

"Hush, Uncle!" warned Fred. "Someone is here."

The plan had been for all to wait until the intruder reached the cabinet where contracts were kept, and thwart him in the act of rifling through the documents. To that end they waited while the lock was snapped and the door slowly creaked open. Homer saw a man's silhouette hunched in the doorway, then it entered and, after a brief pause, the door was swung mostly shut. The dark figure felt its way cautiously through the front clerks' stations, toward the interior of the building.

The specter worked its way slowly, feeling for guidance, while Homer tried to make out its movements. Since he believed himself to be the sole occupant of the building, the intruder didn't bother to stifle his "Ow!" followed by a string of profanity when he bumped into a heavy stool. It was an old stool with high unsteady legs, and it had a habit of sharing its imbalance with anyone who dared to make contact. Before he could right himself, he fell to the floorboards with a clatter, dragging the stool with him. The crash resounded through the office, and both Scrooge and Fred mistook the racket for Homer being locked in combat.

They rose awkwardly, forcing their stiff joints to support them as they determined to play their part in apprehending the intruder.

Homer, however, had not moved from behind his high desk. He was waiting for the culprit to regain his footing when, like hounds on the scent, Scrooge and Fred bounded from the back, banging into each other as they charged through the hallway, creating a commotion that would have alerted a burglar across town. As the man tried to untangle himself from the stool in order to escape, Homer leapt from his post, landing squarely on his back. They struggled until the burglar managed to pull one arm from his coat-sleeve and drag Homer with him as he made for the door. The room was filled with grunts and other noises but Homer somehow managed to shout, "Quickly men, lend a hand – I've got him!"

Halfway to their prey Scrooge was felled with a severe cramp to his right calf. Paralyzed, he howled, "Curse the luck – see to it, my boy!" and Fred bounded ahead into the front office to join the melee. He dived onto the two wrestling bodies like a four-year-old into a feather bed and fought for all he was worth. Within seconds Scrooge limped in, his leg muscle still in knots, and energetically joined the fray. No one could see beyond his nose as each tried to match flailing fists and boots with equal vigor.

Scrooge grappled with what felt like an empty sleeve just before a solid set of knuckles met his cheekbone under his eye. An uppercut to Homer's chin spun him around so that he struck his face on the corner of his work-stand, knocking him silly. Blood spurted from his nose as he sat shaking his head to regain his senses. Fred, meanwhile, found himself locked in a choke hold from which he could not escape. He kicked wildly to free himself, his foot connecting with flesh, and he heard a loud grunt. He realized who had his head in a vice when Scrooge gave his neck a yank and yelled, "Take that, you spawn of Perdition!" To save himself from real harm, Fred gurgled, "Uncle!" but Scrooge was too busy to listen. He continued to twist his nephew's jaw into an unnatural angle until Fred finally managed to cry, "UNCLE!" and Scrooge realized he had the wrong man.

With that, the two relaxed their thrashing and the fighting ceased entirely. During the last few seconds of tumbling around on the floor and knocking each other about, their quarry had escaped. They slowly untangled themselves and got up from the floor to assess the damage to the room, and to each other.

Favoring his right leg and gingerly touching his cheek-bone, Scrooge limped over to close the door and said, "Homer, light one of those lamps and we'll put things to rights here." Still holding his handkerchief to his nose, Homer stood, retrieved a lucifer, then removed the kerchief long enough to strike the match and light a lamp. The scene was worse than they expected. It had been admirably ransacked and resembled a bear-baiting ring after a match. Furniture was overturned, their clothing was torn and in disarray, and blood from Homer's nose had spattered an area the size of Southwark. Amid the rubble also lay a torn black overcoat. "It would seem," remarked Fred, "that our miscreant is, at least, a little colder for our efforts."

"You might search the pockets for clues," suggested Homer, sounding a bit nasal through his pinched nostrils.

Fred dug into one of the coat's pockets and found a large number of matches. A folded packet of something resembling blasting powder was in the other pocket.

"I do believe," announced Fred, "that, unless that fellow was planning to smoke a colossal segar, he meant to reduce our business, and perhaps half of London, to a glowing heap of rubble!"

They were returning furniture to the proper places, gingerly touching their injured flesh and straightening their clothing, when someone pounded loudly on the door.

"P'rhaps it's our miscreant, come to retrieve his overcoat," remarked Fred sardonically. Scrooge sullenly jerked the door open to find the policeman, Rollo Norris, wearing a grin that did not fit the situation.

"Good evening, Mr. Scrooge," he said a little too pleasantly. Giving a hard yank with his right arm he pulled a scruffy looking man into the doorway. "Are you looking for this fellow, by chance? I caught him scurrying from here like a rodent from a broom, and since I knew what you were about, I grabbed him on the off chance he was your man. He says his side hurts, that someone kicked him and cracked his ribs, and he complains of at least one loosened tooth." Giving a chuckle, Norris announced, "Allow me to introduce the dishonorable Willie Higgs, who is totally unworthy of his company."

The man, who was already trussed in iron cuffs, twisted in Rollo's grip and cried, "I ain't done nuthin' – you've nabbed the wrong man!" Rollo gave him another jerk and said, "Here you, stop your struggling – it won't do. I know you. You've been caught proper and you might as well settle down and take what's coming to you, which will only be transportation, if you're lucky!" With that, he shoved him into a chair and proceeded to ask questions of the others. Trying not to fabricate, they gave the basic outline of the story, glancing at each other occasionally to ensure that they were in agreement about leaving out a few unimportant details regarding their ineptitude and precisely how they may have received their bruising.

"But Constable Norris," said Fred. "How on earth did you come to be here at this time of night, and what did you mean when you said you knew what we were about? We made a particular secret of it and we certainly did not include the police in our plan!"

"I am aware of that, Mr. Symons," replied Rollo, "but I learned of your escapade through a mutual friend." Leaning back against the wall, he glanced quickly toward Homer, then back to Fred. "I happened to call on Miss Cratchit earlier this evening, and she told me of the goings on." Homer glared narrowly around the bloodied kerchief with which he was now squeezing his nose a little more tightly than was necessary. Rollo failed to notice and continued with his explanation.

"It seems Mrs. Cratchit told her daughter of your trap for this fellow and Miss Cratchit was concerned." Gripping the burglar by the handcuffs he pulled him to his feet and added, "I came by to offer my services just as this accommodating fellow flung himself through the doorway and straight into my welcoming arms." It occurred to Homer that Rollo may have visions of someone else in his arms, but by heaven he'd accomplish that only over Homer's dead and already bleeding body.

In fact, Homer was feeling anything but a champion. Come morning, he was sure to resemble one of those North American raccoons, whereas Norris, unscathed, would no doubt still be sporting that impertinent grin and be hailed as a hero by all concerned. Even Martha Cratchit might cast adoring glances his way. Homer felt completely ridiculous and had a fleeting thought of booking passage to India.

Rollo interrupted Homer's imaginings by saying, "I'll take this fellow now, and I assure you he will be persuaded to tell what he knows – rely on me for that." His threat to make his captive talk by whatever means necessary brought a loud whine from Higgs.

"'Ere now, govn'r. There in't no need for that sort o' thing – no need for violence. I'll tell you what I know right enough, but it in't much 'cause I dunno who hired me, not direct-like, anyways." Pointing to each of the men, he demanded, "First off, though, get me away from these 'ere lunatics. They might 'a killed me if I 'adnt made me escape. Not a one of 'em knows his 'ead from me ol' Gran's teapot!"

Chapter Fifteen

Thursday Morning, November 28, 1844

It was a subdued group that met in the offices of Scrooge and Symons the following morning. Homer's fears about his appearance were predictive since he did, in fact, resemble a raccoon. Both eyes were blackened into a mask and his swollen nose punctuated the effect of having been thoroughly thrashed. Several lacerations and bruises dotted Fred's face, as well as a few knots on his head. Scrooge sported a black eye, which had caused Mrs. Dilber to let out a horrified yelp when she saw him. She attempted to order a beefsteak for his face, but Scrooge wouldn't hear of it. He insisted he hadn't the time and needed to be at his offices as quickly as possible.

Upon each man's arrival, their meetings included apologies to each other for the previous night's fracas, while Bob and Peter Cratchit tried in vain not to stare or ask too many questions.

Before they could ask, at any rate, Scrooge announced the obvious.

"Men, I am forced to admit that our attempt at crime detection and apprehending criminals last evening was a partial failure. There would be no use in denying it since I'm certain it will be common knowledge throughout the business community by the noon hour, particularly since we are walking proof of what occurred." Turning to Bob and Peter, he continued in a slightly abashed tone.

"As you can see, we have been beaten and battered and are totally unsuited to the job of policing. Sadly, we inflicted more injuries on each other than on the culprit."

Scrooge made the mistake of looking from the Cratchits, who were literally gaping, to Fred, his mouth forming a silent "Ooh" as he absentmindedly felt a tender lump on his head, and at Homer, whose visage reminded him of a stuffed animal he'd once seen in the museum. Without warning, Scrooge surprised himself and everyone else by abruptly doing what was least expected. He burst out laughing! He couldn't help it. Mrs. Dilber's early morning squeal at the sight of him, their ridiculous antics of the previous evening, the would-be arsonist's belief that they were all mad as hatters and the fact that today they resembled a gang of fist fighters was suddenly too much. He leaned back and let out a whoop that shook the rafters. Within seconds they were all hurrahing and laughing until their sides gave them as much pain as their injuries.

Finally, Scrooge blew his nose and, folding his handkerchief back into his pocket, explained further to Cratchit, "In spite of us, Bob, our man was caught, but it was only because of the police – specifically, Constable Norris."

"Preening peeler," muttered Homer, to no one in particular.

"But Uncle," remarked Fred, who was, at the same time, gingerly exploring the ache in his wrenched neck, "We still have no idea who these people are or what they are about."

"No, my boy, we don't, but we're going to find out, by Heaven, and I mean that literally, since we need all the help from on High that we can get!"

At that moment Constable Norris himself wandered into the counting office of Scrooge and Symons, whistling a chipper tune. He greeted Homer, who was less than pleased to see him, and asked for Mr. Scrooge. Homer knew he shouldn't be so put off by Norris, but there it was, and there was little he could do about it. It was true that only one thing stood between them – the lovely person of Martha Cratchit – and it kept him from warming to the fellow, for certain. Trying to look and sound more friendly than he felt, he announced Norris to Scrooge.

"Ah, Constable!" said Scrooge, looking up from some figures. "Have you news of our incendiarist?"

"I can bring you up to date, after a fashion," said Norris, taking the seat that was offered. "I left our felon to stew overnight, and that loosened his tongue. Old Willie Higgs is an odd old job, that's certain. He's been up to no good for years, mostly as a lockpick, which is no doubt why he was chosen for this caper, but he's never before come up for a felony. He told me as much as he knew, I would swear to that, but it isn't much and not enough to point the finger at who is behind this."

"You know," interjected Scrooge, "I've been considering this fellow Higgs and I must admit I have a bit of mercy brewing in my chest for the old fellow. We will no doubt be testifying at trial and I sincerely hope he is transported, rather than hanged." Not particularly caring whether he would receive an argument from the Constable, he added, "After all, nothing of value was taken and the poor wretch did not actually set anything aglow. I hope it's possible that his sentence will not include a rope around his neck, and I plan to say so at the hearing."

"That's well and good, Mr. Scrooge," said Norris. "He claims he doesn't know about the burglaries of Mr. Symons' home, nor this office, and he can't identify who really hired him, either, but that may not help his case.

"In fact," continued Norris, not realizing he had reverted to street jargon, "his story is that he was contacted by a chavey he'd never seen before who ran notes between him and someone who was most likely out of twig, so he could never be identified. Higgs would get another prig, who could read, to tell him what each note said, and Higgs would then tell the chavey what to tell his contact. This happened two or three times until Higgs agreed to do the job and was paid half up front with a promise of the rest when the job was done."

Scrooge was totally baffled. He hoped he would never have to testify to what Constable Norris had just said, because he had no idea what it meant. Norris noticed Scrooge's blank expression and returned it with one of his own until he realized what he had done. Embarrassed, he apologized and explained.

"Sometimes I forget that I speak two languages, Mr. Scrooge. Please excuse me for using slang. What I meant to say was that Willie Higgs was contacted by a street urchin who was the go-between for Higgs and a representative of whoever was paying him. He's certain whoever contacted the urchin was using a disguise because the boy told Higgs the man looked different each time they met, and that it might even have been more than one person. Since Higgs can't read, he had another thief tell him what the notes said, but we can hardly charge that other fellow with reading notes, can we?" Here Norris sighed and said, with resignation, "No, Mr. Scrooge, I fear there is little chance we will be able to trace whoever is behind this."

Brightening a bit, and with a mischievous grin that stopped just short of impertinence, he couldn't help but add, "Still, Gov, at least we do 'ave the cove what was willin' to strike the match in return for some chink!" Scrooge had to laugh, in spite of himself.

CHAPTER SIXTEEN

Saturday, November 30, 1844

Scrooge had accepted an invitation to dine with the Purtell-Smythes and was not particularly looking forward to it, simply because his mind was elsewhere. He had been preoccupied for at least two weeks now. Although he, Fred and Homer had caught their attempted incendiarist, they still did not know the secret behind the break-ins. More importantly, Scrooge continued to be eaten away with the need to know about Fan's death. The load of guilt and uncertainty encased him like the thick London smoke, making him lose his bearings. Yet he knew he must attend the dinner. They were expecting him and he thought it might even do him some good. Perhaps an evening of congenial company would take his mind off of things, at least for the amount of time it took to enjoy a good meal and a few hours of pleasant conversation.

As Scrooge entered the home, his host greeted him with a hearty, "There you are, Scrooge! I've wanted to get a look at you since I heard you were playing fisticuffs with burglars!" Scrooge struck a good-natured pose, letting Purtell-Smythe give him a thorough look-over. Laughing a bit, he looked at Scrooge's healing blackened eye and said, "I see they got at least one good punch on you, but I'll assume you gave better than you got!"

"Well, my friend," said Scrooge, relaxing his stance, "I'm afraid I can't account for who gave which blow, because the entire incident was far too confusing to attach a punch to a particular person." That was as close as he was going to get to admitting that the bruise on his face may have been delivered by his own dear nephew!

Embarrassed, Scrooge waved the subject off good-naturedly and the two wandered up to the drawing room where the guests were assembling. It was to be a small group of ten persons.

"I hope you don't mind, old fellow," said the host, "but my wife has partnered you with my cousin, Mrs. Langstone. I assure you she will hold her own in any conversation and – Oh! That's right – you've met. Well that's even better. Meanwhile we are awaiting two more guests, and – ah – they've just arrived so I'd best see to them since my wife has been cornered by the town gossip."

Scrooge had not had the chance to respond to Purtell-Smythe and was about to seek out Mrs. Langstone when, without warning, from behind came an outburst that was all too familiar and sent chills up his spine. It was the last thing he needed.

"Ha-HA! Why, Mr. Scrooge!" blared Honora Purdy. "We are together again. We travel in the same circles, I see, and that's as it should be." Through her nose she exhaled a loud, "Pheh!" and continued. "Now, tell me, what have you been doing with yourself since we last saw each other, and *do* tell me all about that bruised face of yours. I'm all ears! H-EEH-hah!!"

"I am well enough, Mrs. Purdy," bowed Scrooge almost politely, "considering that I am growing older, am somewhat acerbic and most likely very unpleasant company. That being the case, I would suggest you avoid me as you would the pestilence." The words popped out of his old nature before his new nature could prevent it, but he wasn't sorry. Not a bit. He had too much on his mind to be corralled by this noisy woman and horse-whipped by her effrontery on top of it all. Never mind that she had the best of intentions. Unpleasantness, by whatever motive it was delivered, was still unpleasantness, and he had had quite enough of that for the time being.

Mrs. Purdy was not easily put off because such statements tended to roll off her back like dust under a grooming comb. However, before she could reply, which she was rearing up to do, Scrooge was, for the second time in a fortnight, rescued from her advances as dinner was announced. From nowhere a balding Mr. Blythe slid silently up to Mrs. Purdy's side, offered her his arm and she, somewhat confused and disappointed, took it with an unhappy backward glance at Scrooge as she was ushered, unwillingly, downstairs to the dining room.

Relieved, Scrooge heaved an audible sigh, located Mrs. Langstone near the fireplace and offered her his arm. "I believe we are partnered tonight," said Scrooge pleasantly. "I hope you don't mind."

"I should say not," replied Mrs. Langstone, smiling pleasantly. "I welcome the opportunity to continue our previous discussions." Realizing the partial content of those exchanges, she quickly added, "Do not be alarmed, Mr. Scrooge, I have no intention of revisiting that sad topic. I mean to speak only of interesting and congenial subjects throughout the meal. Will that do?"

Laughing lightly, Scrooge replied, "It will do very well, Mrs. Langstone," and with that he escorted her downstairs. He would not bring her up to date on his current investigation regarding

Fan tonight, at least not unless the moment was right. Some weight was being lifted from him and he felt himself begin to relax for the first time in many days.

They reached the dining room, which was well-lit and inviting. The table was attractive in its settings of china, service, and glittering lights. Dinner would be *a la Francaise*, with a tureen of turtle soup set before the hostess and a fish dish before the host. They would serve themselves before handing the dishes to servants, who would distribute the food to their guests. Other dishes were placed at the sides and corners of the table and would be carried to each diner.

Scrooge seated Mrs. Langstone, and looked around to ensure that all the ladies were situated before sitting down himself. He helped Mrs. Langstone to the wine and they began with the soup.

Two chairs away and across the table sat poor Mr. Blythe, who was saying not a word but was, instead, bravely ignoring Mrs. Purdy without appearing to do so. He gave an occasional grunt or nod of his head, which apparently satisfied her idea of conversation since she spoke and brayed to those on each side of her without need of reply. Occasionally her laugh would penetrate someone else's exchange then be quelled long enough for her to place another spoonful in her mouth. Neither Scrooge nor Mrs. Langstone appeared to mind the noise, so engrossed were they in each other's company.

Following the first removal, more dishes were served and the side dishes changed. Throughout the bustle the men teased Scrooge good-naturedly for his bruised eye. One fellow to his left loudly announced, "If you were a married man, Scrooge, I would say you'd said the wrong thing to your wife!" and everyone, including Scrooge, laughed. Mrs. Langstone asked what had caused the bruising, and he gave her an abbreviated version of the attempted arson. When she realized he was skirting the issue somewhat, she asked, instead, about his taste in music and entertainment and that exchange took up the whole of the second course. Mrs. Langstone mentioned that she and her late husband greatly enjoyed the theatre.

In between bites of a tender cutlet, Scrooge replied by saying, "I do not believe I knew your husband, madam. May I ask you to tell me about him?"

"Certainly, Mr. Scrooge, I would be pleased. Avery Langstone was a very unusual man. It was widely assumed that I married him for his wealth since he was nearly twenty years older than I, but nothing could have been further from the truth. I loved him because he was kind and generous – with both his time and energy – toward his friends and anyone he felt he could help. That is one of the reasons, after his death nine years ago, I became so interested in the plight of the poor, particularly the orphans."

With her last statement Scrooge recalled the boy and girl described as "Ignorance and Want" who had peered from beneath the skirts of the Spirit of Christmas Present only last year. Because those pitiful images were burned so effectively into his memory, he did not scoff at her statement. Instead, he said, "I believe the need is real and I have absolute faith in your sincerity and dedication to the cause." He was not sure why he felt or said so, but it was the truth. He was not, however, aware of the depth of her sincerity with regard to this issue.

The table was again cleared for the third course and Mrs. Langstone continued her line of thought.

"I help support a house where street children can go for shelter, food and a certain amount of education." Sensing his unasked question, she said, "Yes, some run away, but some stay. I have to thank God for those who remain because the few successes make it worth the effort. It would be worth it for only one child, you know." She took a sip of the very good claret, and continued.

"I was certain Avery would not mind me using a portion of his wealth to invest in the betterment of humanity – especially in rescuing street children. We had discussed social conditions in London many times, since we had endured our own particular pain in that regard, and I knew he believed private individuals should be taking a more active part in improving the lives of the poor. He was very conscientious and he believed that having wealth brought with it more social responsibility." Scrooge was curious, but did not ask to what she referred when she spoke of her "particular pain."

Without warning, Scrooge was unaccountably jealous. He also felt belittled, even though he knew she meant no such thing. It was ridiculous, but he could not help himself. He barely knew this woman and here he was resenting her dead husband's philanthropy and, if he were totally honest, even her love for him. Two things struck his watchful mind – the first that he could once again have these sorts of feelings for a woman, and the second that the contrast between her generous husband and himself, who had been so thoroughly miserly for most of his adult life, made him feel grossly inadequate. He knew he was being extremely foolish. Just then a loud "Ha-eeh-haw!" rang out from the direction of Mrs. Purdy, as if to underscore that point.

The evening passed quickly for Scrooge and he was surprised that it was already the third removal of dishes. The tablecloth was taken away and the dessert arrived. There were apples, pears and walnuts, as well as finger bowls for each guest.

For the most part, the group was a delightful mix. Conversation was easy and flowed well enough that even the host and hostess enjoyed themselves. After the fruit and nuts had been picked over, Mrs. Purtell-Smythe rose and led the ladies to the drawing room for tea and coffee, leaving the men at table for their segars, port, and a bit of masculine conversation. Initially Scrooge's burglary with its attempted arson was the topic, and that eventually led to a discussion of the new Metropolitan Police Force.

Taking a puff of his segar, Purtell-Smythe said, "Sir Robert Peel has the right idea, I believe. Greater London has been living with his experiment for some time now, and I say it's working."

A guest replied, "I don't think I can argue, but it was a rum go at the beginning. No one trusted the 'Peelers.' Everyone was afraid of even more graft and more corruption."

"I don't believe that has been borne out, by the way," said Scrooge. "Certainly you have no quarrel with the police being able to inspect vessels for smuggling and unlawful cargo, can you?" By now the room was filling with smoke, which made it the perfect setting, according to those who were present.

"No, I can't," said Purtell-Smythe, "and I am in total agreement with the section of the Act that prohibits nuisances such as furious driving, selling or distributing obscenity and discharging firearms. It's only civilized behavior, I say."

One guest could not resist another good-natured jibe and added, "But Peel says he wants to prevent crime, and I'm not sure that's happening. Scrooge's bruised face can attest to that!" They all gave a hearty laugh, including Scrooge himself, before he added, "Well, at least we didn't lose half of London to a pocket full of blasting powder."

Eventually the men joined the women in the drawing room where conversation once again centered largely on the mundane. At eleven o'clock Mrs. Langstone announced she would be leaving and Purtell-Smythe's carriage was called. She offered Scrooge a ride and he accepted before he realized he lived in the opposite direction from Russell Square. He did not want to take Mrs. Langstone out of the way, leaving her alone for such a long return drive but, upon hearing the conversation, the carriage driver suggested he could deposit Scrooge last. The plan was agreed upon, they settled themselves inside the carriage, and the driver started for Russell Square.

Scrooge asked, "Are you quite comfortable, Mrs. Langstone?" as he handed her a lap robe. Having been assured that she was, he realized he was not accustomed to being alone in a carriage with a woman. Surely it hadn't been as long ago as the ride home from school with Fan, but it was possible. Being in such confined quarters alone with Rebecca Langstone was somewhat intimate – and very pleasant.

They had traveled a short distance and he was about to share with her his search for Fan's murderer when Mrs. Langstone spoke.

"Mr. Scrooge, I realize I piqued your interest when I referred to an incident that brought pain to me and my husband, but you were too polite to pry. I do not know why, but I feel I should make you aware of what occurred since it is that which makes me so passionate about trying to help street children. Perhaps my inclination to tell you is due to your current search for answers to those painful questions regarding Fan."

Scrooge sensed her difficulty in opening the discussion, and soon realized why. After a brief hesitation, which he did not interrupt, she began.

"I feel very strongly about street children, Mr. Scrooge, because our only child – Peter – disappeared to the streets of London when he was six years old. He was with Nanny, a very responsible woman, on an outing to Regents Park. A stranger approached her to ask his direction and she turned her back for a moment to point the way he should take. When she turned back around, Peter was gone. She, and everyone else, including the police, searched every inch of the vicinity, without success. We later realized the 'stranger' was most likely in concert with whoever took Peter because a six-year-old could not have wandered away and disappeared so completely, by himself."

"No, I am certain he would not have," said Scrooge, "and I am aware there are men who perpetrate that very thing." Although Scrooge was pleased and complimented to be in her confidence, he was taken aback. He had not expected such a horrifying event. With some hesitation, he turned his head a little to the side, as if to soften the blow of the truth, and asked, "And was he never found?"

"He was," she murmured, staring at the carriage floor. "His body was recovered from the Thames about three weeks later. He had a head wound that I prefer to believe gave him a quick and unanticipated end. The police concluded he was abducted by men who use young boys to commit crimes that an adult could not perform without being seen. That was my first realization that there were actually two Londons – the one in which I live, and the other, where children are not safe and life is very cheap."

"I'm afraid that is the case, Mrs. Langstone," remarked Scrooge. "I wish it were not so and I am truly grieved to learn of your appalling loss. Time, it seems, cannot totally cure all things. At least you have not wasted yours, as I seem to have done for so many years."

Without realizing he had shared a personal tidbit which she could actually pursue, Mrs. Langstone continued. Her eyes held a mother's infinite grief as she gathered her composure and said, "There was not only the aberrant physical loss of my beloved offspring, there was also that nagging torment over how his last days were spent – and yes, how his death occurred." She shuddered slightly, rubbing her arms as if to warm herself from a chilly draft. Scrooge knew not to press and, instead, let her impart the information at her own pace. She soon continued.

"We suffered dreadfully, Mr. Scrooge. I refused to leave my home for months. I did not want to see the sunlight, nor those terrible streets that had ripped my boy from me. Then, one day – I don't know what possessed me – I called for the carriage and asked the driver to take me aimlessly about town. When a church appeared, I made him stop and somehow managed to get myself inside, not knowing what I hoped to accomplish.

"Inside, however, I met the Rector, who spotted me at some distance away and recognized my emotional state. He spent two hours talking to me even though I was a stranger to him. I will never forget his kindness and his wisdom, not to mention his guidance, and we have remained friends to this day even though I do not worship in his particular parish."

Scrooge was genuinely curious, as well as concerned. "It was fortunate for you that he was available and that he was the sort of man who cared about your grief. If you don't mind telling me, how did he help?"

"I don't mind at all, Mr. Scrooge. It was a very subtle assistance, I would say, because he did not lecture. In fact, I don't recall much that was said, but I know he did not recite clichés and homilies. The one thing I do distinctly remember was a question he asked. He asked if I thought I was helping my son in any way by concentrating on his death, instead of his life. He somehow reached into my heart and wrapped it in hope, as one would staunch a bleeding wound. We even discussed forgiveness, which I could not even consider at the time. That was thirteen years ago, Mr. Scrooge, and in the interim my ability to forgive has grown, eventually displacing the hatred I harbored, leaving room for pity and a deeper love for mankind in its place. It has also freed me to continue living.

"Until the Rector and I talked, I did not realize that my faith had wavered so, but I believe that particular conversation was the turning point for me and I began a slow crawl back to life. Unfortunately, in contrast, my husband began a slow crawl toward his own death. He seemed to recover emotionally and we returned to our normal lives, but his health declined thereafter and he died less than four years later." Here she hesitated, and Scrooge spoke.

"I am so sorry to hear it and I wish there were something I could say or do that would help, but I know too many words can be as empty an assistance as can be too few." He meant it and it was evident in his voice. Even though it was staggering to hear, he wanted to learn every detail about her. They slid to one side as the carriage turned a corner, sending them closer together. As they righted Scrooge put more distance between them, wishing he were not required by good manners to do so, and Mrs. Langstone began speaking again.

"Were it not for my faith, Mr. Scrooge, the entire episode would have broken me, I can assure you, but I truly believe we are placed in a certain space and time for a specific purpose. Some of us are here longer than others." She heaved a sigh, smiled a sad smile and added, "Whatever happened to my child is over now, for him, at least, and I have no doubt he is in Good Hands. My husband and I were able to go on only because of that conviction, although the actual grief did, I am certain, contribute to my husband's weakening health. He was never again as hearty, nor quite as optimistic."

Scrooge nodded his understanding and said, "Losing his only son like that . . ." and could think of nothing else to add. He was humbled. Not two hours ago he had envied Avery Langstone, and now he felt nothing but sorrow for him, as well as for her and their lost child. He did not want to cheapen the exchange, however, and could think of no further comments that wouldn't sound insipid or commonplace. Neither of them spoke for several moments until, abruptly, they both began talking at once. It somehow cleared the tension and they laughed easily. The short remainder of the trip was spent in lighter conversation.

Too soon, Mrs. Langstone was safely put down at her home in Russell Square, the carriage turned carefully around in the street, and Scrooge carried on. He had not told her about his ongoing investigation and his strange conversation with Dr. Devitt, but it could wait. They had shared enough pain for one evening.

CHAPTER SEVENTEEN

Monday, December 2, 1844

On Monday, at some minutes past three, Dick Wilkins appeared at Scrooge's office with a summons for the man, himself. Standing over his desk, Dick said to Scrooge, "I am here on a mission, Ebenezer. Priscilla will not rest until she has heard every detail of your row with a criminal, and she must hear it from your own lips. I have given her the information but she does not credit me with the intelligence, nor the talent, to deliver the facts truthfully, and certainly not with enough élan to keep her interested throughout the entire narrative. She requires your storytelling ability and therefore I am come to drag you to her table. She will ply you with the best tea and cakes she has to offer, for which you must pay by delighting her with a recounting of your recent adventures."

"Dick, my friend," replied Scrooge, "With my turn of mind, at this moment the last thing I am is entertaining." Dick's expression and his arms folded over his chest indicated he would brook no refusal and after several seconds Scrooge sighed, slapped both palms on his desktop and said, "However, as your wife sets one of the finest teas in the Realm, and since I need a reprieve, I will obey her command." The Wilkinses were good company and fast friends, so he might even share his current search regarding the facts of Fan's death. For that reason, he added, "There is a subject on which I may request sage counsel from you both." Wilkins cocked an eyebrow at this statement, but did not pursue it.

Priscilla was thrilled to see Scrooge and thanked him for consenting to be pressed into service. In spite of himself, he was suddenly glad he came. It was good to be among friends just now – people he could trust and with whom he could let down his guard. He sat in his usual spot near the fire as Priscilla alerted the servant that her guest had arrived, then turned to Scrooge and asked him to begin his exciting tale, all the while begging his forgiveness for the summons.

"I simply cannot get a decent story out of this man," she said, gesturing toward Dick, "and I know it must have been very exciting. Do tell me, please – from the very beginning!"

So Scrooge commenced his narrative. He told of the break-in at Fred's, and how their counting house was made "extremely untidy," according to Bob Cratchit. He even included, between bites of very good sandwiches and pastries, the apparent rivalry between Homer and Constable Norris for Martha Cratchit's attention. Priscilla was fascinated by it all, as was Dick, although he pretended not to care quite so much about the romantic bits.

Since they were such close associates, Scrooge also included an unedited version of the fiasco the night the attempted arsonist was taken by Constable Norris. He regaled them so well with his and the others' clownish efforts that Dick once choked on his tea and Priscilla had to wipe her eyes during the telling.

Prior to 1844 Scrooge and Dick had not associated since their time together at Fezziwig's, and Priscilla had only met Scrooge within this past year, so neither of the Wilkinses had any idea how different the man before them was from what he had been for so many years in between. They simply accepted him as a generous friend, full of laughter and concern for others. The conversation became a little more serious when Dick asked, "But have you still no idea who is doing this, or why?"

"I'm afraid not," said Scrooge. Pulling on his ear, he said, "This thing has me flummoxed. I can only hope we figure it out before anything else occurs. I pray whoever it is has been frightened off, at least for now, with the capture of his arsonist, but I admit it's been weighing heavily on me, knowing someone, somewhere, is determined to get his hands on something that is evidently valuable, or possibly dangerous. It is apparently in my possession and I have no idea what it is!"

Scrooge had been wondering whether to expose to them his recent quest regarding Fan, and decided to share at least some of it. After all, who better with whom to discuss it since they were part of Fan and Geoffrey's society so many years ago?

"As I mentioned to you, Dick, there is something else I'm wrestling with these days," said Scrooge, "and with your permission, I will tell you both some of it. You may have insight that will point me in the right direction, to solve what has become a very troubling, and possibly tragic, puzzle. I rely, of course, on your discretion."

"Of course, Ebenezer," said Dick, as Priscilla nodded her agreement while she poured more tea. "Please enlighten us."

"I have recently been informed," began Scrooge, "by someone who did not know I thought otherwise, that my sister Fan did not die as a result of complications from childbirth. In fact," how he hated to say this part, "I did a little digging and I now believe she may have died by someone else's hand." Priscilla gasped.

Both she and Dick were shocked, and appalled. Speaking at the same time, they demanded to know more.

Scrooge continued by saying, "I must be blunt. I suspect Fan was given poison and, even though no one has anything to gain by discovering the truth, I am completely unable to let the thing rest! I must do what I can to uncover the facts, even though I realize there is nothing I can do at this point in time. I am like a man possessed! Even if both my sister and her killer are both in their graves that does not put an end to it, at least in my mind, and I cannot stop asking questions." He hated to impose, and said, "I apologize if I'm placing you in an awkward position, but did either of you see anything untoward during your visits to my sister?" He knew he was astounding them, but could see no other means of approaching the matter. He admitted, "I fear, and it pains me to say this, that I was not in her company enough during those years and I do not know as much as I should about her activities, her friends, or even her marriage."

"Well," said Dick, "we were not present for Fred's birth, nor were we there when Fan died, so we have no first-hand knowledge of those particular events." He looked at Priscilla and said, "I think I speak for both of us when I say we would have no evidence of anything sinister ever touching your sister. Everyone loved Fan and thought her the most wonderful person. I simply cannot countenance anyone wishing her harm!" Priscilla nodded her head in definite agreement and said, "Oh, most certainly so."

"But what about her society?" asked Scrooge. "Who were her friends, her companions, or those with whom she spent most of her time? Was there anything noticeably improper or amiss with anyone in her company?"

Dick frowned and slowly wagged his head as though searching the past and finding nothing, but Priscilla, who was quicker regarding the intricacies of relationships, recalled something.

"I don't want to misrepresent anything Ebenezer, but there was one thing that concerned me during our association, which spanned almost two years." She folded her hands in her lap and took on a very serious expression. She was ordinarily not one to repeat unpleasant things.

"Please do not think me a gossip, but there was a young man who seemed very attracted to Fan even though she was a married woman and several years his senior. He was relentless in his attentions and, at times, I thought, very inappropriate." "Neal!" cried Dick, slapping his knee and startling Scrooge. "Neal Edmonds! I'd forgotten that swellhead, for sure! What an immature and overbearing whelp he was." Dick turned to Scrooge. "His father was Geoffrey's godfather, I believe. I recall that whenever he visited he would spend a good portion of his time chasing after Fan like an adoring lapdog and he even had the effrontery, once or twice, to be openly jealous of Geoffrey, of all things! No one took it seriously, of course. We put it down to the reckless attachments of youth, particularly with older women. After some time, we simply ignored him, as did she."

"That is true," said Priscilla. "However, I happened upon him and Fan once when Neal had her literally backed into a corner and was making some very familiar statements. She seemed anxious to escape and I made it possible by interrupting them. His back was to me as I crossed the room, so he was still speaking as I approached. I heard him say, 'I'm old enough to know,' or some such thing. Just before he noticed me he said, 'I will see that you regret that!' I recall thinking it sounded like a threat, even though, coming from him, the effect was more like a child spouting off in the playroom."

"You never mentioned that to me, Pris," accused Dick. "I wonder you didn't."

"I wonder at that, too," said Priscilla, frowning. "I believe I was torn between loyalty to Fan and the fear that I had got it wrong. I discussed it with no one, including Fan. I was discomfit-ed to have witnessed the exchange and I did not want to embar-rass her. I thought she would broach the subject herself, if she wished to discuss it, and she never did. I was also fairly certain that Neal was basically a harmless young popinjay, full of himself, and she would not be easily intimidated by him. There was, too, the possibility that what I thought I heard was not what was re-ally said, or perhaps I had totally misinterpreted the meaning. I did not want to be the means of spreading something that was untrue and, until today, had forgotten the incident altogether."

"What happened to him?" asked Scrooge. "Do you think he was capable of doing harm?" Both he and Dick were staring at her.

"I have no idea as to either of those questions," she replied, with a slow wag of her head. "He lived somewhere south of London and I did not see him after her death since we never again visited the Symons' home. I must suppose he kept in con-tact with Geoffrey, however, because their family association was close and one of long standing."

"Well," said Scrooge, setting down the cup he had forgot-ten he was holding, "at least I may assume Fan's marriage was a happy one, since she did not indicate otherwise in her cor-respondence." He looked up in time to catch the glance that passed between Dick and Priscilla and his business nose told him it was significant.

"What is it?" he demanded, leaning forward. "You must tell me if there is something I should know, or should have known, had I been paying attention. I beg you! Do not withhold even one simple fact from me, if it may be significant!"

Dick interlaced his fingers, resting them on his stomach, looked again at Priscilla, and said, "This particular thing is not a very pretty picture, but since you ask, we can shed some light on Geoffrey's character." He looked apologetically at Scrooge.

"There were some aspects of Geoffrey that were not entirely pleasant. I am certain Fan did not know, and it took me some time to discover it."

"I, myself, had no idea," put in Priscilla, "until Dick made me aware. Once he did so, however, it was easy for me to pick up the signs as I observed Geoffrey's behavior in the company of others."

"This sounds ominous," said Scrooge, who was now leaning forward in his chair, "but please tell me."

"It had mostly to do with his habit of gambling," said Dick, "although, in addition, he was, to state it plainly, very selfish. He was, in spite of that, quite personable, and his charm was his means to using people. I will not say he was totally untrustworthy, although gamblers do often live from one 'win' to the next, not attending to the realities of life as they ought. Because they need a constant 'win' in order feel good, their perceptions are often not grounded in truth. Geoffrey was definitely a gambler and his habits affected his worth as a husband." It was more than he had ever said, even to Priscilla.

"Was he losing a great deal of money?" asked Scrooge.

"Geoffrey lost on several occasions that I know of and I believe that was one reason he allowed your father to live with them. I understood from Geoffrey during one of our week-ends at their home that the 'Old Man' could stay there as long as he kept out of the way and as long as he sold his own residence and allowed Fan to use any funds she required for herself. I wondered, at the time, whether he meant to access the money through Fan." He suddenly realized that Scrooge was the Old Man's son, and would surely have known of such an arrangement.

Scrooge shook his head with an expression that spoke volumes. "I was not aware of any such financial arrangements, which is remarkable, is it not, since my nose was so deep in money at the time." Dick could not know that Scrooge was annoyed with himself, more even than with Geoffrey, for being unaware, or for ignoring, the situation. His thoughts were interrupted as Dick continued.

"Since Geoffrey was a fairly constant gambler, he did lose on many occasions. I know of at least one such occasion when he lost quite heavily and sold a prized piece of family jewelry to cover the debt. He tended to play with men who were high betters and was not above staking some of his most valuable property. I recall one night – I heard about it third-hand from a mutual friend – Geoffrey reportedly put up his best mare and, thankfully, won. I believe I am fairly astute and a handy enough card player that I can say I never knew him to cheat, which is probably why he seemed to lose at least half the time."

Scrooge was unsure whether to ask, but must do so, since she seemed to play a part in the story, "And what about Rebecca Sotherton – Mrs. Langstone? She is mentioned in Fan's letters. I met her at your last evening entertainment and I assume you knew her through my sister, as well?"

"We did," said Dick before Priscilla took up the reply.

"She was Fan's particular friend and very devoted," said Priscilla. "We all liked Rebecca because she was such fun and so natural, yet she wouldn't say anything ill about anyone. That isn't to say she wouldn't laugh with the rest of us when someone else made an unkind yet witty remark, as Geoffrey was so prone to do, but she would never do so herself and she always defended any unfair attack on a friend's character." Here Priscilla paused then said, quite seriously, "Yes, I liked her very much then, and I still do. She has been through some personal tragedies since then, but she has not changed."

CHAPTER EIGHTEEN

Tuesday Evening, December 3, 1844

On Tuesday evening Scrooge was again on Doctor Devitt's doorstep when Mrs. Cooke came around the street corner, carrying a few sad vegetables. She recognized him and wordlessly bade him follow her inside, shaking her head at what she viewed as foolhardy stubbornness.

Once inside, she said, "I dunno what you 'spect from the old doctor, I really don't," but she agreed to announce him, if Scrooge would wait in the hall while she did so. Within two minutes she returned.

"'e don't rightly want to speak with you, nor no one, for that matter, but says 'e will since you'll no doubt jus' keep comin' back if 'e don't." With that, she ushered Scrooge once more into the miserable room where Doctor Devitt was holed up. He was again – or still – under the influence of cheap gin. The doctor looked up at Scrooge wearily, motioned him into a chair with a less than welcoming gesture, and took a drink. Scrooge did not hesitate.

"I do apologize, Doctor, but as you know, this ambiguity is wearing on me and I am once again petitioning you for some answers concerning my sister's death. I am certain I speak the obvious when I say, simply put, my sister did not die from child-birth and her symptoms have been described to me as suspect. I described her symptoms to you during my last visit, at least as they were reported to me. I have no one else to whom I can apply for answers and I beg you to tell me how she died."

"And why do you think I have your answers?"

Willing himself to be tolerant and remain calm, Scrooge replied through tight lips, "You were her doctor. You cared for her on her deathbed. You have at least some of the answers, and I need to know – desperately."

"Pray, tell me, precisely, why it is you need to know, Mr. Scrooge? Are you able to change any of the past? Are you able to resurrect your sister from her grave, if only you have enough information? Or are you simply in need of a bone on which to gnaw?" There was an edge to the doctor's attitude, but Scrooge was unable to discern the emotion behind it and was rapidly losing patience.

"Doctor, I do not recall that your nature was so mulish when you treated my family, and I find your unwillingness to provide a few simple answers inexplicable."

"Ah," said the doctor, "but I was an entirely different man then, Mr. Scrooge. You are not speaking to your old family doctor, you are speaking to a hollow, wasted shell, wherein an easily frightened man once lived, and I do not wish to share my pain with anyone."

Scrooge had had enough. He wanted to shake the man like a straw doll until his stuffing fell out. Instead, he stood to leave, looking down on him.

"That is an absurd reason to refuse my request, doctor. You are not the only one in anguish. I am feeling pain of my own, and if you are attempting to save me from more, your immovability is increasing my agony more than would a straightforward answer, no matter what its content!"

Something in Scrooge's tone and in what he said struck a chord with the doctor. He recognized in Scrooge a fellow sufferer and, like a small spark, it ignited what little charity remained in his breast.

As if dealing with a pesky gnat that cannot be got rid of, the doctor waved his hand in front of his face, then capitulated. In his weakness he had been worn down.

"Sit down, Mr. Scrooge," motioned the doctor. "Sit back down. I do not believe I shall tell you why she died, but I must, I suppose, tell you how." His words were slurred but understandable. In spite of his level of inebriation, his mind was acute.

"Those symptoms you described during our last conversation are, indeed, as you put it, an indication of something 'untoward.' In fact, you needn't have recited them. They are the symptoms of a very common poison – arsenic. I should know. I have lived with them for decades."

He had Scrooge's attention. He had also placed Scrooge in a quandary. He did not want to insinuate that the doctor had been careless or negligent, yet he had just this minute confirmed that Fan's symptoms resembled arsenic poisoning.

"So she *was* poisoned." It was a statement rather than a question. Scrooge bit his lower lip and held it between his teeth, waiting.

The doctor slowly poured more gin into his cup. "I can assure you it is unlikely anyone would be able to ingest arsenic accidentally in circumstances such as your sister's. As to my care of her, that should be obvious, since she died. So, in answer to your question, yes, I am certain your sister was poisoned." There.

He had finally said it out loud. He had actually shared it with another human being, after all these years!

Scrooge had known that might be what the doctor would say, but he was, nevertheless, dumbfounded. It was not what he wanted to hear! He had suspected it, or he would not have asked. Yet, truth be told, he came here to have the doctor say he was mistaken, that Fan had not been poisoned and that Scrooge's imagination had run away with him. He wanted reassurance. He needed to be told his sister had not had an enemy who would be willing to kill her. Not Fan!

Standing, he faced the wall, then turned suddenly and wailed, "*Who*, Doctor? Who would have done such a thing? Have you any idea? Can you tell me anything that will help me make sense of this? What do you know that will help me with this terrible possibility?" His voice sounded like someone else's, and on the verge of hysteria, at that.

The doctor thought for several seconds. Sounding extremely weary, he heaved a sigh and said with resignation, "You need look no further, Mr. Scrooge. You have cornered your quarry."

It took a moment for Scrooge to understand the words. When he realized what the doctor was saying, he could not believe he had heard correctly. No! Such a thing would be insupportable. It was totally unthinkable that this gentle man, into whose hands the entire family had, for years, placed their physical well-being and shared their lives, could be a murderer. Surely he would be incapable of such an act. Surely he would have no motive for killing Fan. Surely the doctor had misunderstood the question, or Scrooge had misunderstood the answer.

"I . . . don't . . . understand you, Doctor."

The doctor stared directly at Scrooge, yet his expression was vacant. He said, almost without emotion, "I do not know what inner forces are requiring my admission on this occasion Mr. Scrooge but, as I said, you need hunt no further. Like an astute hound with a keen scent, you have pinned down your fox and you are welcome to tear him to shreds. It was I who killed your sister."

Scrooge gasped. All of the old ungoverned and destructive emotions exploded, blasting Scrooge's newer nature to pieces. Before he knew what he was doing, he had closed the distance between him and the physician and was choking him with the power of an uncontrolled rage. He was a large man and the sense of loss and his own guilt combined to give him the strength of a Titan.

"You filthy reprobate!" he screamed, as his hands closed around the doctor's scrawny throat, lifting him from where he had been sitting. "Why in Heaven's name would you perpetrate such a despicable crime?" At that moment he fully intended to snap the doctor's spindly neck.

Dr. Devitt gurgled, both eyes bulging as he flailed aimlessly, his natural limited strength diminished further by years of drink and the quantity of gin he had imbibed only this evening. Within a second of actually fracturing the doctor's feeble spine, Scrooge's newer and more merciful personality overrode his frenzy. He released the doctor as if tossing a filthy rag, flinging his body back into the chair. He took a deep breath as his fingers continued to work into fists. Stretching himself up to his full stature, he looked down on the sordid heap of sin and studied the doctor with loathing. He had no words for the disgust and cold hatred he felt for this worthless creature.

The doctor wiped his nose with his sleeve, gave a shallow hack and croaked, "It's not what you think, Mr. Scrooge. I gave her the poison, yes, and for that I cannot forgive myself, but I was an unwitting tool." Then, almost to himself, he looked down and repeated, more softly and sadly slurred, ". . . unwitting, careless, foolish . . ." As if reciting a phrase long practiced yet still ineffective he muttered, almost to himself for no doubt the thousandth time, "But how could I have known? How could I have known the evil that was present in that house?"

Evil in that house? Evil surrounding Fan? Dear God in Heaven. And I was busy making money!

Scrooge continued to stand, his knuckles taut.

"Are you saying you poisoned her without knowing it? Are you actually saying you administered poison that someone else put into your hands?"

Sucking in a rattling breath, the physician pulled a grubby handkerchief from his pocket, coughed again into it, tried to sit up and added, more fiercely, "Yes, that is exactly what I am saying, although I did not actually administer the dose. Nurse Weeks did that, and I'm certain she suspected what she had done. Someone used us to kill that poor lamb." *So THAT was what I saw in her eyes when I asked about anyone wishing Fan harm,* thought Scrooge.

Scrooge slowly sat back down, and the doctor continued.

"The fiend placed arsenic in her laudanum, knowing I had prescribed it as a sleeping potion. Your sister had most likely already taken some and I told Mrs. Weekes to give her a bit more, to help her sleep. She had been restless in her mind, which she found very disturbing. I didn't think to inspect the contents of the bottle and realized too late what was happening – that I had been a pawn in a murderer's game. By then there was nothing I could do but watch that sweet creature as she was torn from this world. Within a day she had suffered convulsions, and was gone." As if he were giving testimony, he added, "I did not tell anyone she had been poisoned. Instead, I let them think she had been taken with an infection and I recorded it as such. It was cowardly, but I did not report the death as a poisoning since I believed I would be a suspect. I believe Nurse Weekes recognized the symptoms, but I would not allow her to speak of it and she was Loyalty, itself. I am certain she never shared her suspicions with anyone."

"You are saying you watched my sister die of a murderer's poison, then added to that offense the self indulgence of covering it up?" Scrooge could barely contain his fury as the doctor shifted his wobbly frame.

"Try not to be too hard on me, Mr. Scrooge. You were not there." As he realized the absolute truth of what he had just said, he added, "In point of fact, Fan's Brother, you were never there, even though I know she beseeched you, time and again, to be at her side. Where were you that entire period? I did not see you once!" Looking as censorious as his inebriated state would allow, he added, "Yet you sit there, so pious, seeking the truth of her death when one of the truths was your total lack of involvement – your total self-serving absence, as it were."

Scrooge felt as though he had been kicked in the stomach, and he nearly doubled-up from the pain of what the doctor said. It was true. He was guilty of neglect and was, perhaps, guilty of giving opportunity to her murderer. He had no retort, which did not matter since the doctor was not finished.

"But there is more to the tale, and I believe I am at a stage in my doomed existence when I may share a piece of it with you, else it will accompany me to my grave. Perhaps it should, but the graves surrounding this incident are growing rather crowded with secrets. You see, your sister's death was accidental on my part, but it was not accidental the second time I killed." Gazing up through rheumy eyes, the doctor swayed somewhat and looked back down into his cup as if searching for courage as well as more gin. He took another swallow before replacing the cup clumsily on the desktop, nearly tipping it over.

"That's right, Mr. Scrooge," said the doctor, his mouth twitching in an ironic half-smile, "I have killed twice, and the second killing was quite intentional, I assure you. You may abhor me, and you certainly have every right, but your censure of me cannot equal the tumult I have suffered these many years for intentionally taking a human life – I, who was sworn to protect it." He gave a pitiful sniffle and weakly gripped the arm of his chair.

Leaning back, the doctor closed his eyes and whispered, "You see, over time I deduced how I had been used, and by whom, and I vowed to set things to rights. So I did, Ebenezer Scrooge – by all that's unholy – so I did. The sorrow I suffered over her death, for which I was technically responsible but did not plan, was somewhat assuaged by my second deed, which I planned with precision. There was also the fact that I had wished him dead many times for his treatment of her and for what I knew of him as a man, and this gave me the excuse I needed, to rid the world of him." He grimaced, as if he were sneering and weeping at the same time.

"Once I knew for sure, I designed my crime. In fact, my strategy was so precise and coincided so perfectly with chance, that it is only this many years afterward that you, by sheer accident, have happened upon the more obvious portion of the truth. Even now, I am certain I tell you more than you suspected." He shifted uncomfortably in the chair, sending a sad squeak into the dark corners of the room.

"I rejoiced then in what I claimed was a justified assassination. The felon deserved to die and at the time I was glad to be his executioner!"

Scrooge was watching the man with a mixture of repulsion and pity but dared not interrupt. He was too hungry for information and was leaning forward.

"I will not enlighten you by giving you every distasteful detail, nor the identity of my second and very deserving victim, for it is no longer of any consequence and the complete truth would not be edifying to you. Were I to make you aware of the entire set of facts, I would be putting you in an untenable position, and that I will not do. No, I refuse to do so. These things were long ago, yet the first death – that of your lovely Fan – was such a loss to everyone who knew her that I could not believe I had been a pawn in such a sport! In the end, however, it was I who checkmated my opponent. I won the game and dispatched him to Hell."

Scrooge's jaw was working.

As if answering an unspoken question, the doctor said, "It was not difficult. I simply administered a similar potion as the one poor Fan had imbibed. I wanted it to be the same death, you see, so I slipped it into a sleeping potion that I, myself, prescribed, and ensured the dosage would take some time to have its desired effect. Then I spoke to him as he experienced the agonies of dying. My heart, by then, was as cold as his soon would be.

"'Look, you!' I taunted him, and I actually laughed as he begged me to end his suffering. I had become such a monster that I mocked him as he writhed in agony. I said, 'This is not the end you had in mind, was it?' Then I told him all that I knew, as well as the facts I had surmised and, since he was dying, he did not deny it. After he took his last breath I almost laughed and simply recorded his demise as a cessation of the heart following a digestive disorder, which I could do in all verity." The doctor sighed. "What I did not record, of course, was that I had been the one to make his heart cease."

Taking the final remaining swallow of gin, the doctor held his cup in both hands and sucked air through missing teeth. He looked at Scrooge shrewdly.

"There are two ironies in all this, Mr. Scrooge. The first is that we all three died of that evil incident, but the death of my body has taken the longest. My spirit, nevertheless, went with both of them." Scrooge shifted uncomfortably in his seat, wishing he could stand and move about, but he did not dare disturb the doctor's account. His eyes remained fastened on the older man and he felt oddly compassionate, although the coldness in his expression belied it. The Doctor noticed and made his own interpretation.

"You may look at me with as much disgust as you wish, Mr. Scrooge, for I am long past being judged by anyone. I face only one Judge now and I pray He will be merciful. But I admit to you, as I must soon to Him, that I have never repented playing executioner, and I never shall!" Then, in a more subdued tone, he added, "I suspect my eternal damnation will be owing more to my refusal to repent, than to the very act, itself."

The doctor looked Scrooge in the eye with a clarity that could last only an instant, and added, somewhat reluctantly, "I will tell you the second irony, Mr. Scrooge. There is the possibility that I may not have executed all of the guilty parties. He may have had an accomplice who procured the poison or actually placed it in the laudanum, but it is too late for me to know. My body is giving out quickly and I haven't long to live. I will, in truth, be pleased to cease this wretched existence. I find it humorous that I managed to take two lives – one without guile, and the other with satisfaction – yet have never had the courage to take my own. Perhaps I have simply done it more slowly, with gin and a general neglect of my health." His words were, by now, extremely slurred and difficult to understand.

The physician's eyes were drooping and, as Scrooge attempted to question him further, he murmured, "Please leave me now, Mr. Scrooge. I can do nothing more for you and I fear I have already injured you beyond repair." With his last few words he slumped slowly onto the desk, forehead on his arms, and passed quickly from inebriation to unconsciousness.

Scrooge would get no more from the doctor that night. To the insensible doctor he murmured, "I truly believe you are attempting to retain a shred of decency by not burdening me with the identity of my sister's murderer, but it will not do." In any event, the doctor had already taken it upon himself to execute him for the crime. At least Scrooge now knew how Fan had died and his knees were weak with the knowledge. How could he accept the fact that she had been poisoned by someone who knew her and whom, very likely, she had trusted? Who would kill her, and why?

Much as he detested his murderous behavior, Scrooge truly pitied the doctor. He had been ill-used and it had led him, albeit voluntarily, into a state of mortal sin from which he appeared unwilling to be absolved. There was also the possibility that the doctor had executed only one of perhaps two who were responsible. How would he ever ferret out the truth if the doctor refused to share it?

Scrooge stood shakily, slid some coins into the destitute doctor's pocket, and stumbled from the house, gulping down sobs that threatened to choke him. His mind was in such turmoil that he took each step as if he might topple into the street.

Oh, my poor, poor Fan. I cannot leave it be, not like this! I must pursue the truth and lay this thing to rest, once for all, and I cannot do that with only half the story.

As he reached the corner Scrooge gained his legs and decided to walk, rather than hail a hansom. He needed to move about and think, so he opted for the cold night air, to clear his head. Recounting the conversation over again in his mind, he asked himself, *but why do I want to know?* He could do nothing about his sister's death, nor bring her killer or killers to justice. As he progressed down the street, he silently admitted, *I have already found myself blameworthy for circumventing my sister's needs. I long ago missed my chance to intervene in her difficulties and must face the fact that I failed her. I ignored her predicament and, in so doing, allowed my Dear One to die!*

His fury against himself and her faceless murderer – or murderers – rose to a degree he had not known for nearly a year, but was experiencing once again this night. Be it guilt or a twisted sense of justice, he *must* know the name of the man who killed Fan! In angst once so well practiced, he swelled his chest with frustration and roared a grief-stricken and devastated, "BAH!"

CHAPTER NINETEEN

Wednesday, December 4, 1844

On Wednesday Scrooge said, "Fred, may I impose on your wife for some supper tonight?" He did not want to be alone this evening and he needed privacy to discuss Doctor Devitt with Fred. Fred was delighted.

"Of course you may, Uncle. Catherine would love to have you, as you well know. You are welcome anytime, and the sooner the better!" Fred smiled as he spoke, reminding Scrooge of how blessed he was to have a nephew who was like a son, and who loved Scrooge without limits and truly wanted him in his life.

That evening Scrooge did, indeed, dine with his nephew and niece. Dark circles under his eyes made him look worn and he was not his cheerful self. He was polite enough, but tended to answer questions with a simple "yes" or "no," rather than provide the animated conversation to which they had become so accustomed.

As usual, Catherine provided an excellent supper, but she sensed that their uncle was preoccupied, so she busied herself elsewhere following the meal, leaving Scrooge and Fred to their own devices. She was constantly amazed at their ability to carry on business together all day and still have plenty to talk about after hours, but she rightly assumed they were catching up on the many years they had been apart.

The men retired to Fred's study where he poured them each a brandy as they sat in comfortable chairs near the fire. Each took a satisfactory sip before Scrooge spoke.

"I saw Dr. Devitt again last night. The man is in a terrible state and there are good reasons for it. He gave me the worst possible report regarding your mother's death and it pains me to deliver it to you." By now, he had Fred's total attention.

"Plainly stated, my boy, your mother was murdered." With that sentence Scrooge's voice broke. He took out his kerchief, blew his nose, and continued while Fred stared in disbelief, aching for his uncle. Tucking away his handkerchief, Scrooge picked up his glass and continued, rolling the glass back and forth between his palms.

"I cannot conceive of such a thing happening to the dear creature! Who, and why, would anyone want to poison Fan? Yet she was given arsenic in her sleeping potion, which the doctor himself administered. No, I see your expression. He did not murder her – not intentionally – although he admits he gave her a second dose after she had evidently already taken one, and that sealed her fate, for certain. He normally did not do that, but she had been restless of mind and he believed she needed to sleep. He of course had no idea the potion contained poison until she began to exhibit symptoms, and he blames himself for not inspecting the jar of laudanum. When he realized what was happening, there was nothing he could do since the poison had been in her system for some time. He did not tell anyone, at least until last night, when he unburdened himself to me."

Fred leaned forward, uneasy. "You suffer more than I, Uncle, and I grieve for you. This is a terrible blow. It is extremely unpleasant news to me, too, but you must remember that my mother was a stranger to me. I do not feel, I admit, the same loss I would feel, were something such as this to befall you."

"I appreciate that, Fred," said Scrooge, as he patted Fred's arm, "but there is more, much more, BLAST it all!" cried Scrooge. In frustration he leapt up, still holding his glass, and began to pace the room. Fred remained seated, but followed with his eyes.

"Fred, the doctor knows who killed Fan." In response to Fred's reaction of surprise and disbelief, he said, "Yes. It's so. The man told me, himself. He says he worked it out by watching and listening and putting things together. Then," said Scrooge, shaking his head, "that poor wretched man committed murder himself." He stopped pacing, turned to Fred. "He murdered Fan's killer, or, at least, the man he believes killed her." Fred sat up, shocked, and their eyes locked – Scrooge's haunted and Fred's unbelieving. "I'm afraid it's true. He actually used the same poison to, as he put it, 'dispatch the sinner to Hell' – and said he was glad to do it."

Scrooge was still standing. "Dr. Devitt would not tell me the identity of the murderer before he fell unconscious from too much gin. The poor sot's life is ruined and he says his health is in tatters, which it certainly appears to be. I could not press him on the matter at the time, but I intend to – I intend to! The doctor will tell me all and, even though he has already applied his own punishment to the man, I want to know his identity. I *need* to know!"

"A man?" asked Fred. "He said it was a man?"

"He did, and it brings home just how little I was paying attention during those years. I have no personal knowledge of who her male associates were at the time."

Fred slapped his hands on his knees. "Well, it's settled. I will go with you and we'll convince the good doctor that we, as her brother and son, have a right to know. Surely, between the two of us we can loosen his tongue."

They would go within the next few days, when it could be arranged between their many business meetings and the demands of their clients. They could see no other approach but to play on what remained of the doctor's seared conscience and convince him of the rightness of revealing the murderer's identity.

Once home, Scrooge could not stop his brain from churning with what he knew so far, although it told him little enough. What if the doctor got it wrong? What if Fan's murderer were still alive? It was unlikely since the doctor said he took so long to work it out, but if he *were* still alive, it could be Ira Thorne, or that man Edmonds, wherever he was, or someone else, entirely. Scrooge could not approach Thorne on the matter, although any connection to this awful business might account for his coldness toward Scrooge. Perhaps it wasn't coldness, per se, but was, instead, guilt – even fear?

∽✿∽

Another meeting with Doctor Devitt had been secured for Friday afternoon, but on Friday morning Toby Veck delivered a message to Scrooge at his office. Peter gave Toby two coins for his trouble and immediately took it to Scrooge. The note was apparently scrawled very quickly and said, simply,

> *"To Mr. Scrooge from Mrs. Cooke. The doctor dyed last nite so he won't be seeing no one."*

No! It was incomprehensible! Once again Scrooge had "put off" doing something because of business demands, and look

what happened. A fleeting thought had him wondering if perhaps the doctor had been free to die once he had unburdened
himself to Scrooge, and Scrooge offered a short prayer for the
man's soul. He asked, also, that he not end up like poor old
Marley. Come to think on it, he would be quite put out were the
doctor to join Marley in his nocturnal visits! Unless, of course,
he had some truth to impart that was less circumspect than some
of Marley's stingy information. He swiftly pushed such frivolous
thoughts aside with a shake of his head and jumped into action,
calling to Peter to hail a cab immediately. Peter was quick about
it and the driver even quicker. Within twenty minutes Fred and
Scrooge were on the doctor's front step. Mrs. Cooke saw them
arrive and greeted them at the door.

"I sent you a message that the doctor'd passed on. Tsk, tsk.
They've already took 'is body so he in't even 'ere for you to 'ave
a look at."

"We realize that, Mrs. Cooke," said Scrooge, "and we appreciate you sending us notice of his death. However, there are some
matters of great importance we were planning to discuss with the
doctor. Now that he's gone, perhaps we could view his records."
She seemed hesitant, so Scrooge quickly assured her by saying,
"The information we seek would not harm the doctor now, nor
will we damage his reputation with anything we might read."

"Well . . . I dunno," worried the housekeeper. "He were always that protective of 'is notes, y'know. But I s'pose it's okay,
seein' as it's you. Come on in then." It was obvious she was making the attempt to continue to be a reliable employee, but with
the doctor's death it suddenly occurred to her that there was no
longer any real need.

Once inside, Fred asked Mrs. Cooke to tell them what
happened.

"Tsk. It were pretty much the same as usual," she said. "He often fell asleep from the drink, 'is head on 'is arms, an' that's 'ow

I'd find 'im in the mornings. Only this time, 'e weren't asleep – leastwise, not the kind 'o sleep 'e'd be wakin' up from this side of the Hereafter. Tsk-tsk. It's a pity the way that man went down'ill these last number o' years. When I found 'im I called for the local police 'n they brought all sorts of folks, 'n they come 'n grabbed 'im quick 'n took 'im away without so much as a by your leave. Tsk-tsk."

"It is a sad thing, Mrs. Cooke," agreed Scrooge. Then he asked, "What will you do now?"

"Why, bless you fer askin'. I've got me daughter in Folkestone, so I reckon I'll be goin' there. She's bin askin' for me, so I'm thinkin' now's the time. Dunno what I'll do with all o' his things, though. 'e did 'ave a niece, so if I can contact 'er, that's who'll take it all, I'm sure." Then, as if she had just recalled their request, she added, "Now, gentl'men, if you'll come with me, I'll show you 'is books. Take yer time, I'll be around." She turned to go, after depositing them in the study, and gave a final "Tsk" as she shook her head.

Scrooge and Fred were overwhelmed. Ledgers and record books sat in stacks or had been tossed helter-skelter onto shelves and were in no order – at least not after the year 1824. There was nothing to do but dig in and hope the doctor had at least kept some decent notes prior to that year. Unfortunately, the records were not kept according to the patients' names. Instead, there were books for each year, with entries chronologically by date. That meant more time would have to be spent going through them, day by day, to find any entries that might prove pertinent. But they must do it. They had no choice.

"Uncle, it occurs to me we need to begin our search with the year of my birth and my mother's death, up to the year 1824. To my mind, that is the logical thing since the doctor's bookkeeping, which is no doubt a reflection of his state of mind, appears to be in disarray after that year." Fred thought of another question.

"Uncle, when did my grandfather die?"

"He died in – oh – I believe it was 1823, not that long after your father. He died of a condition that had plagued him for years. I believe it eventually reduced his movements and he was housebound for months, perhaps a year, before it actually took his life."

Regarding Fred's suggestion of narrowing their search to a few years, Scrooge said, "You're quite right about the books and the years, Fred, and that is exactly what we'll do." They did not expect to come across a notation that read, "Today I poisoned —— for killing Fan Symons," but they hoped to glean some sort of information that would lead them to who had, in fact, killed her. There was nothing on earth they could do with the information, unless, of course, the murderer was still alive. Nevertheless, Scrooge wanted to know – he had to know.

The dust was making Scrooge sneeze and it wasn't long before he said to Fred, "We cannot accomplish this today. I am going to tell Mrs. Cooke we need to borrow several of these tomes for a few days. My bet is she'll allow it if I place a quid in her fist."

And so the transaction occurred. They left the doctor's house toting books from 1819 to 1824, leaving Mrs. Cooke satisfied with their largesse more than their honesty, and a good deal happier than when they had arrived. She was pleased enough that she did not murmur even one small, "Tsk."

Having returned to the counting house, Scrooge began with the record for the year 1819, and found Fred's birth easily, since he knew he was born on May 30th. According to the doctor's notes, Fan had been delivered of a healthy male child and suffered no complications. She was declared fit and was recovering nicely. Entries noted that she would soon be up and back to a normal life. A few pages later, the doctor was called to her bedside for what everyone assumed was a problem with something she had eaten. After recording one or two symptoms, the following day the doctor finally noted, *Patient convulsed and died due to a digestive ailment.* He wrote nothing else regarding her death. There was absolutely no indication of what he knew to be the truth – that she had been given arsenic.

Eventually Fred approached Scrooge's desk, looking discouraged.

"What are we looking for, Uncle?"

"That, my boy, is part of the problem. From what I recall of my conversation with the doctor, whose faculties had been dulled with drink, we are seeking a man who died after Fan died. He was poisoned, but the doctor recorded the death as a cessation of the heart. I believe he also mentioned a digestive order, or some such thing. We also must assume this man knew Fan, although that does not help either one of us since we do not know the whole of her society at that time."

"Very well. We'll search, but I hold out little hope of finding anything definitive."

"I understand, Fred, but we must make the attempt," replied Scrooge as he returned to the records for 1819.

Fred sat at his own desk and began to search the year 1820. After an hour of reading about broken limbs, gout and fevers he began to grow weary. Three men had died of digestive disorders, and several had died of a cessation of the heart, but none had died of a combination of the two.

Then Fred began to notice a trend. A Mr. F. Bally (age 52) died on September 14, 1820, of a cessation of the heart due to chronic stomach ailments and black vomit. Mr. Woodsong (age 28) met his Maker on November 3, 1820, with a cessation of the heart as a result of ingesting an unknown element. On December 30, 1820, Elias Hammersham (age 40) suffered cessation of the heart due to stomach tumors. What was happening? Could the doctor have been preparing his books to cover the murder he was planning? Or was it coincidence – merely a habit the doctor had developed in his record-keeping.

Fred finished the book and found no more similar deaths recorded. In order to stretch his muscles, he stood and walked to his uncle's office, where he found Scrooge just opening the book for the year 1821.

"What did you find, my boy?" asked Scrooge.

"Very little, I'm afraid, other than three adult males' deaths toward the end of the year that mentioned the combination of a cessation of the heart and digestive problems. It may have been the case with each of them, but it seems somewhat odd that such descriptions would suddenly appear. I also noticed the doctor referred to many deaths as 'a cessation of the heart.' That being the case, that particular phrase may not turn out to be much of a clue, after all. He may have used that term in all of his books, most of which we have not seen."

"Here," sighed Scrooge, handing Fred the records for 1822. "You look through this book while I finish up with 1821 and I'll give 1823 a glance, then we'll put these books aside and go get some punch. Perhaps an idea will occur to us that will help."

Fred sighed. "Yes, Uncle." He took the record book, brushed some dust from it and returned to his desk, not in the least hopeful of finding anything useful.

It was more of the same. Broken bones were set, torn flesh was sutured, and childhood diseases treated. The doctor attended various common complaints, women's complaints, births and deaths. His notes must have been a matter of habit, because most of the causes of death now included the term, "A cessation of the heart." Then, in February there was a spate of illnesses and deaths due to some contagious infection. Among the deaths were three women and two children, which did not fit the criteria of their search. On February 15, 1822, a cooper by the name of Adam Hetcher (60) died of a cessation of the heart following stomach complaints and, on February 27, 1822, a gentleman by the name of Neal Edmonds (22), who was visiting G. S. passed into the Hereafter with the same cause of death – *Unable to digest food, two servants also abed with lagrippe. A cessation of the heart, with digestive complications.* Neither name meant anything to Fred.

Fred was thinking how he could never have been a physician if this were the daily pattern, when he flipped a page and saw his father's name. The date was September 20, 1822. Although the man was, for all intents, a stranger to him, Fred's blood ran cold as he read: *Attended Geoffrey Symons.* Two days later the doctor's entry read, *Patient deceased from a cessation of the heart due to a stomach ailment.*

Surely it couldn't mean anything, thought Fred, assessing it slowly. Surely it didn't indicate his father was guilty of killing his own wife – Fred's mother. Fred tried to apply reason to what he was reading. The doctor used that same terminology with too many deaths, some of them with chronic stomach ailments – two, in fact, that same year! Fred refused to accept the obvious possibility. As he sat, staring at the page, Scrooge entered, looking frustrated.

"What is it, my boy? What has you looking so shaken?"

Fred showed him the entry regarding Geoffrey Symons and was unaccountably relieved when Scrooge said, rather matter-of-factly, "I wouldn't jump to any conclusions, nephew. I have just finished perusing the book for the year 1821 and found nothing but more of the same. The doctor repeated the terminology for patients' deaths in 1823, which included your grandfather's in March, who may have died of any number of things, given his state of health." Crossing his arms, he said, "No, my boy, I think we may have reached a dead end in our search. I suppose that is the literal truth, since the people who know the answers are either long gone, or have managed to die before telling us what we need to know!"

Scrooge saw no need, at least at this point, to share with Fred the several other entries regarding Josiah Scrooge. Apparently the doctor had attended him many times in an attempt to control his increasing madness, with virtually no success. Nevertheless, his continued efforts correlated with Fan's mention of the fact that the doctor and the elder Scrooge had been friends for many years. Scrooge suspected, however, that the doctor's resistance to commitment to Bedlam was more in line with Fan's wishes, than the doctor's. His notes seemed to indicate a belief that everyone would be better off were the man removed from society altogether.

An entry dated January 10, 1823 noted:

Josiah Scrooge continues to worsen in his delusions. Tonight he barricaded his door and carried on a conversation with the late Mrs. Symons. He was weeping and telling her he loved her. I eventually convinced him to open the door and gave him a potion to calm him.

February 22, 1823 was more of the same:

Mr. Scrooge's distemper worsens. He is sometimes unmanageable – taken with gross catalepsy and general decrepitude. He is, for most purposes, not ambulatory and requires more care. I have secured Mrs. Weekes to nurse him at times of an evening, but the end should not be long in coming.

CHAPTER TWENTY

Sunday Evening, December 8, 1844

F red finally began a more detailed search of his parents' belongings since he had only explored one of his mother's
trunks in a very cursory manner, having suspended his efforts
when he found his uncle's letters. His plan had been to continue last night, but those horrid Rumblowes came to supper
and stayed for hours, and then Catherine's dog was fussy and
demanded attention. Why couldn't the blasted animal simply
lose its voice? It was highly unlikely they would ever have another
intruder, so his infernal barking really was no longer required.

Finally, on Sunday evening Fred told Catherine he must
search his parents' things for something his uncle needed. She
was not aware that these were the first times in his life he had
opened any of the chests and she did not ask for further explanation. They had been married almost two years now and she
knew him well enough to know he would tell her when he was

comfortable doing so. She could be patient. However, if he took too long to enlighten her, she would resort to whatever means it took to make him tell all!

Fred suspected he would be searching for a speck in a feather duster, but, like his uncle, he could not seem to let it go. He was, by now, too intrigued. He had earlier had a cursory look through his mother's things, discovered his uncle's letters to her, and returned them to him, but he knew he needed to do more digging. This time he would begin with his father's belongings. He was not looking forward to it, yet he did have a certain interest – there was a magnetic pull to the trunks, as if they were ready to make some meaningful statements that had long gone unsaid.

Fred gave in to the pull and began a serious search of one. It was odd how he could see exactly the way things had been placed in the trunk, having been untouched for twenty-two years. Beneath some letters and books was a stack of what appeared to be business papers. They were not neatly ordered but looked to have been gathered up in a clump, probably by a servant, and tossed in first, to be buried by whatever followed. How he hated the thought of going through them, one at a time, to most likely end up with nothing in the way of pertinent information. Then he reminded himself that any information about his father was more than he now had, so the effort would, in that way, be beneficial. It was as if he and his sire were finally meeting – not in the usual way of child to father but, instead, man to man.

There were a few articles of clothing. They were well-tailored and of good fabric, so Geoffrey Symons was evidently a man of good taste and apparently had the capital to keep himself and his household well. The books were first editions and included modern poets and Shakespeare. Fred picked up several other volumes, to see what they were since there was no writing on the spines and, as he turned one over, he realized they were diaries – his father's. They would no doubt prove interesting as well as informative, although he was not certain he wanted to become that intimate with the man via such a personal, and ordinarily private, means just yet. Perhaps later. For now he could give them to his uncle and let the two of them become better acquainted.

The removal of the diaries left only the papers on the bottom of the trunk. Fred reached in to pick them up in a bundle, but since they were not secured in any way, the act of lifting them out shifted the stack and a good portion of it tumbled to the floor, sending papers flying in every direction. Fred let out an oath he was glad Catherine hadn't heard, heaved a sigh, and sat down to go through them. This was going to take a while, so he might as well begin.

First was a receipt for some gardening equipment. Then he found an order for feed mix for the horses. Next he unearthed a flyer for *Liar* and *The Coronation* at the Theatre Royal, Drury Lane for August 29, 1821. Shaking his head over what was turning out to be such a waste of time, Fred picked up a paper that appeared to be a shipping order for several cases of Spanish wine. His father's name was not on the invoice, so there seemed no reason for it to be among his belongings. Turning his face into a thoughtful pout, Fred flipped the paper to its backside and moved to toss it into the dust bin. As he did so, he noticed handwriting on the back.

Fred read it twice – more slowly the second time – before grasping the truth of what the paper represented. Once he understood, he jumped up, quickly stuffed it in his pocket, grabbed the diaries and ran in search of Catherine.

"My Dear," he shouted as he donned his overcoat, gloves, and grabbed his hat, "I must see Uncle Scrooge immediately! I will share all with you at some point, but for the moment I must be out the door! I will return as soon as possible." With a quick kiss to her cheek, he was gone, almost at a run. He found a cab and, within an unheard of amount of time, was loudly and repeatedly banging on his uncle's door.

"Uncle!" exclaimed Fred, out of breath, when he located him in his study. "Here are my father's diaries," he said, dropping them on a table as if they were extraneous baggage. "They are for you to read whenever you wish, but there is something else. I believe one of our mysteries may be solved!" With that he slapped the paper into Scrooge's hand, plopped heavily into a chair and leaned forward as if to scrutinize his uncle's every movement.

Scrooge looked up. "Remove your coat, Fred, and take a deep breath." Whatever it is can wait until you have done so." Fred quickly obeyed, threw his coat over the back of a chair, took the breath he had been ordered to take, and assured his uncle he would wait until he had read the thing before uttering another word. Scrooge began to read.

1 Sept 1822
Victoria, etc. To all, etc.

Whereas, Ira S. Thorne does grant this deed of transfer of ownership of Thorne Shipping Company on this first day of September, 1822, to Geoffrey L. Symons and his heirs and assigns for and in consideration of payment of a debt owed to Geoffrey Symons, Ira Thorne does warrant the property aforesaid from the claims of himself or any other person or persons claiming through or by him whatever.

By my hand this 1st day of September 1822:
Ira S. Thorne

Witnessed by: Silas Bengough
Albert Carroll
George Danmock

Scrooge looked at Fred, speechless. Shaking his head in disbelief he eventually managed to say, "I am astonished. This is truly mind-boggling, yet it answers so many questions." He stood up, striking his left palm with his right fist. "Of course! Now the pieces of the burglaries fall into place! Thorne is our man and he is behind these searches – and even, God forbid, the attempt to burn us out, the conniving blackguard! So that's his game! Well, by Heaven, we'll see about that!" Scrooge was enraged and now had an actual person on whom to heap all of his deep displeasure of the past weeks. In addition, he was furious and disgusted with Thorne as a man, considering his behavior toward Fan so long ago. Scrooge would enjoy knocking the man down a peg or two. Heaven knew he deserved it!

"But Uncle," asked Fred. "How on earth did this occur? What could Thorne have possibly owed my father?"

Scrooge paused, trying to grasp the enormity of the situation, and decided to share some facts. He began by telling Fred about his conversation with Dick and Priscilla Wilkins. He could see no reason, however, to share the fact that Thorne had been enamored with Fred's mother so long ago, even though they both were married.

"Do you recall when I left with Dick last Thursday afternoon? Of course you do. That was the day Priscilla insisted I take tea with them. While I was there I shared my concerns about your mother's death, and of course I asked several questions about your father."

"They knew my father?" he asked, somewhat surprised.

"They did. Dick and your father had met through mutual friends so, over the course of time, they became well-acquainted with your mother too. She welcomed them because of Dick's earlier connection with me as an apprentice at Fezziwig's, having heard of him and, I believe, having actually met him once or twice. Naturally the Wilkinses were invited to several house parties and got to know the other people who were in your parents' society. They say it was a high-spirited group and that everyone continually laughed and played jokes when they weren't up to some sport or simply gossiping.

"You know, Fred, Dick is an honest sort, and when I asked about your father's habits, he said he was a gambler. Not a rake, because Dick insists your father did not cheat at cards, but he was evidently someone who gambled even when he shouldn't. He played with men whose stakes were high, and he tried to match them. Dick believes that may be why he allowed your grandfather to reside with them, selling his own estate and making the capital available to Fan, through whom Geoffrey could, of course, have access to the money.

"Given that information, Nephew, I begin to get a picture. I can see – show me that paper again – yes, five men drinking heavily, and at least some of them wagering more than they should." Scrooge tapped the paper with his forefinger and said, "Here! Here is Danmock's name, and I see his hand in the writing of this thing. He is a solicitor – ours, in fact, as you know – and was involved in handling your estate after your father died. Yes, as slap-dash as it is, someone acquainted with the law helped draw this thing up, and that's why I suspect it would very likely hold in Court.

"Thorne must have run out of money, and put up his shipping company, whatever that was, being assured in his mind that he would win. However, since you are now literally holding the deed, it appears that he lost. The date was shortly before your father's death so I suspect that, rather than pay the debt to his estate, Thorne waited, hoping it would not come to light, and it did not. No doubt a servant gathered the deed into the stack with the inconsequential papers and tossed them into the trunk, rather than send it with other estate documents to Danmock. I am going to assume that Danmock had forgotten about the wager by the time the estate was settled. I suppose it is also possible that your father thought of the deed as a prank and had no intention of collecting the debt."

"Uncle!" said Fred suddenly, as a thought occurred to him. "You don't suppose Julian Thorne was in on these attempts against us, do you? I would hate to think that. He was always such a straight fellow and I've always been right fond of him."

"I certainly hope not, Fred, for your sake, but there is only one way to find out. We will handle this as a business transaction, since that is what it is. We must see Danmock first thing tomorrow!"

⟡

The next morning did find them in Danmock's chambers. Danmock recalled the evening in question, basically confirming Scrooge's suppositions regarding drinking and reckless gambling and, being furnished with the deed of ownership, was astonished that, after so many years, it should reappear.

"Aye, it's official alright," he said, after looking it over. "It should be." He chuckled a little and said, "I assisted Thorne in writing it! He wrote up the deed in his own hand, aided by me as much as I was able at that hour, having over-imbibed somewhat. Well, we all had, hadn't we? After he had written it, Thorne took the thing, tossed it on the table, and promptly lost the bet. Fred, your father simply scooped it up with the rest of

183

his winnings. I doubt he ever thought of it again. It's too bad, too, at least for Thorne, for it looks as if you are the owner of a very prosperous shipping company!"

Fred gawped at his uncle, who was suddenly struggling with his old greedy and even vengeful way of thinking. Meanwhile, Danmock stated, "We'll contact the attorneys for Thorne – I believe it's Phineas Goodby and his partners – and arrange a meeting as quickly as possible. I am certain I do not need to remind you men to keep this thing quiet. They both nodded, neither of them admitting they had already blazed word of an undisclosed "discovery" throughout the entire commercial world of London! "Meanwhile," added Danmock, "we'll make a copy and hold the original in the Bank for safekeeping."

"Now," he said, leaning forward, "stay where you are. We must put our heads together on this."

CHAPTER TWENTY-ONE

Tuesday Evening, December 10, 1844

Since he was, at this point, well into the habit of looking through old epistles, that evening Scrooge sat by his own fire, picked up Geoffrey Symons' diaries and began to thumb through them. He expected to find nothing but dull notations of horses bought, wine drunk and a recording of various daily duties, and that is what he found in the first volume. The second book was a little more interesting because it described meeting, courting and marrying Fan, whom he described as a "lovely, sweet creature of good nature" who "pleased" him with her innocence and concern for others. Symons also noted the difficulties of her father's behavior, but that seemed not to overly concern him. One entry mentioned Scrooge himself, calling him a "stiff-necked miser, a tightfist and a penny pinch," who would no doubt do very little interfering in their lives since he was wed to a very demanding spouse – his business! Of course it was true at that time.

Nevertheless, Scrooge found himself a little piqued on reading his brother-in-law's astute assessment.

It was getting late and as Scrooge gave one last yawn he picked up the third and last diary and began to read. He did not read each entry, but skipped around from date to date. Most were tedious, but a few caught his eye.

12 April 1818

I am no longer a bachelor and it suits me well. I have a very pretty wife, a very pretty property and, thank goodness, I still have my pretty mare, since I did not lose her, after all. I must have been insane to put her up in last night's game, since I had been losing steadily, but I won the hand and was the better for it. It's a good thing Queen Bea is not aware of how I gambled with her fate. I wager she would have given me a rough ride this morning, had she known!

16 June 1818

Our guests have remained for several days this round and it has been very jolly for Fan and me, as well as for them. We have jokes and games and Fan is setting a very good table. Her friend Rebecca Sotherton enjoys my humor, so I tell her she is welcome to remain as long as she continues to laugh at my witticisms.

17 June 1818

That young pup Edmonds continues to make a nuisance of himself around Fan, but no harm done. Ira is almost as bad. He comes to play cards but first spends time loitering near my wife, at least until she shoos him back to the game. Something in his demeanor toward her is too overbearing and I wonder his own wife hasn't got wind of it. Fan really must control things better than that – his behavior is an insult to me, his host.

7 July 1818

Doctor D was here. The Old Man is behaving peculiar again and thankfully he at least keeps to himself when he's in these moods. It troubles Fan, but she carries on. I cannot say so, but I sometimes wish he were on his own. Impossible, I know. His property is being sold and he will remain with us. I won't mind the additional income.

20 Sept 1818

Rebecca and I played cards tonight. She is a very enjoyable companion. I'm glad she is here again since Fan is taken ill these days and does not care for me as she should do. Rebecca's company always lifts my moods. I wonder that she is not yet wed, for she is a very desirable woman.

28 Sept 1818

I am to be a father! I want a son. Fan is ill of a morning and R has already returned home. I miss her lighthearted humor and her grace. I will ask Dr. Devitt how long Fan will be so devilishly ill – perhaps he can do something to end her dreadful retching, poor wife.

25 April 1819

R is back! The sun is shining again in my life. It is infinitely more pleasant when she is here.

29 April 1819

R and I went riding this morning. She is everything a woman should be and I am totally content in her company. She has no equal! She leaves tomorrow, but Fan has asked her to return soon and to be here for her confinement. I will want her here!

30 May 1819

I have a son.

2 July 1819

Fan is gone. R will depart after the funeral and return to her parents' home in London. I needed her with me for this and do not know how I will carry on once she has gone. It will not be forever.

21 Jul 1819

I can wait no longer and will see R in London. Am in raptures of anticipation! Hopefully we will have time alone, to discuss plans.

There were no more entries.

Scrooge slammed the diary shut and threw it down with a thud. *What an odious excuse for a husband!* Without realizing it, he began to speak aloud, using the present tense as if Geoffrey were still alive.

"Despicable being! He treats Fan with less concern than that mare of his, and holds her responsible for the behavior of men who should have known better." Standing up, he began to walk back and forth, and kicked the diary across the room. "He believes himself insulted by their behavior and discounts the insult to his wife! It is he who should correct those men, not his poor wife who has to tolerate their unctuous attentions. Contemptible worm!"

At once Scrooge realized one of the names mentioned was Ira. There it was again. What had really happened between Fan, Ira and Geoffrey? What had happened with that young man Neal? Once more he rebuked himself for being so removed from his sister during this time. It was becoming very clear she had been in need of more support than he gave her and he reminded himself – again – that it was no wonder she wrote to Marley instead of himself. As Scrooge considered these new revelations he wondered if Fan's letter to Marley was a result of having received a threat from one of those two men. Could one of them have done her harm?

He had not expected this, nor had he expected the revelations regarding Geoffrey's affections. No, it was not absolutely spelled out, yet anyone with a scrap of brain could deduce what it meant. Geoffrey had betrayed Fan, even before Fred's birth, and fallen in love with Rebecca Sotherton – Mrs. Langstone! Had Rebecca also betrayed Fan? It certainly sounded as though she had. Was there more to it, wondered Scrooge as he ruminated on the information. *He shows no feeling for Fan during her pregnancy and did not write even a line during her lying-in, other than that HE had a son!* Nor did he seem grieved at her death, which earned only a passing entry of three short words. It was apparent that, by then, his feelings had been transferred to Rebecca Sotherton, which suggested the unthinkable possibility that he found Fan to be an impediment to his happiness. Was she an impediment he was willing to remove by poison?

Could Geoffrey's love for Rebecca have been the motive for him to commit murder? Did she, herself, take part? She certainly had the opportunity. But if that were the case, why did she mention to Scrooge that Fan's death resulted from something other than childbirth? She had no need to do so and would surely have been more cautious, had she something to hide. It had been a long time and perhaps, with Geoffrey gone, there was little fear of a finger of guilt being pointed her way. Perhaps she thought Scrooge knew more than he did and she was clever enough not to be caught in a lie. She had, at one point, suggested he knew more than she. Was that a ruse?

This line of thinking was disturbing to Scrooge, since he had thought Mrs. Langstone a very straightforward woman and attractive in all ways. In fact, the possibility of Geoffrey having a hand in Fan's death, and Mrs. Langstone's possible collusion, came as a horrid blow. Should he ask her outright? Nothing could ever be proven, so she would be safe in telling him anything. But if she had no part in it, asking her would forever doom any relationship Scrooge himself may have otherwise had with her.

Suddenly another possibility occurred to Scrooge. Perhaps Geoffrey murdered Fan for Rebecca Sotherton without Rebecca's knowledge and she had then spurned him. Or "they" may have killed Fan and she could not live with it and had ended their relationship. There was nothing to do, but ask, even though he might not learn the truth. He would rely on his business acumen and hope to be able to discern the truth from whatever she did, or did not, say.

How he dreaded the encounter.

☙

The next day Scrooge stood at Mrs. Langstone's door, and wished to Heaven he were anywhere else. He was promptly let in and waited only a few minutes before she joined him in the drawing room.

Mrs. Langstone offered Scrooge a seat, then sat across from him. She knew he had no idea how pleased she was to see him and perhaps that was best. He did not appear to be the sort of man who sought feminine company, nor all of the superficiality that seemed to accompany a gathering of most women. Nevertheless, she found his companionship much more compelling than most other successful businessmen. He had a way of reaching out to people in accordance with their pursuits in life. If he happened to be speaking with a woman, he was able to converse on things she found of interest, without condescending or belittling what was generally women's rather limited exposure.

Mrs. Langstone, however, was not one of those women. Nor did she know that Scrooge thought her more interesting than any other female of his acquaintance. He was pleased with her directness and her ability to meet men at eye level, figuratively speaking. She read the papers, discussed politics and business, and had decided opinions on most topics of interest to the adult male population.

Today Scrooge seemed preoccupied with this own thoughts and was, she guessed, somewhat agitated. She did not know that simply being in her presence was somewhat disquieting, which made him regret the conversation he must initiate. Perhaps he should leave it be. Perhaps he should forget the entire thing, set it aside and simply make this a social call, although that would be a bit unconventional. He was a single man calling on a single woman and, even though she was a widow who required no chaperone, it was a relatively early hour of the morning to be knocking on one's door. He admitted, though, that Mrs. Langstone was not particularly conventional and her position in society was secure enough that she did not need to bother with such trivialities.

Scrooge knew this was something he must do, or forever let it sit like a barred door between them. If it proved to be an obstacle they could not overcome, or if it pointed to her culpability, so be it. He had always been a man to take risks if the possible gains were great enough. This time, however, the threat of loss might be too great. Nevertheless, he pressed on. He had no choice.

Clearing his throat, Scrooge began rather weakly. "Mrs. Langstone, I have come to discuss further with you the situation regarding my sister's death." Seeing her shift a bit, he raised his hand slightly and said, with some resignation, "I realize I am imposing on you and you are no doubt fatigued by the topic, particularly since you were there, but I must ask you one further question and I apologize in advance for its impertinence." He was clearly uncomfortable and in a state of consternation. Mrs. Langstone sat comfortably, waiting for the question, although he felt, rather than saw, some apprehension on her part.

"Mrs. Langstone," said Scrooge again, swallowing uncomfortably and unaware that he was repeating himself, "It has come to my attention – through some letters and diaries – that Fan's husband was, how shall I say . . . that he felt toward you . . . that is to say, that you and he . . ." With that last comment he saw her stiffen and she stared at him with a coldness he would not have expected. It surprised him and his disappointment was palpable. He knew she could read his reaction but he was unable to control his expression of dismay. Even though he believed he knew what she was about to say, it placed him on the edge of an emotional precipice from which he was about to topple. He must hear the answer and he prayed she would have the courage to tell him. Please God, he would be able to absorb the unreasonable and unbidden loss it represented to him, as well as to Fan, who no longer cared.

Mrs. Langstone's body was rigid and as she spoke he knew he was intruding. She hesitated, then said, simply, with an edge to her voice, "I suppose I can understand, based on what you are citing as your sources, why you would think such a thing." As if deciding something, she put her shoulders back, sat up a little straighter and, her voice like ice, said, "Mr. Scrooge, I will say to you that you need not concern yourself, for there was nothing of consequence between me and Mr. Symons." Her expression dared him to contradict or question her statement, but it was also tainted with fear.

"Aaa-ah," said Scrooge slowly, his heart in his throat. She had hedged the question and was not at all believable. Mrs. Langstone was withholding something, which only increased his suspicion that Fan had met her death at the hands of her own husband, and that Mrs. Langstone had perhaps played a part. He must get out of this room, and this house, as quickly as possible. He already reproved himself for his feelings for this woman, and hoped to never see her again. He was reaching for his gloves when she continued in a softer voice, yet still guarded.

"I wish I could assist you, Mr. Scrooge, but I cannot see how further conversation would be helpful. Please forgive me for being so intractable, but I have no answers for you and see no reason to continue with this dialogue."

Scrooge slowly and silently nodded his agreement, unable to account for what felt like a shattered ideal. He began to put on his gloves, stood and made for the door. Recalling his manners, he abruptly turned back to her, his face unreadable. He hated to go, yet he could not wait to be gone.

"Good day, Mrs. Langstone," he said politely. "I will take my leave and I thank you for your time." Then he added, "I sincerely wish you health and good fortune."

He did not see that her face was in her hands as he closed the door between them.

⚭

Scrooge made his way toward his counting house, desolate. He was disillusioned and miserable to the core. His renewed character, only eleven months old, was threatening to come apart in shreds. It was all he could do to keep from jumping into the street to lie beneath all those hooves and carriage wheels. Even if he didn't die from the pounding, it would certainly impart less pain than what he was now feeling. How on earth had he come to this? More importantly, where would he go from here in his search for Fan's murderer? He had gone beyond the point of no return long ago and felt, at this juncture, he had nothing left to lose by continuing, but perhaps that was because he had already lost. He could see no means of rescue from his despair.

St. Michael's Parish Church was in view and he turned in, instead of walking left, to his offices. An organist was practicing and he would have enjoyed the recital at any other time, but today he barely heard it. The interior was cold, but it mattered not because it matched his mood. He wasn't sure why he was here, although he supposed he had been drawn as a matter of faith. Perhaps he should pray. It could be something simple – a straightforward cry for relief?

Scrooge trudged a third of the way down the center aisle and plopped despondently into a pew under one of the grand arches. He often admired the round stained glass in the front, but today he paid it no more attention than the strains emanating from the organ. Yet he remained. He sat long enough to actually discuss this thing, albeit one-sidedly, with the Almighty. He asked. He pleaded, and he tried to listen for a reply, but he might as well have had rags in his ears, for all he was hearing in response.

No. Wait. One thing did come to mind. A Scripture verse he had memorized as a child – from the Gospel of Matthew. Yes, that was it. *Blessed are they that mourn . . .* What was the rest of it? *For they shall be comforted.* Perhaps that was what he was finally doing – mourning all that had gone before, so long ago. He certainly had not allowed himself the comfort of mourning when his sister died. Truth be told, he had tried to ignore the fact that Fan was gone by scratching harder to obtain wealth, and he couldn't generate any feeling at all, even simple pity, for his father, either before or after his death in 1823. They had been estranged for such a long time that he did not miss him in the least. Perhaps it was precisely the absence of a relationship that he had never properly mourned.

The music was over, the organist having completed his practice and departed through a side door, but someone else had approached silently and was standing in the aisle, looking down on Scrooge. He glanced up to see a familiar round face that smiled at him. With a voice like warm oil, Rector Colin Gifford asked, "Can I help you?" It was a very sincere face, with eyes full of genuine concern that was magnified by the lenses of his spectacles. Scrooge gave a slight groan and said, "How I wish you could, Rector." Suddenly the man said, "Why, it's Ebenezer Scrooge! I see you are in a bad way, my good fellow, and that is not the man I have come to know and admire these past few months."

Scrooge nodded an acknowledgment and muttered, "Rector, I have been thrust back to a state of mind that finds faith a little difficult. It is almost too much to expect at this point."

The Rector carefully took a seat in the pew directly in front of Scrooge. With his arm on the seatback, he turned as much as possible to face Scrooge, and said something Scrooge would never forget.

"My good fellow, I do not know what your current troubles are and I certainly will not pry, but it might help if you were told what your name means."

Scrooge looked up with a slightly cynical smile, and the Rector continued. "Oh, yes, Mr. Scrooge. It is a Biblical name and you can find it in First Samuel. Your name – Ebenezer – means, 'Hitherto hath the Lord helped us'. He does help us, you know, and with a name like that, surely He's been helping you all of your life. He is bound to do more – just when you need it, and perhaps when you least expect it."

Scrooge thanked him even though it did not, at that particular moment, bring a lick of comfort. Sensing that, and not wanting to interfere, the Rector stood and politely took his leave, but not before extending an invitation to Scrooge to return at any time if he wished to talk.

After several moments Scrooge rose slowly and made his way to the exit, gripping the backs of pews for support as he went. Outside he proceeded to his office, hoping that the Scripture verse and the words spoken by the Rector were real promises he could count on. Even with that faint hope, he was very much the picture of a dejected and fallen man.

CHAPTER TWENTY-TWO

Thursday, December 12, 1844

Thursday morning Scrooge awoke with the thought that, so far, December had been a bleak month, full of discouragement, and he continued to be totally disheartened. Not only had he learned that Fan had been murdered, he had become aware of a romantic attachment between Geoffrey Symons and Rebecca Langstone. God alone knew what part that may have played in the game. Not since Fan's death had he felt so bereft. He was in a constant bad humor and it wasn't going away. Perhaps Marley had been right and he shouldn't have meddled. Perhaps ignorance was bliss, after all, but it was too late to return to ignorance.

"Good mornin', Mr. Scrooge," said Mrs. Dilber brightly as she entered with his tray. She was annoyingly chipper this morning as she brought her employer coffee, instead of tea. She knew he liked some variety in his morning drink but she absolutely refused to tell him which he would have on any given day, preferring, instead, to surprise him. Since she had taken over the actual running of the house, she insisted on exerting power in some of the smallest things, unless she was overruled by him, of course. In those cases she quickly acquiesced since her main goal was to manage things as her employer required, and to keep him content. The latter had not been easy for several days now.

This morning it seemed to Scrooge that Mrs. Dilber was over the top with glee. He found it most irritating, particularly when she opened the window drapes to invite in an uncivil amount of sunlight that was far too bright and far too contrary to his dark mood.

"Mrs. D.," snapped Scrooge, "Can you provide any reasonable evidence as to why you should be so full of cheer this dismal morning?"

"Cheer, Mr. Scrooge?" responded the housekeeper with some defense. "Why, I can't say as I'm any more cheerful 'n what I normally am, come to think on it. It's a fine day – not dismal at all – an' Christmas is comin', Sir. That's enough reason to brighten up, I'm sure."

Scrooge wasn't sure of any such thing. In fact, he wanted to roll over, pull the bed curtains tight and remain cataleptic until summer. At this point he did not care if he never woke up, or even if he woke up beside Jacob Marley, to wander forever in a state of conscious non-existence. This past week had been extremely difficult and he was on the edge of being thrust back into his old attitude. Truth be told, that's exactly where he was headed. He was quickly backsliding to his old character, even though he desperately wanted to retain that bright hope that had been so miraculously rekindled last Christmas Eve.

If he were totally honest, Scrooge was suffering another loss. When his interest in mankind was initially revived, he found he actually liked people, enjoyed their company, and expected the best from them. It had been so with Mrs. Langstone. Much more, in fact, and that was the difficulty. He had allowed himself to become too quickly attached – more than was prudent – and had received, in turn, the sort of revelation that would not have surprised him a year ago. It was a blow to his New Man and was threatening to weaken the foundation of charity on which he had been standing for the past eleven months. No, it was more than that with Mrs. Langstone. He had liked her better than most people of his acquaintance and had been let down. He was confounded and he was disappointed, curse the woman!

"Mrs. Dilber, just set the coffee on the table," instructed Scrooge. "I will take it when I get up, whenever that may be – if ever."

"It will get cold if you wait too long, Mr. Scrooge," instructed Mrs. Dilber, but he couldn't have cared less. He simply replied, with dramatic affect, "No colder than my soul, Mrs. D. – no colder."

Mrs. Dilber sniffed in disapproval. "You have some mail already, Sir, and I've left it on your tray." Her remarks were delivered in a tone that clearly indicated she was being ill-treated. She was also genuinely concerned about her employer's disposition since it was so foreign to how he had been behaving for, oh, so long, now. She certainly hoped she wasn't going to have to search for another position. She was too old for that. Besides, she was happy here – or had been. Surely this indisposition of his was nothing serious. Surely he wouldn't chuck her out . . . surely . . . Oh, my . . .

She continued to worry as she made her way back downstairs.

Five minutes later Scrooge rolled over, reached resentfully for the letter and ripped it open. It was a note from Rebecca Langstone, of all people, requesting that he come to her that afternoon. He was flabbergasted. What could the disgraceful woman possibly want? She was the last person of the entire population of London whom Scrooge wished to see, and he would like to reply to the summons by telling her to go to the Devil. But he wouldn't. He was too curious as to what she would say after that terrible ordeal yesterday. He would go. He must, but he would be wary and would not be mesmerized by the Siren's song again.

Throughout the day Scrooge was unable to concentrate on anything, but managed to slog through the hours, not noticing that his employees, as well as Fred, tended to back out of his way whenever he moved around the rooms. As he left for his appointment with Mrs. Langstone there was an audible sigh of relief from the occupants of the offices of Scrooge and Symons.

It was precisely two o'clock when Scrooge rapped on Mrs. Langstone's door. He was let in by a servant and, this time, deposited in the morning room, where Mrs. Langstone was already waiting. She looked exhausted but she genially motioned for him to take the other seat by the fire, and he did so. The air was thick with their awkwardness and the emotional remnants of their last meeting.

"Mr. Scrooge," she began, "You are undoubtedly uneasy about seeing me, and this is difficult for us both, but I asked you here because our previous encounter weighed heavily on me throughout last night. It has been almost impossible to bear. I do not expect, nor require, your sympathy, but when we last spoke I did you a great injustice by not giving you the entire truth. My only explanation is that at the time I believed myself to be doing you a favor by remaining silent." Scrooge dreaded her next words and cursed himself for being in the position to have to hear them.

Mrs. Langstone was unaware of his discomfort because she was too consumed with her own.

"The truth is, I have thought of little else since our conversation and I have come to two conclusions, both of which I must share with you now, regardless of how difficult it is for either of us." She looked at Scrooge as if he might interrupt, and saw that he had no intention of saying anything. He resembled a statue that would not be moved, no matter what sort of information she might impart. Nevertheless, she persisted.

"My first conclusion is a revelation. All of these questions of yours have caused me to deliberate on what I know, and my deductions are almost too ghastly to take in." Here she paused before saying, "I find myself suspecting that Geoffrey may have murdered my dear friend – your sister." There was total silence for a moment, before she continued. Then their eyes met, but neither dared show any emotion.

"I am horrified by that thought and extremely grieved by such a possibility. In addition, I am reliving a state of guilt I have not experienced for many years, only more so because of what might be construed as my part in it." Mrs. Langstone shifted a bit and smoothed her skirt before she resumed speaking. Scrooge maintained an outward calm, belying the storm that was within. *Is she really only just now suspecting that it was her lover who killed Fan?*

"My second conclusion is that, in fairness, I must force myself to relate to you the facts of my relationship with Mr. Symons. I believe I should recite those particulars to you, regardless of how difficult it is for me to do so, or even how you may feel about me in the end." Scrooge screwed up his reserves and remained stoic. He could bear to remain long enough to hear this, and then he would bolt.

She held her breath, then released it slowly. "When I initially refused to discuss the matter with you I was misguidedly trying to keep you from knowing the depraved character of Fan's husband. I would like to have saved you from that knowledge since there is nothing you can do now to rescue her from such a union, but your suspicions have already shattered any ideas you may have held regarding their marriage." She heard Scrooge's sharp intake of air and quickly added, "Oh, no, Mr. Scrooge, Fan was not abused, do not infer that. In fact, I am certain she believed her marriage to be a normal one. She was not aware of her husband's propensities." Scrooge relaxed only slightly. He was still wary, and exceedingly unhappy, but managed to say, "I understand, Mrs. Langstone, and thank you for making that clear."

"Regarding your question of my relationship with Fan's husband," she continued, "I would, even now, give anything had you not discovered that such a thing between Geoffrey and me had ever occurred." Scrooge was now thoroughly miserable and dreaded her next words. He was glaring at her with hooded eyes, so she hurried on with her explanation.

"Do not misunderstand, Mr. Scrooge. By 'such a thing,' I do not mean there was a reciprocal attachment between us. Mr. Symons never so much as touched me during my visits to Fan and the most I ever did was laugh at his jokes, for he truly was an entertaining person." With a slight smile, she said, "We all spent a good deal of time in each others' company, along with that of other close friends, reveling in our own cleverness and entertaining each other without let-up. I am certain I need not remind you of how witty Mr. Symons could be, for you were his brother-in-law and knew him much better than I."

Scrooge was desperate to believe her, but was not yet convinced. Nor did he want to disabuse her of the notion that he knew his brother-in-law, for he knew him not at all. Nevertheless, he could no longer remain mute. Before he thought it through, he said, with more feeling than he intended, "Actually, I can recall very little of Geoffrey since I spent no real time with him. We met once or twice but we lived in different worlds and, frankly, I gave him very little thought. Since I rarely saw Fan, I never discovered anything of meaning with regard to her husband, including his character, and I have, in fact, come to know Geoffrey a great deal better during these past few weeks." He had to add, "I do not like much of what I have learned! I have come to believe he was a nefarious person and a most defective husband." They both knew he was also now questioning the verity of her friendship to Fan.

Mrs. Langstone nodded. When she continued, her voice was growing stronger, and sounded somewhat angry. He felt that anger because it was palpable, and he knew a portion of it was directed toward him for requiring this confession.

"Mr. Scrooge, I do not refer to anything clandestine. I refer solely to Mr. Symons' conduct, not my own, although his actions related to me and were, therefore, extremely upsetting. His actions toward me made me feel somehow responsible. Fan deserved much better than he, although neither she nor I had any inkling of such a thing at the time we were all together." Scrooge crossed his arms, torn between what he feared he might hear, yet hoping, now, that it was not what he had assumed.

"Mr. Scrooge, the horrible truth of the matter is that not three weeks following Fan's death that odious man appeared on my parents' doorstep in St. James Square. I welcomed him, of course, as the grieving husband of my dear friend and, therefore, my friend, too. That was not his intent, however – not at all." She straightened as if to steel herself, and continued.

"My mother had been called away from the room momentarily, which was unfortunate, for once we were alone he had not taken two sips of tea before falling at my feet and declaring his adoration. He actually pledged his undying love – and suggested that now that he was free, we could be together!" Scrooge swelled with righteous anger for Fan, sympathy for Mrs. Langstone, hope for himself and hatred for Geoffrey Symons. Mrs. Langstone continued, even though it was obvious she would rather not.

"I remember recoiling from his presence, which seemed not to put him off in the least. He admitted he might be presenting me with a shock, yet he said he had known for some time that we were suited and more deeply attached than either of us wanted to declare. Naturally, I rejected the idea outright and I was no doubt extremely rude in doing so, which I do not regret. Nor do I regret what I did next.

"I rose abruptly, to put some distance between us, which accidentally upset the tea tray, spilling hot tea on his leg." She gave a short humorless laugh as she recalled the scene.

"He let out a howl, but was not put off and quickly rose, grabbing my wrist as he continued his declarations. I pointed to the door with my other hand and ordered him out so vociferously that my mother hurriedly reappeared, to see what could possibly be the matter. She found me beside myself, shrieking with rage and heartfelt injury. I said I had once considered him my friend but that he was no longer, and would never again be welcome in my house. I ordered him out as he sputtered his apologies to my mother and she put forth all sorts of questions for which she received no answers. It was a horrible scene, Mr. Scrooge, and it debases me to repeat it to you now, but you evidently have a need to know." It was clear she wanted to exonerate herself, but she was also trying to be honest as to her role in the matter.

Scrooge waited while Mrs. Langstone took another breath before continuing her narrative, and said to her, "I realize it is costing you dearly to recall something you have worked so diligently to forget and I do regret that I have been the instrument of bringing it about."

Her smile was sardonic. "I have no defense other than that I was ignorant, and did not knowingly encourage such a sentiment in Mr. Symons. Given my lack of knowledge of his true character, you can well imagine how the wretched man's sudden declarations affected me. Not only had I no idea he harbored such feelings, the fact that he believed I returned them was enough to make me physically ill. His unwanted and astonishing pronouncements were added to the deep grief I was already feeling for my dearest friend, and I did not conduct myself well. I am ashamed to say I lost all control over my tongue and, as I have said, reacted in an extremely uncivilized manner. With the help of two servants he was turned out and I recall screaming at the door through which he had just been escorted that I most definitely did not return his feelings and did not welcome them in the least." She leaned back in her chair and lowered her voice slightly, speaking more slowly as she gave an almost imperceptible shudder.

"I immediately called for a bath because I felt so sullied. Somehow his confession and his belief that I returned his affections made me feel I had, like he, been disloyal to Fan. I feared that his beliefs and feelings were somehow my fault, that I had in some way betrayed my dearest friend in the world. It took weeks to rid myself of the residue of the entire episode. He sent several letters thereafter but I have no idea what they contained. Perhaps they were apologies. Perhaps he admonished me for my behavior. Hopefully they were not a renewal of his attentions. I will never know because I took them to the kitchen and burned them, unopened. Eventually the letters stopped coming and over two years later I learned of his death, which did not grieve me in the least. I had, by then, however, managed to at least generate some pity for the man."

Scrooge was speechless, but his jaw was working. He desperately wished Mr. Symons were still alive so he could personally put an excruciating end to his worthless existence. Finally, he spoke.

"It grieves me to realize Fan was tied to a man who did not value her nor honor her as she deserved, and your account only underscores his unscrupulous character. As you say, perhaps she was not aware of his propensities – I can only hope that was the case. Knowing my sister's nature however, I can almost assure you she would have forgiven him any transgression. It is also my belief that such forgiveness would not necessarily have kept him from repeating his sins, whatever they might have been." Mrs. Langstone nodded. Scrooge must ask another question.

"Mrs. Langstone, you say you now suspect that Geoffrey may have murdered Fan. Do you have any further evidence on which to base that suspicion, other than what I told you?"

"I do not, other than his total lack of integrity, which I discovered following her death. In those few moments in my mother's home I saw his true nature and it was enough, when attached to your questions, to make me wonder if he could have perpetrated such a cunning and despicable act. However, I would say his temperament tended more toward cowardice, than craftiness. I am not certain he could have designed, nor carried out, such a scheme."

Scrooge's mind was swimming with anger for his sister's situation and yet he felt relief regarding what he wanted to believe was Mrs. Langstone's inadvertent part in it. He could not deny, however, that doubts remained regarding her behavior as a young woman, as well as her truthfulness at this point. His expression may have given a hint of his ambivalence.

As if in answer to his unspoken question, Mrs. Langsone said, "Mr. Scrooge, I realize you are not well enough acquainted with me to know whether I speak the truth even when it is not flattering to myself, but for the verity of my account you may apply to my mother, Mrs. Adelaide Sotherton, who continues to reside in St. James Square. She refuses to relocate, even though many of her friends are migrating to the more fashionable Belgravia. I will give you her direction if you like. She, of course, knows the entire story because I shared it with her, along with my shame at having been the object of such a sordid attachment. She and I always had an extremely close relationship and even in her old age she continues to be my trusted confidant."

Scrooge thought for a moment . . . Sotherton . . . Adelaide Sotherton . . . Of course! He placed the name at once and rudely blurted, from relief as much as to let out the breath he had been holding in for so long, "So you are *her* daughter! Ah, I see. And she is, no doubt, a formidable woman to have as an ally." After making the statement he realized it might be taken as a criticism, or as a suggestion that her mother would lie for her, but Mrs. Langstone seemed not to hear any insult, and Scrooge decided to forego further explanation.

Mrs. Adelaide Sotherton – independent in both thought and fortune – a woman of timeless beauty and intellect had had en-trée to royalty and political power during her famous youth. She must be in her late 70's by now but was, by reputation, still a wom-an whose word, it was often joked, rivaled the Queen's. There was no way Scrooge would call on her to question the veracity of her daughter's tale, but the idea of spending a few minutes in her colorful company was most appealing. Perhaps he could eventually persuade Mrs. Langstone to take him to her mother's as a guest for tea . . .

What was he thinking! He reminded himself this was no time to be planning any sort of relationship with Mrs. Langstone, al-though the fact that such an idea had occurred to him was no doubt proof that he was inclined to believe her story.

CHAPTER TWENTY-THREE

Friday, December 13, 1844

Mrs. Barnes replied to Fred's letter with a very nice note. She began by saying, "I am, of course, always glad to hear from My Boy," which is how she thought of him since she had no children of her own. She included in the letter, which contained the fact that she had been down with the sniffles but was enjoying living with her sister, the name of the Symons' former housekeeper, Mrs. Jane Asker. According to Mrs. Barnes, Mrs. Asker resided in London, and she provided her direction. Mrs. Barnes also gave the name of the former housemaid, Nora, but she only knew that Nora had married and was residing somewhere outside of London. She told Fred, however, that the information should be easily obtained from Mrs. Asker, who was Nora's mother.

As a postscript, Mrs. Barnes mentioned that Mrs. Symons' personal maid, Sarah, had married and sailed away to live somewhere in America. The Symons' cook "died in 1835 – such a shame," and Mrs. Barnes did not know the names or whereabouts of the cook's family.

It was, by now, late Monday afternoon, and Scrooge wasted no time in calling on Mrs. Asker. After they had introduced themselves she replied that, why, of course she remembered Fan and Mr. Geoffrey and was most agreeable to the idea of discussing the days of her employment with their household. They sat comfortably in a clean yet cluttered parlor, and Scrooge politely declined the offer of tea. Mrs. Asker's acuity was immediately revealed.

"Now, Mr. Scrooge, it's impossible to fool an old duck, like me. You did not come here for old times' sake. What, exactly, is it you are seeking?"

Somewhat taken aback by her frankness, Scrooge nevertheless opened up. It was, in some ways, a relief not to have to ease the conversation into those things he wanted to discuss. Instead, with Mrs. Asker, he could approach the subject without subterfuge.

"Mrs. Asker, I am seeking information regarding my sister's death. I have, within the past fortnight, come across some disturbing information and I believe her death was not as simple as everyone took it to be." In the middle of his sentence he opted for the direct approach which, he gambled after several minute's acquaintance, Mrs. Asker would welcome.

"I have, during the past several days, been impressed with how my sister's existence was a series of paradoxes. On the one hand, she was supposedly happy in her marriage, yet I have learned that her husband was not what he should have been. I am also told she was surrounded by people who loved her, yet someone used arsenic to murder her." At Mrs. Asker's shocked expression he said, "Yes, I am afraid it is so, and I apologize for saying it so abruptly, but that is why I am here. That is why anything you can tell me about my sister's situation – even if it seems insignificant to you – may assist me in my quest for the truth. I would truly appreciate your help."

Mrs. Asker looked squarely at Scrooge, nodding her head. "I see, Mr. Scrooge, I see." She leaned back and took a deep breath, as if she were going to give a speech.

"There are some things about that household, and about your sister's dying, that I've not shared with another soul. Perhaps it is time to do so. As you say, Mr. Scrooge, all was not as it seemed. Oh, I believe Mrs. Symons was happy enough – she was naturally good natured – but her happiness was in spite of many things, not because of them. You see, her husband was somewhat inconstant, or so I believe. Although I attempted to keep gossip among the servants at a minimum, a certain amount reached my ears. Most thought Mr. Symons to be a gambler and to care more for himself than for his wife, or anyone else, for that matter, excepting that special mare of his."

"But his treatment of my sister . . ."

Conscious that she might give the wrong impression, Mrs. Asker added, "No, do not suppose he mistreated your sister – he certainly did not. It wasn't our place to say, Mr. Scrooge, but the problem was that he simply did not pay enough attention, at least it seemed so to those of us who observed him. Mrs. Symons was a beautiful thing and not unattractive to other men, and I say he left her unprotected from at least one young man's advances. Had he been paying attention, he should perhaps have been concerned, but it appeared to the servants that his attention would always be on himself, rather than on his family. He was not one to take responsibility." Mrs. Asker shifted in her chair, preparing to continue, and Scrooge stifled his inclination to interrupt the flow of words.

Shaking her head, she said, "Then there was the matter of your father, Mr. Scrooge. If you'll excuse some plain talk, that contemptible, yet pathetic man was the bane of your sister's existence.

He visited often and then, eventually, came to live permanently with the Symonses. Mrs. Symons mentioned to me once that he was selling his own property. I believe he bequeathed something on her at the time, but if he did so, it was very out of character. I always suspected Mr. Symons had agreed that he could live with them only if he liquidated his own assets and made the money immediately available to assist the Symons household financially.

"At any rate, where your poor sister was concerned, she could do nothing right for your father, and he was never pleased with her, nor with anyone, for that matter. The only peace she got was when he shut himself up for days at a time. We left trays of food outside the door and found them later, half eaten in a very disgusting manner. During those times we could hear him carrying on conversations through the door, sometimes shouting at people only he could see. We knew he was alone, but he actually believed others to be in the same room with him." An uncomfortable and fleeting thought suggested to Scrooge that perhaps he had inherited Marley's visits from his father, but he quickly pushed the idea aside.

Scrooge managed to interrupt long enough to ask, "Did our father abuse my sister, then?"

"Oh, no, Mr. Scrooge," said Mrs. Asker with conviction. "I never knew him to touch her – neither to strike, nor to hold. It was as if she were a shadow of someone, rather than a real person of flesh and blood to whom he could actually give a hug or even a short affectionate pat on the shoulder. He was as cold as an ice pond in January, Mr. Scrooge, much as I hate to say so – and he was just naturally cruel."

"Cruel, you say? I always knew him to be detached and severe, but I never knew him to be cruel to Fan, at least she did not say he was."

"I'll not whitewash it, Mr. Scrooge. That's what I said, and that's what I call it. I heard him ranting more than once to Mrs.

Symons about how she was no better than she should be, and how he deserved better in a daughter. Then he would abruptly change sides, like, and take the opposite tack, throwing her off balance. One day (I'm not proud to admit it, but I purposely eavesdropped that time), he and Mrs. Symons were in the morning room and he was raving on about how she was like her mother. The Missus was in tears but that did not stop him. It only seemed to heap fuel on the fire of his anger. Then, suddenly, he said she was too good for this pitiless world and that she would be hurt. He said she was too good for her husband too, that he knew what Mr. Symons was about, but he would 'take care of it.' After that I expected he and Mr. Symons to eventually come to blows, but they never did, at least not to my knowledge, and certainly not before Mrs. Symons' passing. Then there was that poor orphaned child, Fred. I believe he's turned out well, though, has he not?"

"Yes, Mrs. Asker," smiled Scrooge, "He has turned out right well and I am very proud of him, as would be my sister, were she still alive. He has much of her in him. He is kind and intelligent, and has a winning way with people." That comment made Mrs. Asker smile with relief.

Bringing Mrs. Asker back to the subject of Fan's death, Scrooge asked what she could recall of that time, but her response offered no new information. She confirmed that Fred's birth had been normal, with no complications, and that, within weeks, Fan suddenly became ill with what appeared to be a digestive ailment, and succumbed quickly. Scrooge had fully intended to ask her about how and when Geoffrey Symons died when, without being prompted, she spoke again.

"You know, Mr. Scrooge, Mr. Symons died not that many years after his wife, but I was not there when it happened. I had been called to my own mother's bedside due to her serious illness, and I remained there until she recovered. I was gone several weeks and it was during that time that Mr. Symons contracted some sort of ailment. I never knew quite what it was, nor did anyone else seem to know."

As if the thought just occurred to her, Mrs. Asker added, "There were too many deaths during those years. First, there was dear Mrs. Symons, then her husband and then your father." Suddenly she frowned and scratched the back of her neck. "It seems to me there was another young gentleman who died in that home too, of something that was going 'round, but I can't recall the details." As if putting such a thought aside, she slapped the air and said, "Ah, well, I'm sure it's of no consequence to you."

Scrooge assumed that was so, but was disappointed not to learn more details of Geoffrey's death. The doctor claimed he had poisoned Fan's killer and then abused him as he lay dying, which was why Scrooge needed to know more of the doctor's actions toward Geoffrey while Geoffrey was on his deathbed. Mrs. Asker could see he was dissatisfied with her scant information, and she did want to help.

"It's true I wasn't there when Mr. Symons died, Mr. Scrooge, but my daughter was. Nora was an upstairs maid and did not accompany me to my mother's. She was in attendance throughout his illness."

Scrooge had forgotten about Nora. "Would you be kind enough to give me her name and direction? If you think she would be willing to discuss this topic with me, that is." To himself he thought, *She will! If need be, I'll roost on her doorstep and refuse to move until she tells me all she saw and heard!* As if reading his mind, Mrs. Asker wrote her daughter's direction on a piece of paper and said, "I'm certain she will be happy to discuss whatever she knows."

The daughter's name was Nora Hollis and she was married to a man who was working for the new London and Birmingham Railway. Mrs. Asker was unsure of just what exactly his job was, although she said she knew it didn't matter to Mr. Scrooge one way or the other. Their home was actually in Wealdstone, near Harrow.

"Thank you, Mrs. Asker," said Scrooge as he rose from his chair, "for giving me your time and sharing your keen percep-tions. I'm sure you were a very real comfort and help to my sister when you were in her employ. I thank you, somewhat belatedly, for that." He saw that her eyes were glistening and realized that she, too, had loved Fan.

On the way home Scrooge thought about what he now knew. Fan had been poisoned by someone and the doctor had then poisoned him, although the doctor had, at least at some point in the intervening years, suspected there may have been more than one person involved. The doctor had not given his reasons for thinking that, but Scrooge must not discount the possibil-ity. Not discounting the idea, however, always seemed to lead back to Rebecca Langstone. He no longer truly suspected her but it was clear that Geoffrey had been in love with her and had cooled in his attachment to Fan. Perhaps the doctor knew of Geoffrey's feelings. It was also clear that Geoffrey's character was one of selfishness and shallowness. Then there were those other men who evidently harbored feelings for Fan, and made her uncomfortable, but he first needed to investigate the possi-bilities that surrounded Geoffrey. There was too much evidence against him not to do so.

Fan had thought her marriage a happy one, but her acquain-tances and servants reported that Geoffrey was inconstant and a gambler. Neither he nor Scrooge's father had abused Fan physi-cally, but the senior Scrooge had abused her with his words and his moods. It was no doubt a blessing that he was such a recluse.

Nurse Weekes had been unable to offer any real assistance but when he asked about there being anyone who was unkind or threatening to Fan, she did react with some emotion. Was it fear she was recalling? Guilt, perhaps? Of whom would she have been afraid, for herself or for Fan's sake?

Mrs. Asker confirmed that the Symons home was not what it appeared to be from the outside and there were many under-currents of deception, anger and evidently even hatred running throughout the lives of the family. Was everyone's assumption correct that Fan thought her life was in order, or did she know of the evils by which she was surrounded? Scrooge could only pray that she did not.

CHAPTER TWENTY-FOUR

Saturday, December 14, 1844

It was absolutely the worst possible misfortune that could befall him! Ira Thorne had, this morning, received notice from his solicitors that Scrooge and Symons were requesting a meeting. It could be nothing but that accursed transfer of ownership to the broken-down boat he had so pridefully referred to as "Thorne Shipping" in 1822. So it had finally surfaced and was, by all that was unmerciful, in the hands of Ebenezer Scrooge after all! Why had Thorne's hired professionals not found it during their searches? Bunglers, all of them – inept bunglers, particularly that would-be arsonist. Pah! That idiot deserved a trip to Australia or, better yet, to have his useless neck stretched! They all did, come to think on it. Well, he wasn't beaten yet. He would crack that imprudent document, and do it over their heads. He would find a way!

Thorne hied to the chambers of his solicitor, where he rushed in looking jostled and shaken.

"I must see Goodby immediately!" demanded Thorne of the smiling clerk who greeted him, a freckle-faced young man who was unprepared for the fury that was about to be unleashed. Thorne swung his walking stick toward Goodby's office, barely missing the clerk's ear, and yelled, "I've no time to waste and if you do not take me through that door within three seconds, I shall reduce you and it to splinters!" He then leaned toward the clerk and screeched, "You tell him that, you . . . you . . . paid conspirator!"

The clerk jumped backwards, turned and opened Mr. Goodby's door as he began frantically knocking on it. He was preparing to announce Mr. Thorne when Thorne pushed by him. Already red in the face, he began to roar.

"Now see here, Goodby! I know what this is about and it's nothing more than a barrel full of rotten apples! They can't do this, I tell you. There is no legal claim! They are entitled to nothing and I expect you to see to it that that is exactly what they get! Do you hear me?"

It would be impossible not to. Nevertheless, Mr. Goodby rose calmly, shooed his wide-eyed clerk back into the front office, closed the door, and began ushering Thorne to a chair even as Thorne spat out one last blustery threat. Suddenly he was quiet. His chest heaving, he eyed Goodby ferociously as he walked around his desk and sat down to face his client.

"Mr. Thorne," he said reasonably, "I have been furnished with a written copy of a paper penned and signed by you in 1822, deeding Thorne Shipping Company to Geoffrey Symons and his heirs as payment for a debt. It is also witnessed by three persons, one of whom happens to be an attorney who no doubt assisted in the writing of the document. Although it is brief, it appears to contain the needed wording to make it valid." He glanced away

from Thorne long enough for Thorne to see what he was thinking. Then Goodby looked once again at his client and said, "It
seems iron-clad, Mr. Thorne, at least on the surface, although we
will do all in our power to see that it comes to nothing." He had
no idea how that could be accomplished, and Thorne saw it in
his expression.

Thorne wanted to rail against the man, call him an incompe-
tent bobble-headed fake, to even threaten him with bodily harm
but, instead, he crumpled. He slumped in the chair, head down,
his hands dangling between his knees and said, almost inaudibly,
"What shall I do, Phineas? What can I do?"

Goodby's reply was simple. "We shall do our best, Mr. Thorne.
We shall do our best."

⚜

Later that night, over a glass of port, Thorne tried to explain
the situation to his son Julian. It must be done before everything
came to light. Julian must be forewarned and find out about
this thing from no one but Thorne, himself. He was the only
one who could tell it precisely as it had occurred. He wanted to
present himself in the least damning light, but had no idea how
to do so. It was important that he keep his son's respect for him
intact, if at all possible. Oh, he knew Julian loved him and would
never cease to do so, but to disappoint his only son was almost
more than he could bear. He had always been his son's idol, and
was comfortable with the position.

Thorne took a large gulp of port, letting it burn its way to
his stomach, then began. "Julian, I have something of a rather
unpleasant nature I must share with you and I warn you, it is not
something I can even pretend to make easy, so there is no way
to approach the thing other than to simply blurt it out and hope
you will take it like the man I believe you are."

What an odd forewarning, thought Julian as he turned to face his father straight on. "I hope I'm the man you brought me up to be, Father, and I pray I won't disappoint you, but this sounds serious."

"It is, son. It is extremely serious." Another gulp and he could go on. There! The liquor would fortify him, at least enough to begin.

"Julian, I once did a very foolish thing and you may be the one to pay for it." He hadn't intended to say it quite that way, but it was the truth, so why pretend. It was better that Julian heard it from him, at any rate, although it did sound too close to the truth of the matter. It sounded too much like all was lost, and it just might be. Somehow he managed to continue.

"In my youth I drank too much, gambled too much and generally played reckless with what I had." Then, realizing what that might imply, he quickly added, "No, I did not include your mother in those habits. Not once did I mistreat her or, I believe, gamble with her feelings or her well-being. I prefer to think I have been a decent sort of husband, and father to you and your sister." Since he was sharing so much man-to-man he added, hedging somewhat, "I did, once, fancy myself emotionally attached to another woman, but nothing came of it, so you may consider me unsoiled in that regard." Thorne allowed himself to recall Fan so many years ago, perfect in so many ways, and explained, as he had to himself for at least a year following her death, "It was simply that she was such a lovely person and her husband did not value her as he should." He took a drink and, as he set the glass down, added, "I admired her, and felt for her, as well. I wanted to somehow free her from such an unequal situation." He would not tell Julian that the woman was Fred's mother. Things were complex enough.

Julian felt an odd urge to comfort. Very sincerely, he said, "You are a good husband and father, Sir. I can attest to that because I have seen how you treat Mother and my sister."

Reassured of that, at least, Thorne pushed ahead like one of the new steamships he was considering for passenger travel.

"One night I drank too much and gambled far too much. In fact, I gambled my shipping company, which was, at that time, a simple second-rate boat on which I carried bits of cargo across the channel. It was small, but it was a beginning and I was determined to build up my own wealth, rather than live off of your mother's money.

"I was down in the game but was so certain I would win the next round that I wrote out a transfer of ownership to my boat and placed in on the table. The play was, by then, between Geoffrey Symons and myself." At Julian's surprised expression he said, "Yes, you have guessed it – Fred's father. As fate would have it, one of the players – by then they were all out of the game and were simply observers – was an attorney. He is now Ebenezer Scrooge's attorney, wouldn't you know, and he assisted in writing the thing. He ensured that the wording was legal, even though it was abbreviated in form since we were all far less than sober.

"In my youthful, boastful pride, and because I was so certain I would win, I told the attorney, a fellow by the name of George Danmock, that I would word the deed using the term Thorne Shipping Company! Were it not so tragic it would be laughable. Can you believe my foolish pride? Thorne Shipping Company, indeed!" Julian was paying rapt attention, but took a sip of needed port as he listened. Thorne continued.

"The hand was played . . . and Symons won. My tiny business was gone – lost – due to my foolishness. What would I tell your mother? It was my only asset. Oh, I knew she had no ill feeling about us living on her money, but I felt the blow tremendously. I hated to lose and even though I tried to tell myself it was only one boat, not a ship, and that I could start over, I was devastated.

"Without batting an eye Symons raked in the pot, which included the deed, and the game ended. I do not recall coming home, nor what was said as the game broke up. The only thing I recall clearly was Symons laughing as if the game had been the best joke. I think we may have all treated it as a farce, and perhaps Symons didn't really take the win seriously, but he had the deed and, for all intents and purposes, he now owned my business. I recall he quipped, 'Perhaps I'll do a little sailing this summer'. He had no idea, nor did he probably care, that he now owned my heart and soul – my plans for my future, as well as yours. I think, even then, I was hoping he didn't take the win seriously, and he may very well not have. The one – and only – good thing that came out of that game was the fact that I never gambled again."

"But," said Julian, "you did not lose the Company, so I assume he didn't claim it. Is Thorne Shipping a newer business?"

"No," said Thorne, "although your question is a good one. Had I been astute enough I would have simply started over and changed the name of the company, but it didn't occur to me to do such a thing. Of course he could still have claimed my one boat, except that I listed it as 'Thorne Shipping.' I suppose I didn't really expect him to demand the boat and he didn't immediately do so. At any rate, he died very shortly after that game – within a month, I believe. I waited and no one came forward to make the claim on his behalf, which led me to believe he had either destroyed the paper, or it had been lost in the shuffle following his demise. I thought Heaven had granted me a reprieve – that I was safe – and I proceeded to grow Thorne Shipping into what it is today. Eventually I forgot about the deed as if it had all been a nightmare." He put his empty glass on a side table and leaned forward.

"Then!" he said, with more emotion than he had meant to show, "Last October you mentioned your acquaintance with Fred Symons and, from the information you gave, I deduced he was Geoffrey's son. You also leveled the devastating news that he was in business with Ebenezer Scrooge, who is the sharpest, meanest old miser of business I have ever known. He would ruin his close kin for a farthing.

"I realized they may very well have the deed and I became frightened. I feared losing the entire business – your fortune – and I hired some professional housebreakers to search Fred's house and the offices on Cornhill." Julian managed to hold his tongue but he desperately wanted to ask his father how he could do such a thing. Thorne continued.

"Nothing was found, but by then I was desperate." How he hated to tell this part, but he must, because it might come out, and if he had not previously shared it with him, his son would believe there were other undisclosed secrets between them and would always wonder what else his father was hiding. The trust between the two of them would be forever shattered.

"I might have waited, to see if anything occurred, but it was being put about that they had something that would shake the world of London commerce and they were going to make it public in forty-eight hours. I knew it was the deed and I also realized I must act quickly. I was consumed with urgency. Using a trusted third party, through whom I knew I would not be traced, I hired a lawless man to burn them out."

Julian's jaw dropped and he sat back, too shocked to speak. It pained Thorne to see it and it was almost too much. Theirs had been such a close, honest relationship for all of Julian's life that Thorne realized he would give up every ship in the Kingdom to wipe that expression from his son's face.

"I know, Julian. I am not proud of my actions. They were nefarious and I have no excuse other than that I was terrified. At any rate, I actually thank God at this point that the arson came to nothing and the man was apprehended, because, apart from the damage that was prevented, it is less reason for you to despise me."

Julian leaned toward Thorne and responded sincerely, "I do not despise you, Father, I never could. I don't agree with your actions, but I believe I understand your motivations. In fact, I feel for you and I only wish you had shared this with me earlier. I am certain we could have adopted a better, more reasonable plan. I have known Fred since boyhood and he would have dealt fairly with us on this."

"That's as may be, my son," said Thorne, "but you do NOT know Ebenezer Scrooge! His idea of fairness is whatever will earn him the most money, at whatever cost to anyone else."

CHAPTER TWENTY-FIVE

Saturday, December 14, 1844

While Thorne wrestled with the realization that the deed was actually in the hands of Ebenezer Scrooge, Scrooge continued to investigate Fan's death. He had not yet spoken with Mrs. Asker's daughter, Mrs. Hollis, and wanted to do it quickly. He needed an eyewitness who could confirm that Symons had made a deathbed admission, or could corroborate the doctor's statement that he had derided Fan's killer as he lay dying.

Ever the businessman, Scrooge was also intrigued by the fact that Mrs. Hollis' husband was employed by the new rail line. He had been keeping his eye on the railways and was considering investing in one of the newer lines, but he had never ridden in a rail car. It occurred to him that perhaps he should take the railway to Harrow. Well, why not? Jumping up from his desk, Scrooge called, "Peter! In here, please. Quickly!" Peter appeared, whereupon Scrooge gave him six pence to go to the local bookseller and purchase a copy of Bradshaw's Railway Monthly Guide. Once the Guide was in his hands he found there were three trains down and five trains up each day and three each way on Sundays. That would easily work for him. He would go today!

Scrooge took a hansom to Euston Station. It was the first station to be built in London, having opened in 1837, and it accommodated the London and Birmingham Railway. Scrooge had seen the building many times, but had never been inside. Today he entered and bought a first-class ticket for the next train and walked to the departures platform. He hoped to get a good look at the entire operation. He might not only invest himself, he might also encourage some clients to use the railway to ship commodities, rather than the canals, which were slower and could be more prone to theft and mishandling.

Scrooge climbed into the coach and settled as well as he could onto an uncomfortable wooden seat. As they progressed from London into some fields and countryside, he admitted to himself that he could see no huge difference in comfort between a stagecoach and the railway. However, when it came to speed, there was no match.

In little more than an hour they arrived at Harrow Station, in rural Middlesex. Scrooge enquired within for the direction to Wealdstone and was informed it was about one mile north of the station. He could easily walk, although the sensations attached to a slow walk were much less attractive to him now that he had ridden on the railway. It was also quite cold, but then, the temperature was no colder than the inside of that railway coach!

Scrooge quickly covered the mile to Wealdstone, which was merely a small collection of houses. With Mrs. Asker's directions, he easily located the Hollis cottage. It was modest, but hosted a neatly winterized garden and the house seemed to be kept in good repair. Scrooge had often noted that people who were neat in their persons and their possessions were often of well-ordered minds. Yes, he hoped Mrs. Hollis would be neat in her facts and her memory, for he was counting on her good sense and ability to recall needed information. If she was anything like her mother, she would be sharp enough.

Scrooge approached the home, hoping it would be warm inside, and knocked on the front door. A pleasant voice from within chirped, "Yes, just a moment, I'm on my way." He hoped he wasn't coming at a bad time, but had, after all, given her no warning and was counting on her willingness to speak with him for a few moments.

A woman a few years younger than he opened the door, a pleasant expression on her face and flour on her hands. She was still a very pretty redhead, and smiled at him even though he was a stranger.

"Yes? Can I 'elp you, Sir?" she asked, wiping her hands on her apron.

"I beg your pardon, Mrs. Hollis," said Scrooge, doffing his hat, "but I am Ebenezer Scrooge and I have come from London hoping you would spare me a few minutes." She seemed puzzled, so he explained further. "I am brother to Fan Symons, Mrs. Geoffrey Symons, and I believe you were in their employ at one time." Realizing she might require more in the way of his credentials, he quickly added, "Your mother, Mrs. Asker, gave me your direction." While she was still examining his person, he asked, "Could you please spare me a few moments? I am seeking information about my sister and her household."

"Of course, Mr. Scrooge," she replied. Gesturing to the room behind her she said, "You must come in and warm yourself. We'll have a nice chat and hopefully I can 'elp you." She was not as well-spoken as her mother but was every bit as congenial and forthright in her conversation.

Mrs. Hollis led Scrooge to the back of the cottage, into the kitchen, a sunny room where she was at work with some pies.

The kitchen was modern for a small cottage and contained a closed range, which allowed Mrs. Hollis to do her own baking. Her cooking did not interfere with her hospitality, however. In fact, as far as Scrooge was concerned, it enhanced it.

"Now, then, Mr. Scrooge, you take off that 'eavy coat – that's right – 'n I'll put it aside with your hat while we visit." As if to maintain good manners, she explained, "I 'ope you don't mind, but I'm in the middle of this and I'm sure we can talk while I work." She pointed to a chair at the table and asked him to sit. The tabletop was obviously her work place, but it was otherwise clean and he felt comfortable in her company, particularly in this room. Without asking she had taken the kettle from the hob and was pouring water into a teapot. She took out two cups and set them next to the pot while the tea steeped.

Scrooge said he did not mind at all, which was the God's truth since entering her kitchen had magically transported him back in time to the more pleasant aspects of living in his parents' home as a small child. The wonderful odors reminded him of the hours he spent in the kitchen, where Cook let him stir the Christmas pudding. Sometimes she allowed him to cut short-bread and even sample it, waiting for his approval as if it really mattered. He felt very much at home and Mrs. Hollis, for all her simplicity, was an excellent hostess because she made him feel welcome and at ease. He watched her move competently around the room.

"Mr. Scrooge, could you manage a piece o' cake with your tea?" she asked. He accepted thankfully and she poured him a cup, setting it in front of him as she said, "This should 'elp to take the chill off the day." She cut a wide slice of cake and set it next to the tea. He knew, from the scent of the kitchen, that it would be delicious. Hungrily, he took a bite, confirming his assumptions. He swallowed, said, "This is delicious, Mrs. Hollis," and was rewarded by a smile and a bob of her head.

"Now," said Mrs. Hollis, as she covered the cake with a towel, "it's alright if you call me Nora, since I'm no longer in service. It makes it easier to chat, I always say. Oh, don't worry, Mr. Scrooge, I would never dare call you by your first name, 'specially seein's 'ow I don't remember it!" She giggled at her own joke and waited for him to begin.

"Very well . . . Nora. Thank you," he said as he set down his teacup after taking a long drink. "I suppose you are wondering why I've come to see you, although you know it has to do with the fact that you were a maid at the Symons home."

"Yessir, I was that, for several years. It were a very good job, too. That's where I met me 'usband, in fact. 'E were workin' on the canal nearby and we met through the footman. Took to each other instantly, we did, and that's never changed, even after so many years of marriage 'n three grown children."

Scrooge could understand that and smiled at the image of their courtship. Aware that he was being somewhat abrupt, Scrooge nevertheless asked, "Nora, do you recall the death of my sister, Mrs. Symons?"

She was rolling some pastry but stopped and looked up at him with a solemn expression. "Oh, yessir, I do. It were so sad. We was all weepin' and so upset 'n all. She were the nicest lady I ever worked for, and that's the God's truth." He was surprised at how her simple statement affected him. It was perhaps the fact that he was in the kitchen, amid all of those childhood aromas, with this uncomplicated woman who had tended to Fan. She had even loved her. He suddenly wanted to weep himself, for all that no longer was, and for those events that he could not undo. Instead, he blinked, cleared his throat, and continued.

"Nora," he said, "There were several deaths in the Symons house, and I assume you are aware of them." She was his last hope and he prayed she could somehow confirm his suspicions regarding Geoffrey Symons. As he took his last bite of cake, she nodded in the affirmative. He swallowed and asked, "Were you also there when the master died, and was he attended by Dr. Devitt?"

"Oh, yessir. I was that," said Nora as she prepared the pastry. "O' course, She was already gone by then, bless 'er, but when 'e got sick, Doctor Devitt stayed right with 'im, he did. I know, 'cause I was there cleanin' and keepin' up the fire, 'n other such duties as needed doin'. Sometimes a sick room needs more 'n other rooms – you'd be surprised, I'm sure."

"I'm sure I would, Nora, and it sounds as if you were very conscientious. I'm counting on that, in fact, and I hope you have a good memory, as well."

"That I do, Mr. Scrooge. I remember most things, even when me 'usband wishes I didn't!" She gave another small laugh that made her sound like a young girl.

Scrooge smiled. "So you were kept busy during this time. Was he ill for very long? Did he say anything that seemed at all . . . odd . . . to you?"

"Oh, why, Mr. Scrooge, 'e was in that much pain for two or three days. It were a terrible sight an' it made 'im go right out of his 'ead. 'E didn't make no sense. 'E were goin' on somethin' awful, sayin' things 'e didn't mean, like how he'd done the right thing by lettin' his wife die, 'n all sorts of things about how havin' a son were . . . I don't know . . . somethin' I didn't understand. I couldn't 'ardly stand to be in the same room with the poor man, so I was more 'n happy to be sent away when the doctor told me to go."

Oh, Dear Lord. Scrooge closed his eyes with the revelations of what she was saying. It was as he suspected and having it confirmed was heartbreaking. Still, there was one thing that would prove, for certain, that the doctor killed Geoffrey as retribution for poisoning Fan.

"Nora," said Scrooge, squaring his shoulders. "I have an important question and I want you to think carefully. I know all of this occurred a long time ago, but try to recall the scene as well as you can because anything you know may be important, even if it does not seem so, to you. Please tell me everything you remember that Dr. Devitt said at the time, even if it seemed like utter nonsense."

Nora looked surprised. She thought a moment and said, "It's funny you should ask that, Mr. Scrooge, because it puts me in mind of somethin' 'e did say that didn't make a bit 'o sense." She paused in her work, placed her hands on her hips and looked upward, as if recalling the incident.

"I'd picked up me things to go, an' then I went back to get a rag I'd forgot, an' I 'eard Dr. Devitt say to the poor man as he lay there dyin', 'You're gettin' no more 'n what you deserve, and 'oo should know it better than I, the way you used me for such an evil deed!' 'E were bendin' over the master, tauntin' him like, so 'e didn't see me, and I left quick as my legs would take me, real quiet. It seemed so curious to me that I mentioned it to me mum, but she said I surely 'eard wrong, that the doctor was always compassionate and merciful and must 'ave been talkin' about somethin' else. I s'pose that's why I put it right out 'o my mind, 'til you come 'round asking these questions. In't it odd 'ow easy it is to do that?"

"Yes, Nora, it is odd, and it happens quite frequently."

Rather than feeling furious or elated at hearing the truth, Scrooge was deflated. So it was confirmed. The doctor had cornered his prey and dispatched him to Hell. It was Geoffrey who had murdered Fan after all, for whatever reason, may his soul turn on a slow spit over the fires of Hades. God forbid Geoffrey's reasons had included Rebecca Sotherton. At least Scrooge no longer feared she had been a willing party to the deed. At one time his opinion of her had been so shattered that he was willing to entertain many unflattering ideas, the least of them being that she had encouraged Geoffrey. Still, perhaps it was because of

Geoffrey's love for Rebecca that he had wanted to rid himself of his wife. Perhaps Rebecca had, after all, played an unwitting role in her dear friend's murder. He must ask Nora one more thing.

Toying with his cup, Scrooge said, "Mrs. Hollis – Nora – do you recall whether Mr. Symons mentioned anyone else when he was ranting? Did he mention the name of another woman, perchance, other than his wife, that is?"

Nora hesitated, as if she hadn't heard him correctly. "Mr. Symons?" She looked perplexed. Shaking her head slowly, she said, "Begging your pardon, Mr. Scrooge, but Mr. Symons weren't there." Scrooge himself looked puzzled and she quickly realized what he was thinking. "Oh! No, Mr. Scrooge. It weren't Mr. Geoffrey what was dyin'. He'd passed on the year before. I'm talkin' about the old master. It were your father, Sir. It were Mr. Josiah."

❧

Scrooge stared blindly at the landscape on the ride home, completely forgetting his mission to study the railway. He was numb. Such a thing had never occurred to him. It was insupportable that his father had killed Fan, Josiah's own flesh and blood – the daughter he undoubtedly loved. It was totally unthinkable, yet it was somehow believable. Of course! It made a certain amount of macabre sense, or at least as much sense as anything else in this wicked business. Josiah Scrooge was insane. His reasons for such an act would never be comprehended, but Scrooge could certainly believe that his madness might command him to commit such an ungodly act.

Yet Nora Hollis said Josiah Scrooge had raved of killing his wife – Fan and Ebenezer's mother! Could the truth get any worse? Could the senior Scrooge have done such an appalling thing? Or did he perhaps simply "let her die" as he had said?

The man was extremely delusional by the time of his own death, which made it less likely that he was speaking of real events. Most likely he had done his wife no harm so many years before, but no one would ever know. Perhaps he felt guilt over her death, or his treatment of her during her lifetime, and had formed the idea that her death was in some way his fault. Perhaps he neglected her and harbored many regrets where she was concerned. Scrooge could certainly identify with that particular guilt. One thing was certain, however. The doctor had his reasons for, and was convinced that Josiah Scrooge had killed Fan and he had, in turn, poisoned Josiah. The maid's unbiased report of what the doctor said matched what the doctor himself told Scrooge about having taunted Fan's killer as he lay dying. Thereafter, the doctor's life was slowly ruined by his own vile deed until he died of drink and general neglect of his own body and soul. What a tangled mass of heartbreaking occurrences.

So it was not Geoffrey, after all, who had poisoned Fan, regardless of what he felt for Rebecca. That also proved, once and for all, that Rebecca played no part in Fan's death, either wittingly or unwittingly. Scrooge was unsure whether it was better, or worse, that Fan's father had poisoned her, rather than her husband. She was daughter to one and wife to the other, and both men should have loved and protected her, but perhaps there was at least a particle of an excuse for his father. He did, after all, truly belong in Bedlam.

Scrooge now suspected there were two reasons why the doctor had not had Josiah Scrooge committed after Fan's death. One was that he knew Fan was against such a commitment and he wanted to honor her wishes, and the other was that the doctor, by then, was determined to keep Josiah Scrooge in the home in order to extract his revenge by poisoning him. The doctor's obsession with evening the score would have guided him on that account. Scrooge recalled that one of the doctor's entries regarding Josiah Scrooge had been, *The end should not be long in coming.* It was no doubt a way to cover up the fact that the doctor, himself, would be the means to that end.

Scrooge's heart ached for poor, lovely, innocent Fan. He also pitied their deranged Father – and that pathetic avenging doctor. That Fan should have been surrounded by such men, including himself, who did not give her the care she deserved, was unforgivable. She had even had to tolerate men who wanted – no – demanded her time and attention because they adored her in all of her beauty, gaiety and innocence.

Yet he knew without a doubt that she would have forgiven every one of them, quickly and easily. Perhaps she had done so, after all. That was ever her way, and it gave him a certain amount of comfort to think on that possibility. Scrooge found it more difficult to be sympathetic to Geoffrey Symons and actually thought worse of him than of Josiah Scrooge. Their father was not totally accountable, but Geoffrey Symons was dissolute. In fact, Scrooge thought he might, at some point, ask Marley about Geoffrey's and his father's spirits, and where, exactly, had been their final destinations.

CHAPTER TWENTY-SIX

Monday, December 16, 1844

The puzzle that had started a few weeks ago had almost been Scrooge's undoing. In fact, he was not yet convinced it hadn't been since there were times he felt his reason was hanging by a thread. For all of its convolutions, it had begun so simply. He had attended a party and met a woman he truly admired from the time of their introduction. Then her remarks brought such turmoil into his thinking. Oh, he realized Mrs. Langstone's information, itself, had not been the problem. It wouldn't have been had he simply let it go, as Marley recommended. It was Scrooge's tenacious pursuit of what lay behind the remark that had brought about the problems. He became like a growling dog protecting a chewed slipper because he wanted to prove that nothing had been amiss and he had done no wrong, which soon turned into a determination to solve his sister's murder.

In trying to do so he had uncovered another murder, disclosed the unsavory character of his brother-in-law, discovered that several men had loved Fan and, because he involved Fred in his snooping, they had come across the deed to Thorne Shipping. *What surprising turns our lives take,* he thought. His sleuthing turned up facts that were difficult to bear and was the means of discovering a single paper that could make Fred one of the richest men in England.

Scrooge was an old hand at business dealings and had, at his side, the best solicitors in the City. They had worked together for many years and knew each other's foibles, as well as each other's strengths. That was good, because they were soon to deal with Thorne and his legal advisors, and would, once again, act as a well-practiced and effective team. Scrooge had not lost his touch – oh, no – and he planned to demonstrate it once again. He had gone over the matter thoroughly with Danmock, along with Fred of course, and everything was ready. All that was left was to face Thorne – a nasty piece of work and a troublemaker, at that – who had evidently been in love with Fan and made a nuisance of himself. Did Thorne realize she was Scrooge's sister? Perhaps he was not aware that the connection between Scrooge and Fred was through Fan, although he must know Fred was her son.

Scrooge would put all of that aside however, and simply deal with Thorne in a business fashion – as an adversary, for certain! Thorne might never answer for his behavior toward Fan, but he would, by everything in Scrooge's power, answer for his careless and unscrupulous conceit. He would make Thorne squirm, and skin him – painfully – of some of that arrogance.

※

Scrooge and Fred were comfortably ensconced in Danmock's chambers, discussing the new rail lines and the possibility of investing in one of them when Danmock's clerk announced Thorne, his son Julian, and Thorne's attorney, Phineas Goodby. They were shown in, offered seats, and Danmock opened the discussion. As he did so, Scrooge's expression turned cold. He was the hunter, Thorne was his prey.

"Mr. Thorne," began Danmock. "As you are aware, my client, Mr. Fred Symons, is in possession of a piece of paper which has recently been discovered that gives him full ownership of Thorne Shipping."

"That's nothing but a . . .!" began Thorne, before being shushed by Goodby.

Danmock made a harrumphing sound and began again. "As I was saying, the deed appears to be in order and, although the wording is somewhat abbreviated, it is clearly a document by which you were paying a debt owing to Mr. Symons' father, Geoffrey Symons, on September 1, 1822."

Thorne jumped up without thinking, slammed his walking stick down on Danmock's desk and bellowed, "It was a BOAT! It was one small, leaky boat that was barely large enough to carry a full cargo of wine between the Iberian Peninsula and London!" He looked at Danmock in desperate rage and cried, "Do you expect me to accept this as a valid claim for Thorne Shipping Company? Do you, man? I don't see how you ever could. The very idea is absurd. It is total madness!!" Goodby looked stricken, as if he were holding the reins to an unbroken, bucking stallion. Julian remained unhappily silent as Fred and Scrooge coolly observed the outburst.

"Mr. Thorne," interrupted Danmock, who was seemingly undisturbed by all the commotion, "Please sit down. We will discuss this in a civilized manner or we will not discuss it at all."

His eyes blazing, Thorne glared furiously from one man to the other and slowly took his seat. He could not afford to call an end to this charade just yet, because that would mean the matter would be heard in a court of law and be reported in every newspaper in the Empire. He might be beside himself, but, like any good businessman, he knew when to back down, at least for the moment. That did not mean he was ceding anything. No, sir, he would cede not one sail nor one anchor from his company – HIS company. Not to these marauding thieves!

Working his jaw, Thorne sat, and glared at Danmock.

"As I said," resumed Danmock, "this appears to be a valid title. It does not say it pertains to one boat. It lists Thorne Shipping Company as the payment for a debt. Since the amount of the debt is not given, it could be an amount to cover a small 'boat' or it could refer to an entire shipping company."

"Ah, but you see," cut in Mr. Goodby, "that is the point, isn't it? Since the amount was not declared, we cannot assume the amount was equal to the worth of Mr. Thorne's current holdings. We cannot assume any such thing."

"Nor can we assume it was less, Mr. Goodby," replied Danmock. "In point of fact, an impartial investigator, not connected with this office, has spoken to the other two witnesses and neither can recall the amount of the bet, but they both state the stakes were, as they put it, quite substantial. That may be borne out by the fact that one of the witnesses recalls Mr. Thorne stating he had nothing of value left to wager, without going into his wife's property."

"Father!" yelped Julian, even though he had solemnly promised to keep quiet.

Thorne could not contain himself. Good business head or no, he was in a state of panic. "Symons cheated!" he cried. "The man cheated me. I know he did not play a fair game and the entire thing was a farce! The man was a blackguard and a rogue and he did not win the game honestly."

Scrooge had, by now, leaned his chair back onto two legs, against the wall. His arms were crossed on his chest and his expression was one of mild amusement. It was a pose long practiced and one he often struck in the old days, just before moving in for the kill. He was like a snake mesmerizing its prey, and the prey felt it, but there was no way to forestall the inevitable. Even though it was a tactic he had not used for nigh on a twelvemonth, he found he hadn't lost his touch, for Thorne was indeed sweating. That was as it should be.

"No, Mr. Thorne," replied Danmock calmly. "The two witnesses also insist there was no evidence of cheating by Geoffrey Symons, and they are prepared to testify to that, as well as to the fact that the stakes were extremely high that night. They would testify to all that, were this matter to be taken before the Court for a judgment."

Thorne was speechless. Goodby looked down and began fussily flipping through papers while Julian stared at his father, alarmed. Both of Julian's parents had ensured that he was made of better stuff than his father had been in his own youth and, because of that, Julian's concern truly was more for his father's well-being than for the loss of the Company. Losing the Company would be beyond imagination, but they would not starve and he was certain he would not lose his wife's affection and emotional support. He feared his father, however, might never recover from the public thrashing he was evidently about to suffer. Indeed, it might kill him.

Suddenly Scrooge sat forward. Julian sucked in his breath, Goodby shut his eyes, and Thorne's heart skipped a beat or two. The blow was about to be struck by the meanest man on earth. It was unfair. It was criminal. Thorne wished Scrooge were as dead and cold in the grave as Geoffrey Symons, may both their souls rot in Hell. Scrooge stood and began to speak, staring at Thorne with eyes sharp as steel.

"Mr. Thorne," began Scrooge calmly. "It is lucky for you that the police were unable to trace it back to you, because we believe you hired men to break into my nephew's home, to burglarize our counting offices, and you even had the effrontery to attempt to burn down, or blow up, our offices and most likely take a goodly portion of London with it." Scrooge turned to look out the window, his hands clasped behind his back, and said, "You should be brought up on charges and I suspect that, were such a thing to occur, a jury could be convinced of your guilt, even on our circumstantial evidence." He turned back around and nearly spat, "Those crimes alone have earned us payment from you, Sir!" Looking directly at Thorne, he said, "My nephew, Geoffrey Symons' heir, is, as attested to by your own handwriting, the legal owner of Thorne Shipping!"

Thorne looked, and felt, like a worm that had been squashed under foot. His uncontrolled youth had taken twenty-two years to catch up with him and he wasn't sure he could bear it. That rattle-brained Goodby was no help, either, because he had absolutely nothing to say and would not meet Thorne's glance. Neither of them wanted the Courts involved because too many things would come out and those infernal witnesses would tie things up in a pretty package, to be handed over to Fred Symons as nice as you please. He was ruined. Worse, his son, who sat there looking so bewildered, would have nothing but his mother's and his wife's inheritances, which would have to support them all, and the good society of London would turn their backs on him. The entire family would be consigned to the dustbin. Lost in his own agony, Thorne almost missed Scrooge's next statement.

"Nevertheless, although my nephew may be the legal owner, neither he nor I believe he is the 'rightful' owner."

Thorne's head shot up, as did Goodby's and Julian's. What had the man said?

"That's right," said Scrooge without smiling. "You made him the legal owner when you wrote that note of transfer in 1822 and failed to either buy it back, or give Geoffrey Symons the boat and begin afresh. It was a foolish mistake and one that demonstrates your habits at the time. Were you dealing with anyone other than my nephew, you might have had a serious problem on your hands." Scrooge knew that what he was doing would, in the long run, be a more effective punishment than if he stripped Thorne of everything outright.

Thorne could not believe what he was hearing. Perhaps what he thought he was hearing was not what was actually being said. Perhaps it was another trick – a trap to make him squirm just a little more before the kill – a way to twist the knife before ripping his heart out. He believed Scrooge capable of such a thing. Perhaps Fred's slight smile was actually a smirk. He could not bear to see the sudden hope in his son's eyes erased by such a cruel tactic that was obviously designed to raise expectations only to dash them and watch the suffering. Danmock was again speaking.

"Mr. Thorne, Mr. Symons came by the deed to your shipping company honestly, but he does not want your business. It would give him no pleasure to ruin you. It is Mr. Symons' contention that you have worked hard for many years to grow your company and you, of course, have made it what it is." He pulled some papers toward him and continued.

"Nevertheless, Mr. Symons has been advised by me to propose a settlement between the two of you that will lay this thing to rest, for good. I would like to make that proposal to you now." He looked up. "Will that be acceptable?"

Thorne looked at Goodby, who said, "We are willing to hear it, yes. Then we can discuss the matter. We will accept it, reject it outright, or request time to consider it and make a rejoinder at a later date."

"Very well," said Danmock. "I will proceed.

"You have caused some damage and invaded my clients' privacy, not to mention the potential and intended ruination of their livelihood, and there must be reparation for that. There is also the fact that, in giving up his valid claim to Thorne shipping, Fred Symons lets a considerable fortune slip through his fingers." Thorne opened his mouth to speak but was hushed by a warning wag of Goodby's head. This was not the time to interrupt.

"My client insists he has only the right to claim a boat from you, and that is what he intends to do." Danmock looked up over his spectacles and saw three sets of unseeing eyes aimed directly at him. *They are in shock!* he thought, and continued on in hopes that they could actually take in what he was saying.

"Mr. Thorne, considering the original deed for a boat, which was never conveyed to Geoffrey Symons, and the inconvenience and angst you have dealt to my clients, plus what Mr. Fred Symons is technically owed in interest for all these years, you may either award Mr. Symons a small new sailing ship – not a boat – in good order and fit for the sea, or you may pay him today's cost to purchase such a vessel. I believe he would prefer the money." Fred nodded.

Thorne was totally speechless. He sat, waiting for the other shoe to drop. This could not be all of it. Scrooge was at the helm of this voyage and that greedy miser would never let such a formidable fortune go unclaimed!

As Thorne was trying to discern a trap, Fred spoke.

"Mr. Thorne – Julian. This is not a situation I would have wished on any of us, but we must end it by amicable and rational means, and we must do it as quickly as possible. As Mr. Danmock has said, we will be satisfied and the transfer of ownership returned to you, if our terms are met." As if recalling something, he said, "Oh! There is one other thing."

I knew it! thought Thorne. *Here is where the ax falls.*

"I also insist," continued Fred, "as does my uncle, that this thing not be advertised. In fact, one of the most important terms of this settlement is that the entire transaction must remain forever undisclosed to anyone other than to those of us present here in this room."

Thorne could not believe his ears. It would be ended for the price of a small sailing ship and no one need know. No one, including his wife, would ever learn about his earlier indiscretion, his most recent involvement in illegal activities, nor how close he had come to losing his fortune. He had been snatched from the mouth of Hades, itself! His business would remain intact, and his reputation, as well. Of course, the witnesses were aware of the deed of transfer, but if nothing further came of it, they would assume it had all amounted to nothing. He wanted to shout for joy, but definitely not in front of Ebenezer Scrooge!

After a moment, Danmock said, "Well, gentlemen, where does that leave us?"

Goodby ventured to say, "If my client has no objections, Danmock," looking at Thorne for affirmation, "I would say it is a reasonable offer and we will accept it." Thorne nodded silently and Julian broke into a smile, his shoulders relaxing.

"There is . . . one more thing I would like to say," interjected Scrooge, turning toward them from where he had been standing to the side of the room. He took two steps forward. "Prior to last Christmas I would have treated you much differently, Thorne. I would have ruined you without remedy and not given it another thought. Last Christmas, however, my outlook on life was so altered that I have, since, felt like a new man – even generous in thought and deed. Your actions, however, along with some other recent personal events, made me question the wisdom of that alteration in my character. I am pleased to say my reclamation, at least where you are concerned, is intact."

Thorne made no response, and Scrooge did not expect one. Danmock proceeded with the papers and all was signed. The deed of transfer, however, would not be returned to Thorne until Fred had been recompensed by an amount acknowledged as satisfactory.

Without another word, Thorne abruptly turned and fled the office upon conclusion of the business, while Fred and Julian shook hands gladly. Fred was convinced in his own mind that Julian had played no part in the illegal activities, and this would later be confirmed during their many affable conversations. The solicitors said their professional and cordial good-byes, while Scrooge watched Thorne's departing backside, suspecting that he knew what was going through Thorne's mind. He was right, of course.

Thorne could not forgive Scrooge for discovering his foolishness of so many years ago. He was mortified and hated him more than if he had taken everything. He might never forgive him for being benevolent since it put him in Scrooge's debt. He would never say so to Julian, of course, because his son would be disappointed in him, but his intense dislike of Scrooge was solidified, rather than melted by the warmth of human kindness. *Teach ME a lesson, will he?* thought Thorne. *Never!*

Still, beneath his battered pride, Thorne knew, without a doubt, that Scrooge had done him and his son a decent turn, and done it without rancor. Although Thorne could not abide it, a piece of him respected and even thanked Scrooge for it. The two sentiments would war within his breast for some time to come.

CHAPTER TWENTY-SEVEN

Scrooge had told Thorne he was a new man, but it was no longer the absolute truth. It was true that he was not the miserable miser he had been prior to last year, but there were new dark clouds that had settled in his soul since the staggering discoveries about Fan's death. They were clinging like the yellow London fog, blinding him to the good with which he was surrounded on every side. Being a rational man, he realized all of those dreadful things had happened long before his renewal of last Christmas, but it seemed they were very recent events, since they had only just been discovered. How could he have been so blind to the truth? He could do nothing about any of it, but his optimism and charity were shaky, at best.

At least there was an end to it. Thorne was uncomfortably safe and Fred was the better for it. Fred had been party to conducting business with compassion and fairness and Scrooge had been pleased to see that he was never tempted to ruin Mr. Thorne.

❦

It was later that evening that Fred appeared at Scrooge's home. He encountered Mrs. Dilber on her way out and said he would find his own way, quickly locating his uncle in the library. Scrooge had escaped into another world with one of his old companions. This time it was *Ali Baba*.

"My dear Uncle," said Fred unhappily, as if he really did not wish to disturb him. Scrooge looked up over his spectacles, greeted his nephew and waved him to a chair nearby as he marked his place in the book before setting it down. There seemed no reason to prevaricate so Fred immediately stated his reason for coming, as distressing as it was.

"Uncle . . . I have something here I think you should read. I would give anything not to bring it to you, but in light of our recent adventures, I feel I must." With that, he handed his uncle a letter addressed to Scrooge in the same lovely handwriting he had seen so often during the past few weeks. It was another letter from Fan – her last – one that had never been posted. Fred had uncovered it among the rest of her belongings as he was putting them away and was, now, twenty-five years after it was penned, delivering it to its intended recipient. Fred explained as best he could while Scrooge watched him closely, on the alert to something out of the ordinary.

"My mother wrote this shortly before she died and I suspect it was simply gathered up with other papers from her desk and stored by a servant following her death. No one knew to post it. I hope you will forgive me for reading it." He was visibly upset, more so for his uncle than for himself, and he could not have looked more miserable.

Scrooge frowned, took the missive and turned it over in his hands. What, after all that had happened, could disturb his nephew to such an extent? He unfolded the paper and began to read.

1 July 1819
My Dearest, most Loyal Ebenezer,

It grieves me that I am about to give you pain, and I beg you to forgive me, as I believe you will when you understand. I am like that bird we found in a snare when we were children – so frightened and unable to find a way to escape the situation. There is simply no way for me to accommodate my present circumstances, at least not without giving injury to others, no matter which way I turn.

Since my beloved son's birth I have experienced a mother's love for the first time and have learned that it is protective in a way I would never have imagined. It is truly the most selfless attachment I can imagine and, in light of what I am about to tell you, carries the most responsibility.

Ebenezer, I truly believe my sanity is in jeopardy. Since Fred's birth I have been confused. I cannot control my moods, I am not sleeping, and I feel guilty for what I may have done to my firstborn, no matter how unwittingly. His arrival was such a miracle, and yet I am torn unreasonably between happiness and hopelessness and I cannot seem to pull myself out of this deep pit.

I consulted Dr. Devitt but he did not take my concerns seriously. He simply patted my hand and said not to worry, which gave me no relief. He did, however, unknowingly justify and even intensify my fears. He did not realize I feared a connection between my ungovernable emotions and our father's state. My recent behavior is – I cannot deny it – too similar to our father's for me to dismiss it as a passing ailment.

I am certain the doctor did not know to what I referred when I asked him about madness and its possible transmittal through generations. It was his considered judgment that lunacies can continue in blood lines. He even mentioned our father and said it is probable that some of our forebears exhibited similar symptoms.

The implication was not lost on me, although I dare say the doctor had no idea that he confirmed my worst fear. I refer, of course, to my dear one – my precious newborn son. What have I done by bringing him into the world? Have I doomed him to a life like his grandfather's? I have prayed to what I believe is a compassionate God that it will not be so. I want nothing more than for my son to grow up to be good and kind and "sane," and I trust you will assist him to become that – you and his father, of course, for I will not be here. And that, my Dearest Brother, is the decision I share with you now.

I may have already doomed one child, whom I love more than life itself, to a lifetime of lunacy, and that is a terrible thing to bear. I cannot take the same gamble with more children. Nor can I tell my husband that I will hereafter be a wife in name only, and that he will be allowed no more children. It would be better were he to marry again and enjoy a normal life and provide Fred with a sane and loving stepmother. I have not told Geoffrey the truth of what I believe is happening to me because, as I have mentioned before, he does not operate from the center of things. His character is more extreme. He would either wish – without saying so, of course – that I were gone, or would simply say I was being foolish and that we should have all the children we want.

I cannot, however, bring myself to gamble with the lives of innocents such as my new little boy, whom I love beyond anything I ever thought possible. I admit to you that the heartbreak of leaving him behind is unbearable and I have several times very nearly reconsidered, but I must not follow my own selfish desires in this matter. I would do him more harm by remaining in his life and imposing on him what is most likely to be an insane and very injurious mother.

My plan is uncomplicated and not very original. Since I have again been walking a little, I secured some arsenic from the storeroom and added it to the bottle of laudanum. I will take it late this afternoon, and I pray God will forgive me.

I should only add that I have adored you all of my life and will, if it is possible, continue to do so after I am gone. Look out for my small one, I beg you.

Your Devoted Sister,
Fan

Scrooge sat back as if he had been struck, reeling from the invisible blow. So that was how she died! She had not been murdered after all, although the outcome had been the same because suspicion had run rampant, and more murder had been the result. Surely Fan had written this last letter to Scrooge not only to disclose the truth to her beloved brother, but to prevent exactly what did happen following her death. She assumed, no doubt, that her written confession would insure against anyone being blamed for her death. The fact that the letter was carelessly scooped into her trunk along with other belongings instead of being posted proved catastrophic and there was no way of knowing who did it, since they would not have known themselves. There was too much turmoil at the time. Besides, it was no matter now. It was too late. It was too late for anything but regret.

Unable to speak, Scrooge swallowed heavily, leaned forward and lowered his head, his shoulders shaking as he silently wept. With his free hand he waved Fred away. In the other hand he held the letter and slowly crumpled it, ignoring the hot tears that were soaking his cheeks. Neither he nor Fred could find adequate words, so Fred turned to go. As he

reached the door, however, Scrooge gasped a sob and managed to call his name.

"Fred . . . my boy . . .

Stay."

Thursday, December 19, 1844

Scrooge had conducted his unrewarding search against the
advice of his ghostly friend Marley and finally learned that Fan
had not, after all, died by someone else's hand. The threat
about which she had written to Marley had evidently been re-
solved by Marley, and the unpleasantness she mentioned to
Scrooge was no doubt her fear of going mad, rather than a fear
of another person.

She was not a murder victim but, as far as her brother was
concerned, Fan was, nevertheless, a victim of ignorance and
fear. What else could it be called? There had been hers and
the doctor's ignorance regarding her state of mind following
Fred's birth, and that had caused her fears, for which she saw
only one way out. Her death had been misunderstood by the
doctor, who concluded that someone else had killed her. He
then murdered the person he blamed – Fan's and Scrooge's
own father. Geoffrey was not worth mentioning, even though
he had, at least, left Fred somewhat richer in the amount of the
price of a new sailing ship.

Yes, the earlier discoveries had been difficult to absorb, but
this latest truth, as attested to by Fan's own hand in her last letter, was proving far too much for Scrooge. What little peace he
had managed to recapture before receiving that letter flew like
the Ghost of Christmas Past, and for several days now Scrooge
had behaved abominably, acting out his misery as if his regen-

eration of last Christmas had never occurred. He was in a pit of deep melancholy and hopelessness. When he wasn't brooding he was barking, and when not busy at his offices he sat staring at the wall, ruminating on his own failures. He even upbraided his loyal housekeeper as well as anyone else with whom he came into contact.

Most were giving him a wide berth as they tried to sympathize with what little they knew of his situation. They also wished they could somehow assist. His friends, family and close associates missed the lighthearted, sincere man he had become since last Christmas and they regretted that he had not kept his renewed spirit for even a twelvemonth. He didn't see when they whispered to each other and shook their heads at the loss.

Nighttime found Scrooge lying despondent in his bed, heartbroken over the tragedies of so many lives and filled with regret for leaving Fan to fend for herself when she needed him. He was stunned by the truth of her death and the number of people who had been affected by such a disastrous series of mishaps and misunderstandings. His mind was weary from its own churning and his heart lay like wet sand in his chest.

"SCROO-OOOGE!" blared Marley suddenly, from the other side of the bedchamber. The voice was like a pipe organ on full stops and Scrooge bolted upright as the roar echoed throughout the room. It took him several seconds to realize what was happening.

"SCROOGE!" repeated Marley impatiently. Peeking through his bed curtains, Scrooge saw Marley hovering well above the floor. Had Marley's foot been flesh and bone, he would have been tapping it. His arms were as folded as his chains would allow, and he was glowering. Scrooge slowly rose from the bed and settled on the edge of a side table, as though his legs could not support him.

"Marley, my old partner," whined Scrooge, shaking his head. "I see you have come to rub my nose in my folly, to tell me I should have listened to you in the beginning and not played the detective, but I could not have imagined the findings that awaited me. I am wretched Marley. I am totally desolate!"

In a somewhat more subdued tone, Marley replied, "No new evil has occurred, Ebenezer. You have simply uncovered old events, about which you can do nothing. Yet you are in danger of once again being overcome with ill will, and that is the evil that may destroy you."

"Marley!" exclaimed Scrooge. "Have you not even a crumb of charity to toss my way? Can you give me no words of sympathy to serve as a balm for my suffering? I am no better a man than I was a year ago. In fact, I am in a worse state!" Marley looked at Scrooge with eyes that burned away all but the absolute truth.

"Do you recall how you felt last Christmas Eve, when you saw your name on that lonely headstone on an overgrown and neglected grave? Do you recall how, then and there, you determined to alter your life?"

"I do, I do!" cried Scrooge, "but why do you remind me of this? Why now, when my 'reformation' seems such a shallow and unkind deception?"

Marley looked puzzled. "Your reformation was genuine, but you have allowed your most recent discoveries to once again threaten you with a lonely, wasted fate. You may still choose, as you did then, how to live your life, and your choice will dictate what your end will be." Scrooge opened his mouth to make an excuse, but Marley hushed him by holding up his palm and issuing a terrible scowl. Then he continued.

"The past is unchangeable, Ebenezer, as you have been reminded these past few weeks, but there is more to the truth of your present conduct, and you must hear me out." Marley drifted soundlessly toward Scrooge and leaned over him with a certain amount of authority, forcing Scrooge to cower slightly.

"You were delivered from greed and avarice last Christmas, but they are not Man's only sins, Ebenezer. There is also self-centeredness, even self-pity. Your current suffering is not for the dead – they do not require it. No, my friend, your suffering is for yourself. You are not imparting pity to Dr. Devitt, your father, or even Fan. You are, instead, pitying Ebenezer Scrooge because you were not what you should have been many years ago. You resemble the clean Biblical pig that has returned to its wallowing since your behavior is, once again, concentrated on yourself." With Marley's last statement, Scrooge began to weep, but Marley was not yet finished.

"You, as well as the rest of the human race, always have the ability to choose wickedness over goodness. To think only of yourself is to choose wickedness. Is that the life, and therefore the end, you prefer?" Lifting and displaying his heavy chains and money boxes with a sad clanging he asked, "Is this the fate you wish to choose, after all?"

Humbled and mortified, Scrooge moaned loudly and slid to the floor in a heap. He was trembling, and it had nothing to do with the chill of the room. He knew Marley's description of him was accurate and he was heartily ashamed, as well as afraid. For the second time in twelve months Ebenezer Scrooge sincerely repented and held up his hands in a prayer for a change of heart. Miraculously, as he did so, the weight of his self-loathing and de-pression was gently lifted from him and, as with last year's specter of Christmas Yet to Come, Marley's presence shrunk, collapsed and dwindled to nothing.

CHAPTER TWENTY-EIGHT

Scrooge slept soundly that night. He was still saddened by the events surrounding Fan's death, but was finally, once again, at peace with the present. His delight at being alive had returned because Ebenezer Scrooge was no longer at the center of his thinking. Prior to turning onto his side and slipping into a dreamless slumber he had yawned widely and thought of one more thing he must do on the morrow, to try to set things right.

The next morning, following a heartfelt apology to Mrs. Dilber, which was readily accepted with a great deal of relief, Scrooge appeared on Mrs. Langstone's doorstep. It was much earlier than was generally thought a civil hour in which to call, but he was, nevertheless, quickly ushered into the morning room. It was warmed by a large fire and at his entrance Mrs. Langstone turned to face him from where she was standing. She was polite, but he could see she was wary.

Mrs. Langstone requested a servant bring coffee and rolls, and offered Scrooge a seat on the sofa as she took a chair across from him. He sat, not realizing he was, for the first time in weeks, wearing a very sincere smile. His expression was infinitely more affable than the last time the two of them met. He decided not to open the conversation with small talk since they were both aware of the weather, and neither of them cared a whit for the gossip about the politician's wife who had resumed her habit of removing her clothes in Trafalgar Square. He opted to get directly to the point since he believed she would appreciate that approach.

"Mrs. Langstone," he began, "I do not know where to begin, but I must try. I realize I have caused you pain and I pray I have not done irreparable harm. I am come to beg your pardon and to ask that we be friends, as it seemed we were to be before I set out on my doomed quest for the 'truth.' Your forgiveness and your friendship would mean a great deal to me and I would like to explain the extraordinary things that have occurred during this month of December. If you will allow it, I will begin with our meeting at the Wilkinses' party."

Mrs. Langstone's expression was pleasant, but guarded, yet he sensed that she welcomed his overture. She did not answer immediately. Looking directly at him, she seemed to consider his words. Finally, she spoke.

"Mr. Scrooge, I am very pleased to see you and I gladly accept your apology, although I believe I gave you as much pain as you may have given me. It was, I assume, an equal exchange. Perhaps we should forgive each other and start afresh." He was so relieved he felt an odd sensation with which he was not familiar – his chest gave a slight, merry flutter.

The coffee arrived, she poured, and they both drank while he recounted his extraordinary tale.

"As you know, Mrs. Langstone, it all began with a letter Fan wrote to my old partner Marley, indicating she was afraid of someone. Then, at the Wilkinses' gathering you mentioned your conversation with Mrs. Reynolds and remarked that you agreed there was something mysterious about Fan's death. That, in itself, was enough to pique my interest, but it also magnified the fact that I was not there for her and knew very little of the things you mentioned.

"The next day I read some of Fan's old letters and began an investigation into the past. I believe I initially hoped not only to prove there was nothing amiss in her dying, but also to prove that I was not negligent in my treatment of her. Naturally, my interest gave every indication of being altruistic, but it was in large part selfish, I am ashamed to admit."

Mrs. Langstone began an apology for having initiated the problem when he stopped her by saying, "Do not chastise yourself over the incident, please. It has turned out well, I assure you." He took a swallow of coffee before setting down the cup and continuing.

"My searches during this past month have taken me to the homes of several persons who were once in my sister's employ, and each one was a distinct adventure. At one I actually used my foot to keep a woman from slamming the door in my face, and at other interviews I was subjected to unpleasant revelations and required to maintain my composure in the face of them. In between those encounters I was involved in solving a most perplexing burglary of the counting house with its attempted arson, and I was unintentionally pummeled by my own nephew as we tried to capture the offender." He breathed deeply and admitted, "Yet none of that was the worst.

"After you told me of Fan's symptoms, I visited Dr. Devitt and was given the most astounding news. It seems he recognized that Fan had been poisoned, but he never said anything for fear of being suspected, himself. Then he did the most astonishing thing. The doctor took three years to convince himself that he had found the killer, then murdered him, using the same poison, ensuring that the dosage was at a level that would make him suffer a longer death." Scrooge knew he was heaping a great deal

of information on the poor woman, but he continued, nevertheless. She seemed able to cope, although she had turned a bit
pale and was watching him wide-eyed. He needed to speak it
aloud and recap the entire episode, to be done with it.

"I became convinced that Geoffrey had poisoned Fan and, as
you also know, I feared he did it for love of you. Through an eye
witness I discovered that it was our own father, instead, whom the
doctor 'dispatched to Hell,' as he put it, so convinced was he that
our father was Fan's killer." Mrs. Langstone clapped her hand
over her mouth, stunned, but Scrooge continued. He must tell
all, not only because he felt she deserved to know, but because
she was someone with whom he sincerely wanted to share it.

"Mrs. Langstone, this brings me to the most painful part of my
discoveries. I had requested of Fred that he search his parents'
trunks for any clues they might contain, and he did so. He found
some letters I wrote to Fan, which thankfully confirmed, somewhat, that I was not entirely unfeeling of her situation, but four
days ago he also found . . . this." He handed her Fan's last letter.

Rather than give her a narrative, he simply asked her to read
it with the admonition, "I warn you that the subject is extremely
unpleasant, but I believe you have a right to know, since you were
Fan's intimate friend and were at her bedside during the entire
ordeal. I would prefer she tell you, herself, via this letter." He
watched as she read it, observing her fight to control the tears
that finally spilled. When she finished, she wiped her face with a
handkerchief, making Scrooge wish he could take her in his arms.

"Oh!" cried Mrs. Langstone suddenly, as a thought struck her.
"What about Sarah Reynolds? Have you told her the truth of
these things? Does she know the conclusion of the matter?"

Scrooge shook his head. He had not forgotten Mrs. Reynolds.
"No, I have not, not yet, although I intend to. She has carried a
heavy weight for many years, and she deserves to be told. I don't
know which would be worse for her at this point – having her

suspicions of murder confirmed, or learning that Fan died by her own hand. I will have to go easy in my approach because it will be a great shock, but she must be informed. In fact, she is one of the very few people who need to know."

"Yes, she must," agreed Mrs. Langstone. "If you think it would be of benefit, I am willing to accompany you."

"I accept that offer, Mrs. Langstone," said Scrooge. "It is very kind of you and I am certain your presence will make things easier. She will no doubt be very shaken."

Mrs. Langstone herself was also understandably shaken. "I had no idea such things could take place within my circle of acquaintances," said she, "and I always considered myself to be fairly astute – not at all naïve. Perhaps this is a lesson to me, in some ways."

"I think we have all learned something, Mrs. Langstone."

"To think," she said as she dabbed at her nose, "that Fan believed such a thing about herself and received no reassurance from her physician. Had she even said something to me, or to the nurse, she might have been given better information regarding the state of her mind." Shaking her head, she said, "I am not certain it would have helped, however, since there was your father's situation and she was terrified of being like him, particularly toward Fred."

After Mrs. Langstone recovered and had given the letter back to him, Scrooge admitted, "It was my overriding sense of guilt that not only drove me on, but also made me less than objective in my approach to things. I refer, of course, to my feelings of having neglected Fan and my suspicions of you, which sprang from letters and diaries that led to erroneous assumptions that could not be easily corrected since those who wrote them were no longer alive. I must tell you, Mrs. Langstone, that the entire process has humbled me, but I believe I have become a better man because of it."

Scrooge was very careful not to mention Marley's role in his activities of the past weeks. Even though he did not know whether Marley was a real vision, or a dream conjured out of his own conscience, he feared such an admission might earn him a trip to a small locked room. He would much rather remain here, in this cozy situation, drinking coffee with the very amiable Mrs. Langstone.

"I believe," said Mrs. Langstone pensively, "that you reacted as most people would when confronted with such clues and facts, particularly when they are added to one's sense of guilt, whether justified, or not.

"With regard to Fan's mental state, I am aware that some women have unstable moods following childbirth, and it is likely it was nothing more than that. I am nevertheless convinced, based upon your information, that her circumstances were such that she would not have believed it, had the doctor explained it to her. I suspect, too, that he either did not know of that particular phenomenon of childbirth, or did not take her complaints seriously. You may not realize it, Mr. Scrooge, but many doctors respond to their female patients' complaints as if they are mere hysteria."

"I believe what you are saying," agreed Scrooge, "and I would appreciate hearing any other thoughts you may have regarding Fan's situation prior to her death." She was happy to share them and began with a question.

"I am wondering what it is you think you could have done to alleviate Fan's fears." Scrooge gave a small shrug as she continued, not really expecting an answer. "It also seems to me that the truth of her husband's character and dissipation would eventually have shown itself. That would no doubt have been extremely difficult for her to bear, and for you to change. Do not misunderstand. I am not saying I think this ending was for the best.

It was not. I am suggesting, though, that what she thought of as a harmonious situation would eventually have been revealed to her as something quite the contrary and she would have been very unhappy."

Mrs. Langstone offered Scrooge another roll and poured both of them more coffee. Picking up her own cup, she said, "One other thing I suggest you note is the fact that, by her salutation in her last letter, your sister felt toward you as she always had. Nothing had changed in that regard. Your fears of having 'neglected' her, as you say, were no doubt unfounded in that she still saw you as available to her. Her faith in you had not wavered and she addressed you as her 'Loyal Ebenezer.' You were still her dearest brother. Besides that, Mr. Scrooge, let's do be honest, her circumstances created the problem, not you. You may feel you were not as attentive as you might have been, but she did have a husband who was responsible for her, and a devoted physician. For all you knew at the time, she was being well looked after."

Scrooge was overwhelmed with gratitude and relief. "You are being very generous – and helpful," he replied. "I know that some of my questions will never be answered, yet my emotions have settled a great deal and will, no doubt, continue to do so, as time goes on. I do thank you, Mrs. Langstone, for discussing this with me."

Mrs. Langstone smiled warmly. "Rebecca, if you please, Mr. Scrooge. Call me Rebecca. I believe we have, through all of this, become well enough acquainted that you may use my given name, at least in private."

Scrooge's heart hopped a full beat before he replied, "Very well . . . Rebecca, but if that be the case, I must insist that you call me Ebenezer." She concurred, and they cheerfully agreed they would each do so – "at least in private."

Epilogue

Tuesday, December 24, 1844

Even in his darkest, most tightfisted moments, Scrooge had never forgotten the kindness and generosity of old Fezziwig, to whom he and Dick had been apprenticed in their youth. He could recall it as if it were yesterday. On that Christmas Eve so many years ago Fezziwig noticed it was seven o'clock, rubbed his hands, adjusted his capacious waistcoat, laughed and called out in a jovial voice, "No more work tonight. Christmas Eve, Dick. Christmas, Ebenezer!" With that they put up the shutters and cleared away every movable piece of furniture from the room. The floor was swept and watered, lamps were trimmed, the fire was fueled and the warehouse became a ball-room.

In came a fiddler. In came Fezziwig's family, friends and employees, and the dancing began. There was food and drink and enough merriment to keep them in good stead well into the New Year. After the ball, Mr. and Mrs. Fezziwig bade everyone good-bye and wished them a Merry Christmas. Dick and Ebenezer went to their beds, which were under a counter in the back shop, and poured out their hearts in praise of Fezziwig. The happiness he had given was quite as great as if it had cost a fortune.

This Christmas, Scrooge was set on hosting a Christmas Eve party of his own. He would fashion it after old Fezziwig's gathering and produce the same merriment that had delighted him and Dick so many years ago. Christmas was a joyful season, after all, and it should be appropriately celebrated. Besides, he felt like celebrating – he truly did!

Scrooge would, as with last year, spend Christmas Day with Fred and Catherine, but on Christmas Eve they would gather at his own home to dance, eat and make toasts asking God to bless them, everyone! Scrooge might even ask Tiny Tim to do the honors.

So it was that the morning following his latest visit with Mrs. Langstone, Scrooge rose and dressed quickly before loudly calling, "Mrs. Dilber, my good woman! We need decorations, Mrs. D., and food. We need food and drink!" She ran into the room just as another idea occurred to him. Holding up his right index finger, he cried, "And a kissing ball, Mrs. D.! Make it big enough to be easily seen, with plenty of mistletoe!"

Mrs. Dilber laughed. It was a relief to see her employer once again in such gladness. She knew exactly what he wanted and by Christmas Eve the house was as festive as any in London Town. There were garlands of green, branches of holly, and even a Christmas tree gaily decorated with tapers and all sorts of glistening objects. Bunches of Christmas crackers provided a little more merrymaking and a great deal more noise. The kissing ball was hung in a prominent place, to be admired or employed, according to one's inclination.

Proficient musicians were hired and the food prepared and laid out on cloth-covered tables. Per Scrooge's instructions, in addition to other traditional foods, Mrs. Dilber kept the repast along the same lines as Fezziwig's celebration, which meant there was cold roast, cakes, mince pies, beer and negus – a drink made of wine, hot water, spices and sugar.

Scrooge's employees were there, including Mrs. Dilber and her husband Ollie, who complained only a little throughout the evening. The day cook and scrub woman and their families appeared, as did the Cratchits, every one. Homer Probert, Dick and Priscilla Wilkins attended and, of course, Fred and Catherine. Julian and Marian Thorne stopped in long enough to wish everyone a Merry Christmas and enjoyed themselves so much they were very late in leaving. When they did depart they said they hoped this would be an annual event. Mrs. Langstone was Scrooge's particular guest and deftly avoided the kissing ball since she was of two minds with regard to being kissed, particularly in the presence of so many people.

Carolers appeared at the door early in the evening, singing in as good a voice as any cathedral choir, or so it was said by those of the party. In return for their carols and their wassail punch, Scrooge's guests gave the carolers coins and asked them to partake of the plentiful food. When the carolers moved on, the dancing began.

Toby Veck and Rollo Norris stopped in for a bit of Christmas cheer and were welcomed with a great deal of commotion. Toby took a turn with Mrs. Dilber since Ollie's spine did not allow such exuberance, and Rollo quickly asked Martha to partner him in a polka. Unfortunately, his request interrupted Homer as he was edging her toward the kissing ball. Between Homer and Rollo, poor Martha did not sit down once during the entire time the musicians performed. She did not seem to mind, but Homer minded a great deal.

Scrooge had particularly requested the musicians to end the evening with "Sir Roger de Coverley" as had been performed at old Fezziwig's, and he and Mrs. Langstone played the part of Mr. and Mrs. Fezziwig, as top couple. *Advance and retire, both hands to your partner, bow and curtsey, corkscrew, thread-the-needle, and back again to your place!* Things went well for the first stanza or two, until those old enough to have danced it in their youth found they had forgotten some moves, and those too young had no idea of the moves at all. It became such a confusion of blunders that the company was reduced to helpless laughter and found they enjoyed their mistakes as much as they would have enjoyed the dance, had they only known the steps!

The celebration was deemed by all to have been entirely successful. At eleven o'clock Scrooge bade his guests good-night and sincerely wished each and every one a very Merry Christmas. Mrs. Langstone, Dick and Priscilla were the last to leave and, as she accepted her coat, Mrs. Langstone remarked to Scrooge, "I have been remiss in one of my duties." She was in a playful mood and was unaware of his hope that she referred to the kissing ball.

"I am yours to command," replied Scrooge, unable to hide the anticipation from his voice. Within a few seconds of unwittingly keeping him in suspense, she smiled and said she had been dispatched with a particular invitation from her mother, Mrs. Adelaide Sotherton, who would be pleased with an introduction.

Scrooge lifted his eyebrows in surprise. "I would very much like to make your celebrated mother's acquaintance, Madam, and would be honored to do so." With a wink, he said, "I sense the part you must have played in this."

"Oh, no, Mr. Scrooge," she said, raising both hands, "I deny it. I merely related some of your recent adventures and she is determined to meet the person who, as she put it, can actually disrupt convention, unlike those other 'dullards' who persistently surround her."

Scrooge climbed happily into bed that night, thinking back over the year, mainly this very eventful month of December 1844.

He had come full circle and was again thankful to be alive and rejoicing in the Grace and Hope of the Season. He hated, however, to think of poor Marley still floating in that ether of lost souls, particularly since he had been the means of rescuing Scrooge from a bitter end twice in a twelvemonth. Surely Marley's assistance to his old partner would count for something, unless he really was only a figment of Scrooge's conscience, or a Heavenly vision, after all.

As he relaxed, Scrooge turned over and drifted into a deep and peaceful sleep, but not before he heard the faint echo of chains and money boxes. Perhaps he was only imagining things . . .

AUTHOR'S NOTE

Each time I read the book or watched a movie version of *A Christmas Carol* I imagined what Scrooge's life would have been like after Christmas 1843. What challenges would naturally follow such a massive metamorphosis? Surely the change in lifestyle would not be as simple as it appeared.

In one night Dickens' Scrooge was transformed from a ruthless miser into a paragon of virtue and joy, but he would still have to deal with the man he had been. Even his new, sincere attitude could not instantly expunge the past. It was a past, after all, that had left ruination in its wake. I wanted to see him love, laugh and make up, somewhat, for all that had gone before.

Then there was the ghost of Jacob Marley. Could he still be available to give sage advice? What better quandary for Scrooge and Marley to confront than one that always stood out in Dickens' story, at least for me as a reader. Fan's death was never explained. We assume she died in childbirth, but Dickens left it open-ended. Scrooge would only need a few suggestions of murder and he would be driven to discover the truth, particularly if he felt overwhelming guilt and regret.

Toby Veck is a character from another Dickens' Christmas story, *The Chimes*, and two "real" people also make an appearance – my two grandfathers. Rollo Norris was a building contractor and Homer Probert was a farmer. Both lived in Central California, but their roots were in England and Wales. So I transported them back in time and gave them each a role to play.